CHILLING
EFFECT

ALSO BY MELISSA F. MILLER

The Sasha McCandless Legal Thrillers

Irreparable Harm

Inadvertent Disclosure

Irretrievably Broken

Indispensable Party

Improper Influence

Irrevocable Trust

Irrefutable Evidence

Lovers & Madmen: a novella

A Marriage of True Minds: a novella

The Aroostine Higgins Novels

Critical Vulnerability

Women's Work: Three Crime Fiction Shorts

An *Aroostine Higgins* Novel

CHILLING EFFECT

MELISSA F. MILLER

THOMAS & MERCER

Text copyright © 2015 Melissa F. Miller

Published by Thomas & Mercer, Seattle

www.apub.com

Amazon, the Amazon logo, and Thomas & Mercer are trademarks of Amazon.com, Inc., or its affiliates.

ISBN-13: 9781477829790
ISBN-10: 1477829792

Cover design by Megan Haggerty

Library of Congress Control Number: 2014922712

Printed in the United States of America

*To David, my amazingly supportive husband,
and Adam, Jack, and Sara, our three awesome
children. Together, we can do hard things.*

CHAPTER ONE

Isaac Palmer tried to click the button to save and close the spreadsheet, but his hands trembled too badly.

He stopped and exhaled a long, shaky breath.

When his hands were steadier, he closed Excel and popped the thumb drive out of the USB slot.

Why was he even doing this? Why continue to copy the spreadsheets when he'd already decided not to turn them over to the feds? So much risk, and for what?

The darkest part of his soul whispered, *blackmail, that's what for.* But he pushed the words aside.

No. It was an insurance policy. Just in case.

Just in case what, he didn't know. But he slipped the thumb drive into his pocket before powering down his computer and flipping off the harsh fluorescent light mounted to the underside of his shelf. Then he scanned his cubicle to confirm everything was tidy, picked up his stainless-steel travel mug and jacket, put his head down, and walked through the warren of accounting cubicles and out of the building.

Not until he was ensconced in his red Tercel did Isaac relax even a tiny bit.

He fished his keys out of his pocket then sagged against the driver's seat and just sat for a long moment in the stuffy, overhead interior, reveling in the feeling of safety that eluded him at work. Ever since he'd called the FBI, he'd spent every second of every work day in a state of suspended terror, waiting for someone to call him out on his treachery. Even though anxiety dogged him, following him everywhere—trailing behind his car and slipping into his house each night like an unseen cloud—it was always the worst at the casino. Okay, and, if he was being honest, at night when the sun slipped behind the mountains and darkness fell.

This wasn't how this was supposed to turn out. When he first discovered the dummy transfers, he'd been excited, imagining himself like a movie character bringing down a well-funded, faceless villain. He'd be bold and fearless. A hero. A hero who got the girl through his relentless pursuit of justice.

Flooded with adrenaline, he'd called the Eugene field office and asked to speak to the agent in charge. Carley Whitsome, the agent who took down his information, was enthusiastic and effusive, which only fueled Isaac's imagination. For a few thrilling moments, he saw himself as a man of action, passion, and strength.

But then, while the excitement was still coursing through his veins, he'd bumped into *her*. The gorgeous, kind-hearted girl who always greeted him with a warm smile and some friendly chitchat but had no idea that he loved her.

He'd screwed up his courage and confided in her, certain his cleverness at uncovering the scheme and his bravery in reporting it would impress her. He was sure she'd see him in a new light. He'd no longer be the dorky, good-hearted neighbor who could always be counted on to babysit her kid or jump-start her car's dead battery. Instead, he'd be the strong, smart, hero next door.

Or so he'd dreamed.

But as he recounted his story, her flawless skin turned gray, and her big black eyes lost their sparkle.

"Oh, Isaac, no. What have you done?" she'd gasped.

He remembered how he'd blinked at her, trying to force his racing brain to process her words.

And then tears welled up in her impossibly deep eyes, and she shook her head mournfully. "They'll kill you."

Before he could respond, she'd run off, her hair trailing behind her like a long, shimmering scarf.

He'd stood there dumbly staring after her, as two thoughts tumbled through his mind, one after another, over and over:

One, she cares what happens to me.

Two, what have I done?

That was the moment when the fear grabbed his chest and began to eat away at him like a cancer. And it had settled inside him, buried deep in his chest cavity, and never truly relented. He'd breathe easily—like just a moment ago when he'd settled in his car—but the relief was always fleeting.

Already his pulse pounded in his ears, and his hands shook as he gripped the steering wheel, white knuckled. He gulped for air and prayed he'd make it through the night.

CHAPTER TWO

Aroostine's phone continued to buzz. She continued to pretend not to hear it.

Even though she physically itched to answer it—or at least swipe the bar to wake up the screen so she could take a peek at who was calling her—she clasped her hands together in her lap and forced herself to gaze steadily into Joe's eyes. She focused on the Central Oregon sun warming her shoulders, the morning breeze tickling at her long, loose hair, and the face of her husband, the man she loved, the man who had surprised her with this romantic getaway. She took in the breathtakingly blue sky, the distant mountains dotted with snow despite the fact that it was mid-August, and the soft purple wildflowers carpeting the meadow between the boulder where they'd set up their picnic and the rushing white stream providing the background music for their breakfast. She smiled up at Joe, trying to convey a picture of relaxed bliss.

He squinted at her for a moment then shook his head. "Go ahead."

"Sorry?"

"Go ahead and answer the damn phone, Roo. You look like a constipated dog." He gave her a smile that was half amused, half resigned.

"Way to ruin a moment," she managed to say while smoothing her expression into something she hoped looked less canine. And less constipated.

He laughed. "You get points for effort. You've been trying to ignore that thing for a good three minutes." He glanced down at his watch, her anniversary gift to him. "It's nine o'clock sharp back East, so the first item on *someone's* to-do list was to call you at the earliest decent hour and not give up until they reach you."

He paused and sipped his coffee then placed the thermos on the blanket and continued ticking off points. "So *either* Rufus is sick and my parents decided to call you instead of the vet *or* someone requires the services of my favorite assistant US attorney. As of last night, Rufus was a healthy golden retriever enjoying a week with his grandparents. So I'm guessing it's someone from your office. Just answer it already. Whoever it is obviously isn't going to leave a message."

The phone weighed in with another *bzzzt*.

"Are you sure you don't mind?"

She'd promised not to work during the trip and, so far, had kept her word. But her curiosity was killing her. And if he really didn't care . . .

"Just make it quick."

He stretched over and gave her a small kiss on the crown of her head then stood and headed toward the stream.

Before he could reconsider, she snatched the phone up from the blanket.

"Aroostine Higgins."

"Finally. I hope I didn't wake you," said a familiar voice. The dry tone made clear that whether Aroostine had been awoken at six o'clock in the morning during her vacation was of no actual concern to the speaker.

Her eyebrows shot up her forehead. "Sid?"

Sidney Slater, director of the Criminal Division of the Department of Justice, was not on the list of people she expected to hear from.

Not on this trip.

Not ever.

Her former boss hadn't even bothered to say "don't let the door hit you on the way out" after he'd summarily demoted her from hotshot trial attorney in the Criminal Division to lone AUSA assigned to the backwater outpost of the Johnstown, Pennsylvania, office. Not that she was complaining, exactly. The reassignment meant she'd been able to return to Walnut Bottom, settle back into her cozy, sun-splashed home with Joe and Rufus, and put her ill-fated stint in Washington, DC, out of her mind.

But the circumstances that had landed her in Sid's bad graces still stung. *Some* bosses might have commended her for what she'd done. After all, she'd rescued two kidnapping victims and shut down a vicious plot to control the United States government and private industry by hijacking essential technology.

But not Sid.

Sid had focused on the fact that she'd failed to show up for a court appointment in order to save Joe's life. First he'd suspended her, and then he'd summarily transferred her out of his division.

"I'm awake," she said, ignoring the way the memory of his treatment made her heart race and her palms sweat.

"Good. I need you to do me a favor."

"Pardon?" She couldn't imagine what he wanted from her, but, unless it involved picking up a souvenir mug at the airport, it wasn't going to happen.

His tone softened. "Let me rephrase that. I realize you don't work directly for me anymore, but I'm really in a jam and I need your help."

"Sid . . ." she fumbled around for the words to explain that this was not a trip that could be interrupted.

"Let me finish. We both know you're an exceptionally competent and capable attorney. I also recognize that what you did last winter was a service to the department. Hell, it was a service to the entire country."

Finally, she thought. But in true Slater fashion, he ruined the moment as he kept prattling.

"But rules are rules, Aroostine. And rules governing attorney conduct, in particular, are not optional. I had no choice."

She had no intention of wasting a gorgeous morning listening to this drivel. She cut in, "Come on, Sid. There's always a choice. I made mine, and you made yours. What do you have, almost a hundred AUSAs working for you? Give one of them a chance to shine. There's a mountain here waiting for me to hike it." *And a husband to hike it with.*

She was surprised by the fire in her own voice, but he hadn't supported her when she needed him. Sid could have defended her to the director, but he chose not to. Now he could go pound salt.

"Wait, please. I know you feel betrayed by me, and I understand that. You think I failed to stand up for you. I won't waste your time or mine trying to justify the decision I made. But you should know two things: it was an extraordinarily difficult choice for me. I hated losing you—you're a rising star. But, I'll be honest, I'd make the same decision again. The rules matter. All that said, you're uniquely situated to help me right now, and if you do, I'll make sure it's taken into consideration."

She stared out at the endless sky and watched as a golden eagle stood on a cliff and spread its massive, dark wings, prepared to take flight. The majestic bird soared overhead and circled the meadow looking for prey. She tried to shake the feeling that she was the helpless baby rabbit in this conversation and cleared her throat.

"Meaning what, exactly?"

"Meaning you come up for annual review in October. Because I was your section chief for part of the year, I'll be contributing to your evaluation. And I carry a lot of weight. I can bring you back to Main Justice with the press of a couple of keys."

A shot of adrenaline raced up her spine, but she forced herself to slow her breathing. "I'll be honest with you, too, Sid. I'm not sure I want to come back."

"Fair point. But I presume you don't intend a stint as AUSA in a small, unimportant office to be the capstone of your career. I can help you advance, Aroostine."

She bristled at the description of her current post, but she had to put that aside and deal with the unspoken component of Sid's statement, which came through as loudly as if he'd shouted it. *And I can sink what's left of your career.*

"Why don't you tell me what the favor is? Let's start there."

It almost didn't matter. She'd made a promise to Joe. She wasn't going to work on her own caseload during this trip, let alone take on whatever mind-numbing research task Sid was about to spring on her.

"There's a Native American reservation located about eighty miles from your resort. It's made up of three tribes in the Chinook Nation. Their casino and hotel are the region's largest employers. And they turn a tidy profit, although judging by the poverty level on the reservation, they aren't much for sharing the wealth."

"Tell me something new." She didn't need Sid to tell her about the broken promises and despair that permeated the native populations. She'd lived it—at least until the Higginses had adopted her and saved her from that bleak life.

"In any event, an accountant for the casino, a fellow by the name of Isaac Palmer, contacted the FBI in Eugene about possible embezzlement. As you may know, the Bureau is sensitive about sticking its nose into issues on the reservations."

As far as she knew the Bureau simply ignored the reservations, turning a blind eye to the rampant criminal activity that threatened to destroy so many native communities.

"Sensitive?"

Sid sighed. "It's complicated. The Bureau has jurisdiction to prosecute crimes that occur on the reservations, but the agents are often unwelcome. The tribes resent their presence, and the residents usually refuse to cooperate with investigations."

"Well, Mr. Palmer reached out, so presumably that's not an issue in your case."

"It wasn't. The Bureau forwarded the report on to the Office of Tribal Affairs. The liaison there reviewed the initial information and determined there was sufficient evidence to open a white-collar investigation, so she turned it over to our Eugene branch office. Unfortunately, at that point, Mr. Palmer fell off the face of the earth. He's not returning phone calls. His AUSA sent him a registered letter; it was returned. We're at a dead end—unless you can help us."

"What do you want me to do?"

"I'd like you to contact Mr. Palmer and ask him to meet with you. Go see him and convince him to follow through with the investigation. From what the Oregon US Attorney has gathered, this could be a significant case from a financial standpoint."

"Why me?"

He coughed. "You're uniquely qualified to make him feel comfortable. I think he'll talk to you."

"Because I'm a Native American?"

After a long pause, he answered slowly, choosing each word with precision. The careful speech was a hallmark of her former boss's deliberative thought processes.

"I do think your shared heritage as Native Americans will help to break the ice, yes. But the reason I thought of you was the rapport you manage to build with your witnesses, regardless of their background. It's one of your strengths."

"And the fact that I just happen to be in Oregon right now is gravy, huh? You would have tracked me down in Johnstown and flown me out here for this assignment, right?"

She generally wasn't a fan of sarcasm. She found it petty. But Sid deserved to squirm a little.

"Honestly, I don't know. I'm sure there are other Native American attorneys in the Department who are geographically closer. In fact, there's likely at least one already assigned to the Oregon Office. But yes, I was aware you're out there—thanks to the wonders of our electronic calendaring system I know where just about every assistant US attorney is at a given moment—and I know you're good. So I'm asking you. What do you say?"

She chewed on the inside of her cheek.

Her instinct was to say no.

But.

This could be her chance to redeem herself in the eyes of Main Justice.

So what? Remember, you chose Joe.

Joe, who was this very moment crossing the meadow with a fistful of wildflowers and a smile that tugged on her heart.

"Aroostine?"

"Let me think about it, Sid. E-mail me the file and Mr. Palmer's contact information."

"Thank you. I knew you'd do the right thing."

"I haven't said yes."

"You will."

She ended the call and let Joe sweep her into one of his big, tight hugs.

CHAPTER THREE

Joe cocked his head and appraised his wife. She was curled up in the window seat with a light cotton blanket wrapped around her. But instead of gazing out at the endless mountain vista that stretched across the sky, she had her nose in a book—or her electronic tablet, to be exact.

With the diffuse light behind her, she was a slightly softer, more mature version of the Aroostine he'd dated in college. He could almost always find her studying—engrossed in a book with her legs hooked beneath her, a blanket around her shoulders, and that long curtain of dark hair partially obscuring her face.

He smiled at the memory and crossed the room to stand near her.

She swiped the device to mark her place, pushed her hair out of her eyes, and gazed up at him with an open expression. Not annoyed at the interruption, but curious about what he wanted.

"Are you sure you don't want to come along?"

He tucked a stray strand of her glossy hair behind her ear as he asked the question, just as an excuse to touch her. He still couldn't believe he'd almost lost her because of his pigheaded refusal to meet her halfway. He shoved the thought out of his head and let his hand drop to her shoulder.

She considered him with sleepy, heavy-lidded eyes.

"You're sweet, but that hike kicked my butt. I think I'm going to take a nap and then maybe check out the sauna. You go have fun; you've been excited about this craft beer thingy ever since the concierge mentioned it."

It was true. Oregon was known for its artisanal beers, and the resort had organized a tour of several local breweries for interested guests. Good beer was one of his passions. But Aroostine rarely drank and loathed the taste of beer.

"Are you sure you don't mind?"

He watched her face, searching her expression for a hint of annoyance or hurt.

"Sweetheart, please. We're not Siamese twins. This is something you know you'll enjoy. It's not a personal affront to me if you have hobbies, you know."

"I know. It's just . . . this trip is about rediscovering each other."

She gave him a lazy smile. "So go discover some new beers and then come back here and rediscover me. I'm not going anywhere."

He cupped her face in his hands and kissed her hard.

She leaned into him. Her honey-scented body lotion wafted from her skin and enveloped him. All thoughts of amber ales, extra-hoppy IPAs, and chocolaty porters faded from his mind. He pressed closer against her.

She leaned back and gave him a playful shove.

"Go already. Let me have my nap and recharge."

He sighed in mock resignation.

"Thanks, baby."

"Go."

She waved him toward the door then woke up her screen and returned to whatever it was she'd been reading.

———

Aroostine yawned and switched off the tablet. Her entire body was stiff. A nap and a steamy sauna were definitely on her agenda.

The climb up Broken Top had been worth it—the view from the top was spectacular, breathtaking even, and they'd stood there in silent communion for a very long time drinking it all in—but the hike itself had been strenuous. They'd chosen the more challenging of the two marked paths, and she was paying for it with sore muscles, aching feet, and a serious sense of fatigue.

She was glad Joe had gone on the beer tour. Now she could indulge in a guilt-free nap.

She flopped on the impossibly high, improbably fluffy cloud of bedding that graced the king bed and closed her eyes.

Unbidden, the notes from the electronic file on Isaac Palmer flitted through her mind. The file had been a quick read. Mr. Palmer had spilled a wealth of information during his initial telephone interview and then clammed up. The evidence he had shared was definitely compelling and pointed to a large-scale embezzlement operation. The notes also showed he had that most prized ability in a witness: to explain the minutiae of a complex scheme in clear, easy to understand language. The upshot of the report was Isaac Palmer could tie forty thousand dollars a week, every week, to a dummy accounting entry. Whoever was behind the movements had chosen a number low enough that it wouldn't attract attention, at least not immediately, but high enough that, with consistent transfers, it would drain over two million dollars a year from the casino's coffers. The siphoned funds were redirected into an account Palmer had traced to a bank in the Cayman Islands. It was death by forty thousand cuts.

She saw why Sid was eager to secure the man's ongoing cooperation.

She didn't see why Sid was so sure she was the one to do it.

For one thing, according to his dossier, Mr. Palmer traced his lineage to the Wasco tribe, part of the Chinook Nation. She was Lenape. More accurately, she was white-bread American, but her heritage stretched back to the Eastern Lenape Nation. The Chinooks had settled in the extreme eastern part of Oregon; the Lenape, in the mid-Atlantic region.

It was as if Sid expected a Vietnamese village woman to bond with a Japanese businessman simply because they both knew how to use chopsticks. He didn't mean to be insulting. But he was misguided, at best.

And more important than Sid's cluelessness was the fact that she simply wasn't going to interrupt her time with Joe to do him a favor. She had to admit she wanted another shot at Main Justice, just to prove she had the talent and work ethic to handle complex, high-profile cases. But she wasn't sure her marriage was sturdy enough to weather her return to that environment. Not just yet. She and Joe were still rebuilding. Her energies were better spent on her marriage than on currying favor with the powers that be within the Department of Justice.

She needed to focus on repairing her foundation with Joe. She couldn't afford any distractions—not even a small one that would get her back into Sid's good graces.

She inhaled deeply through her nose and emptied her mind, preparing herself for restorative sleep.

Three minutes later, her eyes popped open, and she sat bolt upright.

Sleep was not going to happen. Not now. Not with the whirring activity in her brain.

She sighed and pushed off the covers. As she paced in a tight circle around the suite, she tried to identify the root of her dis-ease.

Her grandfather's words rang in her ears. *Dis-ease, little one, the word itself means disease. When you're troubled and not at ease in the world examine your heart just as we examine the roots and shoots of a diseased plant. Look for the spots where the disease grows and then you'll know how to cure it.*

She'd been six, and their small vegetable garden had been under siege. Almost overnight, their tall, straight plants had begun to wilt and rot in the ground. They'd meticulously searched every leaf and stalk until they uncovered the source. Late blight, her grandfather had declared, showing her the white fungal spots on the undersides of a tomato plant. They'd mixed up a copper-lime spray and treated the plants, saving what would turn out to be the last harvest before he died and she went to live with the Higginses.

It'd been years since she'd recalled that garden patch. Like every other memory from the first seven years of her life, it had been tucked away in a corner of her mind—the loss of her grandfather was too painful to dwell on. And she'd begun a new life, with new customs and a new culture. The old memories hadn't belonged.

Now she pressed her forehead against the cool window pane and stared out at the late-afternoon sun blazing red over the horizon. She knew the source of her dis-ease.

She didn't want pass up the opportunity for redemption that Sid had offered.

But she didn't want to upset the delicate balance that she and Joe had achieved.

She twisted a section of hair around her finger.

What *did* she want?

She wanted to impress Sid without hurting Joe.

Was such a feat even doable?

Joe would be gone for four hours. Isaac Palmer lived on the White Springs Reservation, eighty miles away. She didn't drive. She'd have to convince him to meet with her, find a way to get to him, and get back before Joe returned for the late dinner he'd promised her.

Her eyes fell on the faux leather binder on the desk. She flipped it open to the local activities section and confirmed that the resort offered car service to the White Springs casino, located just over an hour to the north. She did some quick calculations in her head. Assume a conservative two and a half hours for round-trip travel time and an hour to talk to Mr. Palmer. It would be tight, but the timing could work. *If* Isaac agreed to talk to her.

She pulled her hair back into a sleek ponytail and snapped an elastic band around it. Then she shook out her hands and tapped Isaac Palmer's telephone number into her phone.

CHAPTER FOUR

"You sure this is the right place, ma'am?" the driver craned his neck back to look at her.

Aroostine stared through the town car's backseat window and tried to shake the feeling that she'd been transported back in time.

Isaac Palmer's home sat in the exact middle of a row of five dusty A-frames in varying states of sagging disrepair. In the twilight, the sturdiest of the homes, two houses to the left of Isaac's, could have passed for her grandfather's house. It was the same simple style, made from the same building materials—mainly wood, like a mountain cabin or beachside cottage minus the majestic setting. But the clincher was the straw broom propped against the wall beside the door. Whoever lived in that house appeared to share her late grandfather's habit of sweeping all the bad energy and dust out of the house at the end of each day. Another memory that she hadn't thought of in decades.

She bit down on her lower lip hard enough to draw blood.

"Ma'am?"

She shook herself back to the present.

"This is the address."

She peered at the dark, shuttered windows. Isaac had said he'd turn on the light in the front room. She really hoped the dark house didn't signal a change of heart.

"You want me to wait and make sure you get inside okay?"

"No, I'll be fine."

She wanted the gleaming town car to disappear from this desolate residential area before it drew attention.

"Okay, then like I said, I'll be up at the casino just playing a few hands. You just call the number on my card when you're ready to go back. The casino's up at the far end of the reservation. Call me about thirty minutes before you wrap up."

"A half hour?"

"The reservation's land totals almost a thousand square miles, and the roads are crap. We're easily thirty minutes from the parts they want you to see."

"Okay. Thanks, Tony."

"You're sure you're going to be okay here alone? This place is overrun with criminals." His neck reddened, and he hurried to add, "Uh, no offense."

"None taken. I'll be fine. Hope you get lucky."

She flashed him an insincere smile and stepped out of the car. He drove away slowly, whether because he was reluctant to leave her or because he had difficulty negotiating the bumpy hard-packed earth that passed for a road, she couldn't tell.

Once the car's tail lights had disappeared from view, she smoothed the front of her dress, squared her shoulders, and rapped lightly on Isaac's front door.

While she waited for him to answer, she took in the peeling white paint and the rusted screen door. She wondered why he still lived on the reservation. His file indicated that he'd taken two years of accounting courses at the local community college and had gone on to become a certified public accountant. A job at the casino would come with a decent salary, mandatory overtime pay, and benefits. Surely he could afford to move to the small town on the outskirts of White Springs.

The house was still.

She frowned and rapped again.

He hadn't taken as much convincing as she'd expected. As soon as she'd introduced herself, he'd surprised her by asking if her name was Lenape. Score one for Sid.

Had Isaac's readiness to talk to her been an act? Maybe he'd hung up and hightailed it out of there?

She waited another moment before walking around to the back of the house. She passed beside his neighbor's house, startling a cat that jumped out of the scrubby brush and hissed at her before slinking away.

Aside from the irritated tomcat, she spotted no signs of life. The back of Isaac's house was as dark as the front.

The single small window set into the back wall was closed. Next to it, a plain wooden door hung slightly ajar. Parked a few feet behind the house on a patch of dried earth was a late-model Toyota. He was home.

She eased the door open about a foot and poked her head into the dark kitchen.

"Mr. Palmer? Isaac? It's me, Aroostine Higgins."

She listened as her voice echoed off the silent walls. The faint ticking of a clock and the hum of a refrigerator were the only response.

No other sounds.

Her pulse ticked faster as she stepped inside and ran her hand along the wall until she hit a light switch.

An overhead bulb blinked to life slowly.

As her eyes adjusted to the light, she surveyed the kitchen. It was old and worn, but clean.

Isaac said he'd been eating an early supper when she called. If so, he'd finished and tidied up.

The dishpan was empty. The counter had been wiped down with a wet rag, the circles still visible, and the faded linoleum floor had been swept clean.

"Mr. Palmer?" she called again, louder this time, projecting her voice toward the front of the small house. "Are you okay?"

There was no answer.

Her heart banged in her chest.

Maybe he fell asleep in the front room waiting for her.

It was a reasonable explanation. But her legs seemed to be frozen to the spot just inside the kitchen door. Her hand, of its own volition, clung to the door frame as if she feared being swept out to sea.

Maybe she should walk back outside and try his telephone number.

Don't be ridiculous, she scolded herself. *He's just a room away, probably having a cat nap. Go wake him up and get on with it.*

Finally, she crept forward, through the empty kitchen and a shadowy doorway and into the dark front room. She could just detect the shape of a man slumped in an easy chair by the front window, his head lolling back against the chair's headrest.

Aroostine's hammering heart slowed, and she let out a shaky, embarrassed laugh at herself. Then she crossed the small room to wake her dozing witness.

"Mr. Palmer, wake up." She kept her voice soft as she shook him gently. She didn't want to frighten him.

He didn't move.

"Isaac." She called him a little bit louder this time and gave him a more vigorous shake.

Jeez, and she thought Joe slept like the dead.

She reached over and switched on the small lamp centered on a side table near the chair.

Isaac Palmer's sightless eyes appeared to be staring right at her. The bullet hole between them formed an almost perfect circle. A small trail of congealed blood snaked down his forehead and into his gaping mouth.

Aroostine stumbled out the front door and onto the dusty patch of ground that served as the late Isaac Palmer's front lawn. She fumbled for her phone, trying to pull up Joe's number, but her hands were trembling too much.

Breathe, she told herself. *Slow down. Take a breath.*

She gulped down three long swallows of the cool evening air. Then when her heart had slowed and her hands were somewhat steadier, she tried again.

As the call connected, she scanned the street. No activity. No kids playing a game of pickup. No lovers canoodling. No dog walkers. Nothing to hint that people made their lives here. Maybe everyone was off at some community event or closed up in their houses updating their Facebook statuses. Whatever the reason, the deserted streets felt creepy.

It was just her on a lonely stretch of land with a dead man in the house behind her.

After the fourth ring, Joe picked up.

"Hey, Roo."

His voice was relaxed, inviting. The sound of laughter, music, and clinking glasses filled the background.

"I need you," she said without preamble.

"Are you okay?" he asked, instantly serious.

She ignored the question and plowed right into her story. "I'm on the White Springs Reservation. I came here to meet a witness, but when I got here, he was dead. My God, he was murdered—"

"Whoa, whoa, whoa. Slow down. You're . . . on a reservation? How'd you get there?"

"Shuttle service from the resort. Listen, I'm sorry. I know I agreed not to work on this trip, but Sid asked for a favor and—"

"That's what the call was about this morning?" Irritation seeped through the phone receiver.

"Yes. Can we focus here? There's a *dead* guy. I . . . I'm scared, Joe."

Instantly, the agitation left his voice.

"Okay, right. You're okay? Are you someplace safe?"

She swept the desolate strip of land with her eyes. Was Isaac Palmer's killer watching her from behind one of the other shacks? Or from out in the windswept plains? A red-tailed hawk circled the field, and a shiver ran down her spine. The sight of the opportunistic predator out hunting made her feel as though she were prey herself.

"I'm not sure," she admitted.

"Text me the address. I'm on my way."

"Thank you."

"Just stay put. Don't do anything brave—or stupid."

"Don't worry," she assured him.

"I'm serious."

"So am I. I'm going to call Sid and then the tribal police. Then I guess I'll let the shuttle driver know he can take off. I imagine we'll be here awhile dealing with the authorities." Ever since his kidnapping he'd acted as if her natural response to danger was to rush into it. He didn't realize that her bravery was a direct response to that fact that *he* had been the one in peril.

In any case, he didn't need to worry about her getting adventurous out here on her own—she couldn't shake the image of the dead man slumped in his chair just on the other side of the door.

"I love you," he whispered.

"Love you, too."

She ended the call and texted the address with trembling hands.

The hawk circled again. It called. Its cry chilled her—it sounded like an infant in distress. Another call, and a second bird joined it in the dusky sky.

She stowed her phone without calling Sid or the police and set off across the narrow street toward the field on a hunch.

The hawks perched on two high branches and peered down at something in the far corner of the field.

It's probably a dead rabbit, she tried to convince herself as she tromped through the long grass, sage, and juniper bushes.

The predators continued their calling, louder and more insistent now.

What was left of the sun was dipping behind a distant rock formation.

She wrapped her arms around her torso and bent her head against the wind.

As she reached the spot that the hawks were watching, she saw what was causing their excitement and sucked in her breath. She was right, it was a dead rabbit. But it wasn't *just* a dead rabbit.

An adult black-tailed jackrabbit, its long thin ears spread against the earth like two antennae, stared up at the sky, a single bullet hole between its eyes.

Someone had been practicing.

———————————

The tribal police were unimpressed. Or, at least, the baby-faced Ahmik Hunt, the first officer to respond to her call, was unimpressed.

"Ma'am, we're overrun with rabbits. Everybody hunts them, although it is unusual to see one left for dead like that, to be sure," he said.

Aroostine nodded. Most Native Americans frowned on hunting for sport, and if someone on the reservation killed a rabbit, he would likely eat the meat and put the skin and fur to other practical uses. But this guy seemed to be missing the larger point. She cocked her head and searched his expression, trying to determine if he was being sincere.

"This rabbit wasn't hunted. It was executed. Shot in the forehead, exactly like Isaac Palmer," she explained in the most patient tone she could muster.

"Now, let's not jump to conclusions. We'll have to leave it to the ballistics experts to determine whether that's true."

"You don't find it curious that there's a dead rabbit less than fifty yards from Mr. Palmer's corpse?"

He shrugged. "Tell me again why you were in Mr. Palmer's house?"

She flushed and tried to ignore the heat in her cheeks. She'd called Sid first, before calling the locals, and he'd been adamant that she not mention the investigation.

"Don't lie, Higgins, but obfuscate your pants off if you have to" was his exact quote. Unfortunately for her, she was a terrible liar and, she imagined, an equally bad obfuscater.

"Ah, I'm out here on vacation from back East. So I called Isaac to see if he wanted to get together for a visit while I'm here."

All true.

"You two involved?"

"You mean romantically? No, nothing like that. My husband was taking a tour of some breweries. I don't drink, so it seemed like a good time to see Isaac."

The cop seemed to age before her eyes as he squinted at her, sizing her up. She smiled as convincingly as she could.

"You're not Chinook, are you?"

She shook her head. "Lenape," she confirmed.

"How did you say you know Isaac?"

She stared toward the front door of the house, where the officer's colleagues were struggling through the front door under the weight of a black body bag.

Now what?

She turned back to Officer Hunt with a pained expression.

"I'm sorry? What did you say?" she asked to buy time.

It was his turn to blush.

"I didn't mean to upset you, Ms. Higgins. I'm sure it must have been quite a shock to find Isaac like that."

"That's putting it mildly."

They stared at each other for a long moment. She was about to break the silence by asking whether there were a lot of execution-style murders on the reservation when Joe sped up in the rental Jeep and screeched to a stop when he saw her.

The cop's right hand danced toward his service weapon.

"It's my husband," she hurried to explain.

His fingers relaxed.

Joe ran around the vehicle and caught her in a tight hug.

"Are you okay?"

"I'm fine."

Despite her assurance, he held her at arm's length and examined her, as if he might find signs of injury.

"Are you sure?"

"Yes, I'm fine—now that you're here." She leaned into him and wrapped her arms around his neck.

Officer Hunt coughed awkwardly.

"I'll give you folks some privacy. Ms. Higgins, please make sure you give your contact information to someone before you leave the scene."

She nodded. He touched his fingers to the brim of his cap and walked over to join the cluster of uniforms gathered around Palmer's front door.

She relaxed, sagging against Joe's chest.

"I'm so glad he's gone," she whispered.

"Why's that?"

"Sid doesn't want me to share any details of the investigation with the locals. So I was sort of sidestepping a lot of that guy's questions. And you know how I am with lying."

Under ordinary circumstances, Joe wouldn't pass up a chance to tease her about her terrible poker face. But instead of ribbing her, he frowned and stared down at her.

"I don't like the sound of that. Why wouldn't the Justice Department cooperate with the tribal police?"

She looked up into his guileless blue eyes and crafted a response that wouldn't disillusion him too much.

"I'm not sure Sid thinks these guys are equipped to deal with issues related to a federal embezzlement case, babe."

He stiffened and said, "Why? Because they don't wear two-thousand-dollar suits?"

Leave it to Joe to identify with a bunch of tribal police. His distrust of what he considered city slickers had only snowballed since she'd joined the Department of Justice.

"I'm sure that's not it. Can we drop this? I still can't believe he's dead. I talked to him just a couple hours ago."

She watched his indignation morph—first into sadness for the dead stranger and then into a spark of fear for her safety.

"You don't think he was killed because he was going to talk to you?"

She shrugged as if to say she had no idea. But that was exactly what she thought.

And Sid thought so, too. The last thing he'd said to her had been *"Try to stick around and see what the locals turn up. But for the love of all that's holy, Higgins—be careful."*

CHAPTER FIVE

After the county coroner's van pulled out and bumped along the road with Isaac's corpse secure in the back, Officer Hunt gestured for an older man to follow him and broke free of the various official types milling around the crime scene. They headed across the street to the fallen log where Aroostine and Joe had finally parked themselves, waiting for someone to tell them they were free to leave.

Aroostine rose to her feet and dusted off her pants as they approached. Joe stood up beside her and followed suit.

"Ms. Higgins, Mr. Higgins—" the police began.

"It's Jackman, actually. Joe Jackman."

Joe stuck out his hand. Officer Hunt shook it and then resumed his introductions.

"Right. This is Chief Johnson."

"I appreciate your patience. I know you've been cooling your heels for a while now," Chief Johnson said. He had the tanned face of an outdoorsman and the tired eyes of a bureaucrat.

"It's okay. You've got a murder to investigate," she said.

He flashed her a tight smile.

"Well, currently, it's a death. It hasn't been ruled a homicide just yet," he cautioned.

She felt her eyes widen. She stole a sideways glance at Joe. His face mirrored her bewilderment.

"Uh, Aroostine said the guy had been shot between the eyes at close range. I don't think he died of natural causes," Joe countered.

Officer Hunt jumped in. "I think we're all in agreement that Mr. Palmer died as a result of a gunshot wound. The chief's just saying we need to proceed in an orderly fashion."

"Sure. Understood. Did you tell the chief about the rabbit?"

Aroostine had watched the various personnel come and go from the scene, traipsing through Palmer's house with bags of equipment, cameras, and finally the body bag. At no point did anyone cross the road to examine the jackrabbit that had been shot in much the same way as the late Isaac Palmer.

Officer Hunt scrunched up his face as if he were trying, through superhuman effort, not to roll his eyes.

Chief Johnson turned to the younger man with a questioning look.

"Rabbit?"

"Uh, right. Ms. Higgins noticed some hawks showing an interest in the field back there. She went over to investigate and found a dead rabbit." He waved his hand in the general vicinity of the field.

"I see," the chief said.

Before he could launch into an explanation about the circle of life, she said, "It's not just a dead rabbit. It's a rabbit that was shot point-blank between the eyes, at close range, using a small-caliber weapon. Ring any bells?"

The chief's substantial eyebrows wriggled across his forehead like gray caterpillars.

"You think Palmer's shooter did the rabbit, too?"

"Well, it didn't commit suicide, chief." She managed to keep her disdain out of her voice, but just barely. This guy was a joke.

"Good point. Hunt, go tell one of the forensic dweebs to check out the rabbit before the hawks turn it into dinner, eh?"

Officer Hunt huffed off.

The chief squinted at Aroostine.

"What kind of lawyer did you say you were?"

"I didn't. But I'm the kind of lawyer who's on a romantic getaway with her husband. Why?"

He looked from Aroostine to Joe and then back at her. "That was some detailed knowledge of ballistics for a civilian."

He waited.

Maybe he wasn't such a joke after all. She glanced at Joe, but he gave her an innocent look as if to say, "you got yourself into it, you can get out of it."

"Well, I have prosecuted some crimes back home. And I watch CSI, of course." She smiled, willing him to laugh. Better to let him think she was ditz than to reveal that Isaac Palmer may have been killed because he was cooperating with a federal investigation of crimes committed on the chief's turf.

The short burst that came exploding from his throat might have been a chuckle, but it was devoid of actual humor.

"Let me assure you, there's nothing quite so exciting as an episode of CSI happening here, ma'am. This is a small, if sprawling, community. We're just a big extended family. This kind of violence is rare. And I'm sure there's an explanation." He dug into his pocket and pulled out two card stock tickets. "Now, we thank you for your good citizenship. And on behalf of the police force, we'd like to invite you to head up to the casino for dinner—our treat. The steak house is one of the best in the state."

He extended the tickets. She hesitated. Was the chief of police trying to buy her off with a steak dinner? Or was this just typical resort-style public relations? After all, it wouldn't do for a tourist's only exposure to the reservation to be stumbling on a murder scene.

Beside her, Joe shrugged. She knew he was thinking that they'd missed their reservation and they had to eat somewhere. As if to punctuate the point, his stomach growled loudly.

"Okay, I guess. Um, thank you." She plucked the tickets from the police chief's hand.

Joe watched his wife devour her petit filet as if she hadn't eaten in a week.

"Maybe you should have gone for the New York strip," he observed.

She paused and swallowed then reached for her water glass before answering. "Don't judge."

He smiled and sipped his wine.

"I'm not. I'm just kind of surprised you have an appetite—much less one for rare meat—after what happened today."

She rested her fork and knife on the plate and leaned forward, resting her arms on the black linen tablecloth.

"I know, right? I think I burned a lot of nervous energy or something. I'm famished. But every time I think of that poor man . . ." She trailed off. Her dark eyes threatened to turn liquid.

Crap. He wasn't trying to make her cry.

"Hey, hey. Don't think about that. You need to eat. I was just teasing you." He kept his tone light and looked around the bustling restaurant.

Between the clank of glasses, the chatter of diners, and the din of ringing machines, shouts of despair, and whoops of joy that drifted up from the casino floor below, no one was paying the slightest bit of attention to them or their conversation.

"Yeah," she agreed. But the fork and knife stayed on the plate. She was quiet for a moment, then she gave him a searching look. "Don't you think it's weird that none of Palmer's neighbors came by or even popped a head out to see what all the commotion was?"

Yes, he did. But there was no way he was going to admit that and wind her up. He knew her too well. The last thing he wanted to do was increase her interest in the murder. They needed to eat their steak, tip their waitress, and get off the freaking reservation before she got sucked into the case. This was their vacation, not an opportunity for her to prove her mettle to that jerk Slater.

She was staring into his eyes, expectantly waiting for an answer.

He scratched the side of his neck and jammed a large forkful of potatoes into his mouth to buy some time.

"Mmm . . . maybe a little? But Chief Johnson's glad-handing aside, you don't know what kind of community this is. Not every place is as neighborly as Walnut Bottom, Pennsylvania, Roo. When you were staying in DC, do you think your neighbors would have stuck their noses into a criminal investigation?"

She twisted her mouth into an aggravated little bow. "That's not the same thing."

"Why not?"

"For one thing, nobody's *from* DC. Virtually everyone's a transplant from somewhere else. But nobody lives on a reservation unless they were born there. This place ought to be close-knit. Even if Isaac Palmer's neighbors hated his guts and are having a party right now, they should have been snooping around the scene to see what was going on. That's just the way it works."

He bit down on his lower lip to keep from reminding her that she wasn't exactly the expert on Native American reservations she was pretending to be. For one thing, her tribe didn't even *have* an

officially recognized reservation back home—just a sad little cluster of falling-down shacks. For another, she'd left that life behind
when she was just a kid. She'd grown up in a white-bread community no different from him. Her adoptive parents probably would
have gone out and offered the investigating police officer lemon-
ade if a crime had happened in her neighborhood, but the crime
in question would more likely have been a case of a house being
egged or some kids stealing a case of beer out of a neighbor's garage
than an execution-style murder. But he figured saying as much
would hardly be prudent. And prudence and marriage were two
great tastes together.

"What?" she demanded.

"Nothing. I don't know anything about this place. And neither
do you. What I do know is there's chocolate decadence cake on the
menu. Let's get some dessert and get back to our own hotel, get back
to the point of this trip. What do you say?"

She shook her head and smiled. Chocolate cake was her weakness—shoot, it was more like her Kryptonite.

"I'm onto you, Joe Jackman."

"Is that a promise? Because I'd sure like to have you on me . . ."
He trailed off.

A faint blush crept over her cheeks and she lowered her eyes.

"We'll see. But cake first."

He raised his glass to that.

Joe headed to the parking garage to fetch the Jeep while Aroostine
used the ladies' room. After wending her way through the casino
floor and getting turned around multiple times, she finally managed
to find the cashier's cage and then found a route to the exit and the
valet stand from there.

She was sober and had not been gambling; and yet, her brief travels through the casino had left her feeling overstimulated, dazed, and wrung out. *Or it could be the whole finding-a-dead-body part. Right.*

She tripped out into the foyer and blinked into the obnoxiously bright fluorescent light.

"Can I get your car?" the valet asked. His white smile was nearly as blinding as the lights.

"Oh, no, thanks. We self-parked."

She spotted a bench near the bushes lining the entryway. She plopped down and eased her feet out of her dress pumps, flexed her toes, and was jamming them back inside when a little voice squeaked, "What's the password?"

She started and scanned her immediate surroundings. Saw no one. She must have been tireder than she realized if she was having auditory hallucinations.

"Password," the childlike voice demanded again.

It was coming from the fragrant, flowering bushes behind her. She leaned over the back of the bench and peered down into the shrubbery.

A glitter-dusted face stared up at her. Big brown eyes, pinchable cheeks, and a tangle of wild dark hair, crowned with a wreath of flowers and ribbon completed the picture. Aroostine took in the fairy wings strapped to the girl's back and the wand she waved regally in her right hand.

"Pixie dust?" she ventured.

The girl shook her head solemnly. "Sorry."

"Magic?"

"Nope. You get one more try."

Aroostine considered her next guess.

"Love?"

The fairy girl popped to her feet.

"Close. But it's moon glow."

"Of course," Aroostine said. She tried to keep a straight face, but the girl was so adorable it was ridiculous.

The girl appraised her.

"I've never seen you before."

"No, you haven't," Aroostine agreed.

"I know. I know everybody who lives on the reservation. And the tourists are usually . . . white. Where do you live?"

"I'm from Pennsylvania. It's pretty far away."

"I know. It's near New York, right?" the girl said proudly.

"Yep."

"You're Native, though. Like me," the girl observed.

"Right again. My name's Aroostine." She smiled at the girl.

"I'm Lily." The girl stuck out her free hand and Aroostine took her small palm in her hand and gave it a shake.

"It's nice to meet you, Lily."

"Thanks. My name's a flower. My mom's is a jewel. What does yours mean?"

"It means sparkling water."

"That's pretty."

"So is Lily," she told the girl. Then she asked, "What are you doing in the bushes? Looking for fairy houses?"

The girl shook her head. Her eyes were big and serious. "Waiting for my mom. She works inside."

Aroostine tried to keep her judgment off her face. Maybe childcare was hard to come by on the reservation, but surely there was a safer place for the girl to spend her time than crouching in the bushes outside the casino.

"Do you always wait for her out here?"

The girl answered with a quick shake of her head, tossing her hair over her face. "Oh, no. Usually I stay at our place. I do my homework and get ready for bed. Mom works pretty late some nights. Most of the time we have dinner together and then I see her in the morning."

Latchkey kid.

Aroostine flashed back to a very long time ago, before the Higginses adopted her. A memory of warming a plate her grandfather had left for her in the oven while he was at a tribal council meeting. Eating alone and crawling into bed and listening to the wind blow outside the window. She blinked away the memory.

"So what are you doing out here, then?" she asked.

"Mom said it isn't safe to be home alone tonight."

News of the murder must be making the rounds, if the girl's mother thought she was safer hanging around the casino than tucked in her bed.

Headlights arced over her, and then Joe slowed the maroon Jeep to a stop near the bench.

"Well, I have to go, Lily. It was nice to meet you."

"Good-bye, Aroostine. Have fun in Pennsylvania."

The way the girl said "Pennsylvania," as if it were the most glamorous location imaginable, made Aroostine's heart squeeze in her chest.

She turned as she slid into the passenger side of the car and said, "Moon glow."

She could hear the girl's excited giggling as she closed the door.

They drove in companionable silence for several minutes, winding their way down the lushly landscaped hills that separated the resort from the rest of the reservation. Aroostine couldn't shake Lily from her mind.

"Pull over, okay?"

Joe gave her a curious look but edged the Jeep to the side of the road. He put the vehicle in park and turned on his blinkers.

"Too much cake?"

"Nothing like that."

She unbelted her seat belt and turned to face him full on. She inhaled deeply then exhaled.

"Uh-oh, you're gearing yourself up for a big pronouncement. I can tell."

She ignored the commentary. "Joe, I don't want to go back to our hotel."

"Okay? What do you have in mind? I'm game for a late night of carousing if you are."

"No, nothing like that."

"Well, what then?"

She gnawed on her lower lip and considered what she was about to say. Was she sure about this?

Palmer and his blank, staring eyes. The long-eared rabbit, lying supine in the field. The uninterested police response. Lily's small face, so somber even with all her fairy finery surrounding her in a cloud of glitter.

"I want to stay here and get to the bottom of Isaac Palmer's murder. I *have* to, Joe."

She braced herself for his reaction.

He just sat there, unmoving and staring out into the dark night. Finally, he turned the key and switched off the engine. He checked for cars and then opened his door.

She got out the passenger side.

He headed around the car, head down, and started toward a gravel path near the side of the road. She jogged after him.

"Joe? Where are you going?"

He looked over his shoulder and pinned her with a look that tore at her heart. His face was a study of anguish.

"I need a minute. I don't want to say anything I'll regret. Things have been so good between us. I'm trying not to screw this up. Please. Just go back to the car. I want to clear my head," he nearly pleaded.

"Wait, please. I have to tell you this—it's important. This isn't about Sid or getting back in good graces at Main Justice. This is about me, something I have to do to be at peace with myself." As she said the words, she was thinking of the little girl with fairy wings hiding in the bushes.

He shot her a look that she couldn't read but nodded. "I hear you."

He turned back to the dark path and walked into the woods.

CHAPTER SIX

Joe clenched and relaxed his fists as he trudged along the dark trail. *Clench, relax. Clench, relax.*

His thumping heart and the sweat beading at his hairline were signs either that his body recognized that his nighttime promenade through a strange field was ill-advised or that his anger at Aroostine was bubbling to the surface despite his efforts to quell it. Or maybe both.

He stomped farther along the path and paused near a copse of trees. He glanced back. He didn't see Aroostine's tall, lean figure near the road. He blinked in surprise that she apparently had done as he'd asked and gone back to the car. Not so long ago, she would have pushed the issue and followed him. But not anymore.

He leaned against a tree trunk and focused on slowing his breathing.

It's progress that she's consulting you, asking for your input, he chided himself.

It was true. Ever since she'd returned from DC, she'd been close-lipped—even for her. She was warm and attentive when they were together, but she didn't ask what he thought about anything that didn't involve their shared home life.

Switching Rufus' brand of food? She'd engage in a heartfelt discussion.

Agreeing to the assignment at the US Attorney's Office in Johnstown? She hadn't even mentioned her new position until she'd been working there for almost a week.

And that was the way it had been with everything. If it involved their marriage, their home, or their families, they were a team. If it related to her career, he was persona non grata.

He understood. How could he not? She'd asked him to support her when she'd moved to Washington, DC, for her big break, and he'd agreed. But when the time came to actually put the pieces of his life in the tidy white rows of Bankers Boxes she'd assembled for him, he couldn't do it.

He couldn't leave the farmhouse they'd restored together, room by room, over the early months and years of their marriage.

He couldn't leave his workshop with the table where he'd sanded and carved and shaped planks and doors and boards into their new lives. Every design choice was stuffed full of memories, from the dry sink she'd found at a flea market to the wall sconces he'd rewired to mount on either side of the fireplace mantle. He couldn't leave the creek that ran behind their place, the meadow where they'd said their vows, the diner where they had breakfast on lazy Saturdays. He was paralyzed with grief every time he contemplated those blasted moving boxes, staring up at him empty and reproachful.

Meanwhile, she'd been sitting in a sterile, mostly unfurnished condo, waiting for him to do what he'd promised and come to be with her. Instead, he'd stopped returning her calls then served her with divorce papers.

Stop beating yourself up; look to the future, not the past. He repeated the words she'd said to him so often in the early days after they'd reconciled. And to their shared credit, they had forged forward together, leaving the past behind them, where it belonged. This trip was part of their new life together, a chance to make new memories to replace the ones they'd rather not dredge up.

But now she was going to go off on a mission. He'd known this was coming. He'd seen the excited glint in her eye when she got in the car.

The hill he'd been huffing up crested, and he stood for a minute and surveyed the dark outline of the mountains, the tall trees bending in the wind, and the stillness of the air. The quiet was pierced by a shrill birdcall. Joe started at the sound. Then a dark shape swooped overhead, low and close. He ducked, stumbled backward, and nearly lost his footing.

"A bird must fly."

The voice came from the clearing to the right and scared him worse than the bird had. He grabbed a tree trunk to avoid tumbling off the ridge.

A man stepped out of the dark, holding a lantern.

"Didn't mean to startle you," he said, a smile creasing his tanned, lined face.

Joe examined the man's face in the light dancing from the lantern. He looked to be in his midsixties or so. Long white hair, parted and braided into two neat plaits, hung over his shoulders.

"Uh, no worries, " Joe lied. It was clear the man was a Native American and presumably a local. But it wasn't at all clear why he was traipsing around in the dark while a murderer was on the loose.

The man extended his right hand. "I'm Matthew Cowslip. Everyone calls me Boom."

Joe wiped his sweaty palm on his slacks and then shook Boom's proffered hand.

"Joe Jackman."

"I know."

Joe cocked his head and narrowed his eyes. The hairs on his arms stood up. *Was this an ambush?* The notion never would have occurred to him a year earlier, but being targeted and drugged by a prostitute in a bar, spirited to a remote cabin, and held hostage by a homicidal Eastern European gangster tended to make a guy suspicious of overly friendly strangers.

"You do?"

"Sure. You're with Aroostine Higgins, correct?"

"I'm her husband," he said in a half growl, his worry mounting. He didn't know which direction the man had come from. What if he'd already encountered Aroostine at the car? What if he'd hurt her . . . or worse? He clenched his fists at his side.

"Of course. Ms. Higgins called in the report of the tragic death of one of our young people, Isaac Palmer." Boom gave a sad shake of his head at the mention of Palmer's death but kept his face open and friendly, as if to reassure Joe that he meant no harm.

"Are you with the tribal police?"

"No, no. But I'm an elder and a member of the cultural board. We'll be working closely with the police."

"How?"

"Community patrols, encouraging people to talk if they saw something, that sort of thing." Boom's eyes narrowed and his voice took on a pained note. "And, of course, helping to ensure our guests feel safe."

"Your guests?"

"The white fat cats who want to tour our grounds, gamble away their money in our casinos, and enjoy some overpriced alcohol and meals while they're at it. It wouldn't do for our profits to dip if they get scared off by the death of one expendable Indian." Anger clouded his face for the briefest moment. And then he smoothed it away with a too-bright grin. "Which reminds me, did you enjoy your dinner?"

"Price was right," Joe joked. Boom's mercurial mood shifts were making him uneasy. And humor was Joe's fallback when he was uncomfortable. He wanted to get out of the woods and back to his wife.

Boom laughed and clasped Joe's shoulder with his free hand. "Very good."

"Well, Mr. Cowslip—"

"Please. It's Boom."

"Okay, Boom. I need to get back to Aroostine. She's waiting in the car. I just had to . . ."

Joe didn't intend to tell this guy he just had to get away from his wife before he said something he regretted. Before he could come up with a plausible lie, Boom supplied one.

"Relieve yourself?"

"Yeah, right. Nature called."

"Hmm. Well, yes, hurry back to the missus."

"Nice meeting you," Joe said as he turned to head back down the trail.

"Do you know what happens when you clip a bird's wings?"

Joe turned back, disconcerted by the odd question. "No."

Boom turned the lamp in his hand toward himself. He looked exactly like a ghoulish jack-o'-lantern.

"It doesn't have a way to cope with flightlessness. It becomes irritable, meek, anxious, and fearful."

"Oh-kay." Joe started backing away.

"I hope you and your strong, brave wife will stay on the reservation for a few days."

"Why's that?" Joe wondered where he was headed with this sudden change in topics.

"We need her help. We need an outsider who understands our ways and traditions and can also navigate the federal issues that Isaac's death will certainly stir up."

"What federal issues would those be?"

As far as he knew, Aroostine had honored Sid's request not to mention the potential embezzlement charges to anyone on the reservation. And he couldn't help wondering how Boom knew his wife's heritage. Did word spread that fast? Or was Boom more connected than he was letting on?

"I'm sure you know as well as I do that Isaac found evidence of embezzlement at the casino."

Joe stared at him. "I'm not sure I know what you're talking about," he lied.

"I doubt that very much. Your wife didn't make the trip out here to talk to Isaac about the weather. Don't worry, it's not common knowledge. But as a member of the cultural board, I have to have my finger on these issues."

"Right. It wouldn't do for your guests to get the wrong impression."

"Or the right impression, as the case may be. But in this instance, I think my people have a serious problem." Boom's voice was grim.

"Oh?" Joe said reluctantly. Joe wasn't at all sure what Boom was up to but his desire to end the weird conversation and go find his wife was becoming urgent.

"A fish rots from the head, Mr. Jackman. I'm convinced the information Isaac uncovered traces directly back to Lee Buckmount." Boom dropped this bombshell with a triumphant note in his voice.

It was clear from the way Boom emphasized the name that he expected a reaction. He was going to be sorely disappointed.

"Who?"

Boom sighed. "Right, why would you know? Mr. Buckmount is our chief financial officer."

"There's a tribe CFO?"

"Technically, he's the CFO of the tribe-owned corporation that operates the casino and resort, but that's just a nicety. He is, in reality, basically the CFO of the three tribes who form the reservation, yes."

"And you think he killed Isaac Palmer?" he ventured, not at all sure why Boom would be sharing his theories with a stranger in the woods. Unless their encounter wasn't random.

"I didn't say that. I think Isaac Palmer's death is related to Mr. Buckmount's activities."

"You sound like a lawyer. What activities would those be?"

Boom shook his head, his braids whacking against his neck.

"I'm not sure. Possibly drug activities. I've thought for a while he's had a problem, but I'm not sure. That's why I need your wife's help."

Joe stiffened at the thought of Aroostine wading into a scandal involving tribal politics ugly enough to result in murder. "I'm not sure why you think Aroostine can help you."

"Because our community is small and insular. And because the outside views us with disdain and suspicion. But she understands our ways—and yours. Please. Mr. Jackman, let her do what's in her heart."

Boom's timbre was pleading and sincere. But Joe was just creeped out. It was like the guy had installed a listening device in the car or something. How could he possibly know what was in Aroostine's heart?

"Um—"

"Just spend the night. The cultural board maintains an authentic home we offer to rich, white philanthropists who want to get the flavor of life on the res. You're welcome to it. Stay, watch the sun rise over the majestic mountains and enjoy some of our cook Selena's hand-ground cornmeal cakes for breakfast. You'll be my guest. If you still want to go back to your luxury resort after experiencing all of that, well, then go right ahead."

For a possibly demented old guy, Boom sure was a masterful salesman.

"Well . . ."

"Talk to your wife. See what she says. If you want to stay, I'll see you at the guest cottage. It's just two doors down from Isaac's house."

Joe left the man standing in the clearing and hurried along the trail back to the road. A jumble of thoughts whirled through his mind as he tripped over rocks and roots. Boom's comments about drugs, crime, and profit on the reservation were background noise. Joe kept coming back to the cryptic remarks about clipping a bird's wings. He couldn't be responsible for grounding his wife, flightless and listless. He had to let her fulfill her purpose.

A bird must fly.

He quickened his pace as the ground flattened, running back to her.

<hr />

Aroostine milled around the car for a moment after Joe stalked off. She had no intention of getting back in the Jeep just because he'd told her to. At least he hadn't said "I told you so," in response to her announcement. That was progress of a sort.

Slipping into the passenger seat held some appeal. She was tired. No, she was more than tired. She was drained. She'd started her day with a sunrise hike and ended it by finding a murder victim. Closing her eyes and leaning back against the headrest sounded like a much better way to wait out Joe's fit or tantrum, or whatever he was doing, than pacing back and forth.

She settled into the seat, slowed her breathing, and tried to wipe the image of Isaac Palmer from her mind. She might have succeeded—she might even have caught a quick cat nap—if it hadn't been for a car that pulled up alongside the Jeep, idled for a moment, and then eventually parked, leaving its headlights on. Her eyes snapped open. She blinked into the light and squinted to make out a figure moving toward her car. She tensed and hit the door locks.

Tap, tap, tap. The person was rapping on the passenger side window. A concerned woman peered in at her with wide, heavily made-up eyes.

"Are you okay?" the woman shouted.

She nodded yes, but the woman's forehead was still crinkled with worry, so she gestured for the Good Samaritan to move back so she could open the car door. She unlocked the door, stepped out into the cool night air, and smiled reassuringly at the woman.

"I'm fine. Thanks for stopping to check on me."

"Sure, okay." The woman pulled her jacket closer around her body.

Aroostine noticed she was wearing a sequined leotard under it. Gray yoga pants and flip flops completed the outfit. She examined the woman's face more closely. Thick eyeliner, lots of blush, and bright red lipstick couldn't hide her tired pallor.

"Are you a cocktail waitress up at the casino?" she asked. It was the only explanation for the attire.

"Yeah. Ruby Smith." The woman stuck out her right hand to shake and her coat fell open.

Aroostine took her extended hand. "Aroostine Higgins."

"Are you having car trouble or something?" Ruby jerked her head toward the Jeep's engine.

"No, nothing like that. I'm just waiting for my husband." *While he stomps around in the woods or communes with nature or whatever he's doing.*

Ruby cocked her head and glanced over at her car.

"Uh, okay. Listen, I don't know if you're from around here or what, but a guy was killed tonight. It's probably not safe to just be hanging out on the side of the road, you know?"

So word of the murder was getting around.

"No, I'm not from here. I'm sorry to hear about the death." She considered Ruby's tense face. "Were you . . . close to him?"

"Not like that. He lived next door to me. He was a completely harmless, nice guy, and he took a bullet right between the eyes . . ." Ruby trailed off and took a long, shaky breath. Then she frowned and gestured toward her own car, moving her hand in a downward motion,

"I can see how that would be disturbing—" Aroostine began, then she turned to look where Ruby was gesturing and stopped midsentence.

A tiny face was pressed up against the rear passenger side window, grinning. Its owner waved excitedly at her.

The pieces began to fall into place. She turned back to Ruby.

"You're Lily's mom?"

"How do you know Lily?" Ruby's voice was raw with suspicion.

"I met her when I was leaving the steak house. She was playing fairy in the bushes while she waited for you," Aroostine hurried to explain.

Ruby's posture softened just a bit.

"Oh, okay," she said with a nod. Then her eyes widened and her voice shook. "I don't usually bring her up to the casino. I just . . . I didn't know what else to do."

A twinge of guilt ran through Aroostine for her earlier judgment of the woman. "First of all, you don't owe me any explanations. Second of all, I'd say you did the right thing. Your next-door neighbor was murdered. You couldn't very well leave her home alone after that."

Ruby gulped down air and nodded again. "Yeah."

Ruby's rear car door opened slowly.

"Lily Lotus Smith, don't you dare!"

The door closed. Lily made a sad face out the window.

Aroostine tried not to laugh.

"She seems like a great kid," she told Ruby.

"She is. She's so smart and hardly gives me any trouble. She's a little bit flighty, though. Always living in her make-believe world." Ruby paused for a moment. "I think it's her way of dealing with living on the reservation. She pretends she's in some faraway land or something to escape."

Aroostine thought of another little girl who used to pretend she lived on the moon, under the sea, anywhere but where she really lived—a place of limited opportunity but no end of misery.

"That's normal. She's just creative."

Ruby gave her a sidelong glance, as if she knew she was receiving parenting advice from the childless. "She's got to keep her head on straight. That was one reason I liked her spending time with Isaac. He . . . he made something of himself. He got a degree, had a good job. I thought it would show her that it wasn't a fantasy—a better life was a real possibility for her, even if she never got off the res . . ." Ruby choked back tears.

Aroostine gnawed her lower lip. She had no idea what to say to comfort the woman. She was obviously shaken up enough to be confiding in a complete stranger who she met on the side of the road. Before she had the chance to frame a response, Ruby wiped her eyes with the back of her hand, smearing mascara and eyeliner across her face, and sniffled.

"Sorry. I don't know what came over me." She straightened her back like a woman who was used to doing hard things and pushing back fear and doubt.

"Please, don't be," Aroostine said. Then she plunged in, unwilling to let the opening pass. "You know, I found him."

Ruby blinked. "Found him—Isaac?"

"Yes."

"Are you a friend of his or something?"

"Not exactly."

Ruby eyeballed her. "Then who are you, *exactly*?"

Aroostine exhaled slowly. If she was going to stick around and try to get to the bottom of Isaac Palmer's death, she'd need an ally. And, so far, the cocktail waitress seemed like the most viable candidate, if only because she was actually willing to speak to Aroostine. Her inner lawyer took over and blurted out the words before she could second-guess herself. "I'm an attorney with the Department of Justice. Do you know any reason why someone would want to kill Isaac? You said he was well liked."

Ruby stepped back as if putting physical space between them would shut down the line of questioning. "I think what I said was he was harmless. And he was—he was just a numbers cruncher for the casino."

Ruby's words were neutral, but her tone was saying *I know more about this than I'm letting on.* Aroostine decided to push her, just a little.

"So in his position he had access to the casino's financial information, bank accounts, and a lot of money, right?"

The other woman shrugged and glanced over to check on her daughter again. "I guess. I wouldn't know. In *my* position, I have access to the casino's watered-down rail drinks and domestic bottles."

Wrong approach. Aroostine dropped the all-business lawyer act and appealed to the mother standing in front of her.

"Ruby, listen, you don't know me and I don't know you. I get that. But I can tell you're a good person."

"Oh, yeah, can you read minds?"

"No. But I can interpret what I see. You stopped on a dark, rarely traveled road to check on me. You didn't have to do that. You're worried about your daughter's future. A daughter who, by the way, is delightful. So I can tell you're doing a good job raising her on your own. And you're upset about Isaac's death, which is more than I can say about your tribal police. I don't need to be a mind reader to know that you're a good person. I want to find out who murdered your friend and why. Help me."

Ruby's eyes flitted to her car again. Lily had abandoned her window vigil and was waving her wand around the backseat, probably casting some sort of spell. She watched her daughter for a moment and then glanced back at Aroostine with a hard expression, like she'd made a decision.

"You have to keep my name out of it."

"I will."

"I need your word. I have Lily to worry about." She said her daughter's name with heavy emphasis, driving home the point that Aroostine's promise wasn't for her benefit, but for the girl's.

"I understand. You have my word."

They regarded one another for a silent moment that seemed to stretch endlessly into the night. Ruby gave a small nod, like she'd seen something in Aroostine's face that satisfied her.

"Okay. Isaac said someone was siphoning off money from the casino."

"He told you this?"

"Yeah. A couple weeks ago, I ran into him when I was going to pick up my paycheck. He was all excited about it."

"Do you know who else he might have told?"

The woman shook her head fiercely, swinging her high-combed hair wildly around her head. "No one. No way he would have told anyone else."

"But he told you."

"Right. And I told him that running around saying things like that was a great way to get himself killed. Looks like I was right, too." Her voice cracked.

Aroostine stopped herself from pointing out that if Isaac really hadn't told anyone other than Ruby then she was going to find herself the principal suspect in a murder investigation. "How can you be so sure, though, that he didn't confide in someone else?"

"I think I really scared him when I said that. He started to get paranoid, fearful of everything. I just know he wouldn't have. Plus, who else would he tell?"

"I have no idea. Why'd he tell you? That seems like an odd thing to share with a neighbor."

Ruby pursed her lips and grappled with how to respond. She let out a small sigh. "Isaac had a crush on me, okay? He was trying to impress me. I liked him, I liked how he was with Lily, but I didn't feel that way about him. So I acted like I didn't know about his feelings, even though they were pretty obvious. But he wouldn't have told anyone else. I know it."

"Okay. Understood. Did he tell you any details—how he found out about the embezzlement, who he thought might be behind it, anything?"

Another pause and another breath. Then Ruby said, "Yeah. I'd gotten angry with him about the whole mess and told him not to talk to me about it. Then, about a week ago, Lily was at his house— he was teaching her how to play chess. I went over to pick her up, and I could tell something was wrong, you know? He had this real tight expression on his face. He was a million miles away even though he was laughing at Lily's jokes or whatever. I was worried about him. So after I put her to bed, I walked back over and invited him to my place for a drink."

"And?"

"And he got drunk, sloppy, because he's not—wasn't—a big drinker. And he started running me this wild story about how he thought the stolen money was somehow related to the missing drones."

Aroostine tried to make sense of the words Ruby was saying, but it was as if the other woman were speaking some language other than English.

"I'm sorry, did you say drones?"

Ruby stared at her, disbelief and panic flooding her face.

"You mean Washington doesn't know?"

"Know what?"

"I can't believe they haven't noticed. Listen, I have to get Lily to bed. Come to my house in the morning and I'll tell you all about the military drones that have disappeared from the testing facility here." She started back to her car and her sleepy daughter.

"Wait. Which side of Isaac's house?"

"I live to the left as you're looking at the houses. Lily leaves for school at seven thirty. Come any time after that." Ruby looked at Aroostine over her shoulder and then shook her head. "You really didn't know?"

"About the missing drones? No."

Ruby shook her head again as she slid behind the wheel of her late-model Buick and started the ignition.

Aroostine stood motionless beside the Jeep processing the news that Ruby had just dropped on her. *Missing military drones?*

CHAPTER SEVEN

Joe parked the Jeep two houses to the right of Isaac's front door, with its bright yellow X of crime scene tape. Aroostine made out the silhouette of Ruby's Buick parked in front of the house to the left of Isaac's. Her house was still and dark. Aroostine imagined her sitting on the edge of Lily's bed telling her a story as she smoothed the girl's hair over her pillow.

"Now what?" she asked Joe.

She hadn't fully understood his change of heart—something about a bird and a man named Boom, but he'd come out of the woods with a lead on accommodations for the night and a desire to stay—so she wasn't complaining.

"Uh, I'm guessing it's unlocked," he said defensively.

She arched a brow at that, but the response forming on her tongue melted away when she noticed the sky. "Look up," she breathed.

It was as if someone had thrown a blanket of stars over the earth. Small pinpoints of light stretched overhead, almost dizzying in number and brightness. No moon, no clouds. Just stars, some clustered close together in the black sky and others sprinkled farther apart.

"Whoa."

He reached for her hand, and they stood together in silence—their breathing the only sound—and drank in the sight. Then as if by unspoken agreement, they walked across the road to the meadow where just hours earlier she'd found the dead jackrabbit. They settled on the fallen log, and she leaned back against his warm chest and tipped her face to the galaxies, planets, and constellations swirling above them.

After a long silence, he said, "That Boom guy knew about the embezzlement."

She wanted to pretend she hadn't heard him and just keep basking in the majesty of the night sky, but another person who had information about the funds being siphoned was exactly the sort of thing she needed to chase down. So, with no small measure of reluctance, she shifted her weight and tore her eyes away from the sky to look at her husband.

"He did?"

"Yeah. He said it wasn't public knowledge, but I don't know, Roo. He thinks this thing goes all the way to the top. He made a lot of noise about some Lee Buckmount guy, who's the CFO of the casino, being involved. This could be a real hornet's nest."

She digested that news then weighed telling him about the drones. Her deliberation lasted all of about twenty seconds. She had to tell someone, and she sure couldn't call Sid, not at this hour, and not until she got the full story from Ruby.

"You're telling me. Do you know anything about a military drone testing facility around here?"

He'd been the one to pick Central Oregon as a destination and appeared to have digested whole travel guides, which he'd been regurgitating in bits at seemingly random intervals through the trip. She wasn't convinced a drone testing facility was likely to appear on any lists of can't-miss local attractions, but judging by the way he leaned forward eagerly, he'd heard something about them.

"Sure. It's actually right here on the reservation."

"Shouldn't it be on a military base?" Ever since Ruby had mentioned the testing facility, she'd been puzzling over what possible connection it could have to the White Springs Reservation or any of the tribes living there. Weren't military drones the sort of top-secret weaponry that the Defense Department would eagerly classify as a national security secret? Why would they plop a testing facility onto a residential area that also served as a major tourist destination?

Joe answered quickly, as if he were pleased to know the answer to the question. "Well the original plan was to use the facility for civilian drones."

"Civilian drones? Why do civilians need drones?"

Joe gave her a blank look. "Where've you been? Civilians need drones to take aerial photographs of their vacation homes and to follow their kids to the bus stop and to spy on their ex-wives—and someday to drop their packages of socks and dog toys on their front porches."

She arched a brow. "What in the—never mind. Okay but civilian drones are presumably unarmed, right?"

He shrugged and thought a moment before answering. "I guess, unless you count cameras and surveillance equipment."

"But no weapons, not like the ones that operators in Omaha or wherever control to drop bombs on targets in the Middle East?"

"Right."

"So there's a big difference between testing a flying camera in a populated area and testing unmanned weapons. How'd they get from the first one to the second?"

Back on surer ground, Joe sped up again. "Conservation of resources. The military bases out in Pendleton and Redmond can test the weaponry—make sure the bombs work when they're supposed to—but the politicians decided it was wasteful and redundant to have to continue to maintain its own flight testing capabilities when there was a shiny new civilian one right here. So they entered into a contract with the White Springs Reservation to use the testing facility when the Federal Aviation Administration and the corporate manufacturers weren't using it."

"This was all in a travel guidebook?"

"No, but it was news back when I was researching the area last spring. All of the official Central Oregon websites were making a big deal of the partnership. An innovative partnership between a Native American tribe and the military that would create jobs on the reservation and save the federal government loads of money—what's not to love?"

"Maybe the fact that the military drones have gone missing?"

In the dark, Joe's face was shadowy, illuminated only by starlight, but she could see the shock roll across his expression like a wave—starting at his eyes and moving down until he opened and closed his mouth, gaping like a fish.

"Are you serious?" he asked.

"Maybe. We'll find out more in the morning."

"Why wait?"

"Because Sid's not going to be happy if I wake him to run it down and it turns out to be a baseless rumor," she said.

They sat in silence some more, but this time the power of the night sky was lost on Aroostine. Judging by the way he was fidgeting, Joe was also focusing on something other than the constellations overhead.

He cleared his throat and pulled her closer to him. "I think we may be mixed up in something bad."

The way he said "we" made her catch her breath. She hadn't expected quite so much support. But his point was, unfortunately, valid. "There's no maybe about it."

They lapsed back into silence—not a companionable, awed silence. A tired, overwhelmed, "what now?" silence.

***

They crossed the shadowy road and headed for the guest cottage.

Aroostine didn't need to check her watch to know that it had to be close to midnight. Her fatigue outweighed the horror of the day and the puzzling scraps of information floating in her mind. She ached to crawl into bed, pile the covers over her, and snuggle into the warmth of Joe's body. She'd worry about murderers, and dirty CFOs, and missing drones in the morning. From the silent way Joe trudged along beside her, she sensed he felt the same way.

As they neared the Jeep, a rustling sound startled her out of her tired musings. She reached out a hand to stop Joe, but he'd already frozen in place.

"Did you hear that?" he whispered.

"It's probably an animal."

Of course, out here, it was as likely to be a coyote or a wolf as it was a rabbit or a mouse. Still, she'd take her chances against a wolf over, say, Isaac's killer, any day.

Her dry mouth and racing pulse were making it hard to breathe.

"Who's there?" Joe called. His hand vibrated in hers, pulsing with anxiety and adrenaline, but his voice rang out clear, loud, and true in the darkness.

After a moment, a shape emerged from behind the vehicle. A flashlight clicked on in the figure's hand. He aimed the circle of light at the ground rather than their faces.

"Mr. Jackman? Ms. Higgins? Is that you? I didn't mean to frighten you folks. I'm Lee Buckmount. I'm one of the tribal leaders."

Lee Buckmount, alleged drug addict and potential mastermind behind Isaac's death and the possible disappearance of military drones, was skulking around their car in the dark. Great.

"Can we help you?" Joe said in a hard, cold voice that suggested his internal monologue was about the same as hers.

"Oh, I don't need any help. I'm just glad *you* don't. Boom mentioned you folks might be spending the night at our guest house, so I stopped by to make sure you found everything okay. When no one answered the door, I got a little worried, so I was checking your car to see if you were in there."

In the weak light, Aroostine could make out a distinguished faced, silver hair, and little else. He was neither tall nor short, thin nor fat.

"We didn't hear a car pull up." She scanned the road for a new vehicle but saw none.

"I walked."

"We were stargazing, so we haven't been inside yet," Joe explained.

"While our night sky does put on quite a display, I'm not sure that this is the safest time to go wandering around the reservation in the dark."

"You mean because you've got a murderer on the loose? So you think Isaac was killed by someone from the community?" Aroostine asked. She wanted to push Buckmount a little—just enough to see if she could raise a reaction.

"I'm not saying that at all, actually. Let's get you folks inside, huh? We can talk in there."

Joe gave her a look as if to say "what next?" before he followed Buckmount through the unlocked front door and into the empty house.

She trailed behind them, pausing to peer at the Jeep to confirm that the doors were still locked. Buckmount's sudden appearance put her on edge. She wondered why Joe's new friend Boom, who seemed to think Buckmount was involved in the murder, would have told him they were spending the night

She stepped across the threshold into the small front room. Buckmount was leading Joe from room to room, switching on lights and pointing out where they could find towels, soaps, and extra blankets.

She blinked while her eyes adjusted then looked around. The interior was about the size of Isaac's place but it had been carefully decorated. Native pottery, quilts, and feathered decorations were arranged throughout the clean, freshly painted home. The wood floors gleamed, and the faint, lemony scent of cleaning supplies lingered in the air.

Joe and Buckmount returned from the tour of the small space. The older man made a sweeping gesture toward the seating arrangement near the front window. Aroostine took a seat on the small love seat, covered in fabric the color of red clay. Joe sat beside her, close enough that their thighs touched, and leaned forward slightly, as if he were trying to shield her from something—or someone.

Buckmount wavered between two chocolate brown armchairs and chose the one closer to the door. "I hope you find the accommodations comfortable. I know they're a far cry from the resort where you're staying."

How'd he know where they were staying? she wondered. *Probably from the police report,* she answered herself. A point that only raised the further question of why the casino's chief financial officer had access to the tribal police's internal records. Her uneasy feeling about the man ratcheted up several notches.

"It's lovely," she finally said, aware that he was waiting for her to respond.

"Yes, it's great—nice and cozy. It's frankly more our style than the luxury resort," Joe agreed.

A proud smile played across Buckmount's face as he waved off the compliments.

"Very good." His face grew serious, and he leaned forward to stare intently at Aroostine. "Now, Aroostine—may I call you Aroostine?"

"Sure, Lee."

He continued, "You asked outside whether I thought Mr. Palmer's murder was an inside job for lack of a better way to characterize it."

"Right."

"I don't. I won't pretend that our people don't have brushes with the law—it would be a lie. We have a high poverty rate and the typical attendant high alcoholism and domestic violence rates—both of which we're working to address internally, with programs aimed specifically at our population, programs that aren't necessarily accepted by the outside. But that's why our self-determination is so important. We know our people and our culture. And I know Isaac wasn't killed by one of our own. Couldn't have been." He nodded firmly as if saying it would make it so.

"How can you be so sure?" she pressed.

A small frown knit across his lips. An instant later it was gone, wiped away by a neutral, open expression, but she saw the anger that sparked for a moment in his eyes. And it scared her.

"That's a fair question. And I'm not going to try to cloud the issue with cultural mumbo jumbo or political doublespeak. I'll answer it fairly—even though doing so will require me to speak ill of the dead."

He paused and dropped his eyes to the gleaming floorboards for a beat before continuing.

"I was Isaac's boss. Not his direct supervisor, of course, but as the CFO of the casino, all of the accounting personnel reported up to me." He pursed his lips for a moment. "I have reason to believe Isaac had a drug problem."

"A drug problem?" Boom had told Joe that he thought *Lee* was doing drugs. What was going on at that casino?

"Yes, sadly. His behavior had become erratic, paranoid. I noticed it not long ago. I had planned to have our casino security staff look into it, but I never had the chance. I'm afraid he may have gotten mixed up with a nasty gang of dealers out of Eugene. I believe his murder was a deal gone bad."

He delivered his theory with absolute confidence and finality. He hadn't shared a shred of evidence to support his story, but he looked at them as though it was an open-and-shut case, as if—through the sheer force of his personality—they would agree.

She had a sinking suspicion that tomorrow's news would lead with Buckmount's unsubstantiated belief, and in another day or two, the tribal police would close the case, chalking it up to a murder committed in the course of a drug transaction and that would be that. Isaac Palmer's legacy would be to serve as a caution, a morality tale trotted out for the reservation's teenagers as what could happen if they dabbled in the white man's drugs.

Buckmount was watching her face closely. She smoothed her expression from skepticism to sadness, or so she hoped.

"That's tragic," she said.

"It is. But it's also, sadly, the reality that some of our people, once they come into a little bit of money—whether through a stable, prosperous job like Isaac or through a winning slot machine payout—are ill-equipped to handle that lifestyle change. To combat this, we're going to be piloting a fiscal responsibility program sponsored jointly by the casino and the cultural board. I'm going to propose we name it the Palmer Program as a way to remember our unfortunate friend."

Aroostine found herself nodding along as he spoke, more in response to the cadence of his voice than out of any real agreement with his words.

"That seems like a good program to run, regardless of whether Mr. Palmer's death ultimately proves to be tied to a drug deal," Joe said in a voice that hinted at the conversation being over. Then as if to drive home the point, he stood and yawned widely. "If you'll excuse us, Mr. Buckmount, we've had a long day, to put it mildly, and my wife's asleep on her feet. We're going to turn in, if you don't mind."

Buckmount sprung to his feet. "Of course, of course. You sleep well and, please, call me if you need anything, anything at all."

He pressed a business card into Joe's hands and then strode forward to shake Aroostine's hand with a vigorous pump. She stood and gripped his firm hand with a wan smile on her face.

Joe showed him out and deadbolted the door behind him. He stood, back against the wood-hewn door for a moment and looked at her wide-eyed. Finally he said, "What a creep."

She arched her stiff back, and heard the bones crack in protest. She needed to do some yoga, or stretching, or something. Tomorrow.

Whether Joe knew it or not, he hadn't been exaggerating. She was ready to fall asleep standing up.

"Yeah, he's definitely a creep. Let's go to bed."

CHAPTER EIGHT

Aroostine sat on the fallen log. The orange sun overhead warmed her bare shoulders. The wildflowers danced in the soft breeze, and birds chattered and called from the trees.

Lily was running and twirling, dancing through the meadow with her beribboned fairy wand floating on the breeze. She laughed and jumped and sang a tuneless song.

Aroostine felt herself smiling. It looked like the girl was playing with her shadow. But as she looked more closely through the long, wavy grass that swished with the girl's every leap, she realized that Lily was playing with a large beaver.

She squinted. No, not a beaver. Her beaver. Her spirit guide. As if it sensed her looking, the beaver turned to face her, and the sun glinted off its sleek fur. Yes, it was definitely her beaver with the wise, silver eyes that saw into her soul.

What was her spirit guide doing here? What do you want? she asked it silently.

The beaver didn't answer. It turned and resumed its frolicking with the girl. Aroostine settled back on the log.

Then something blotted out the sun. A dark cloud?

She turned her face upward, as the birds shrieked and fled the trees with a furious flapping and calling. Rabbits thumped by at top speed.

The dark silent shape hovered above, exactly over Lily and the beaver. Then the bottom opened soundlessly and an object streaked toward the earth.

Aroostine's brain processed what was happening just seconds before the blast hit.

"Run!" she shouted, but the sound of her voice was drowned out by the tremendous noise that accompanied the blast. Intense heat baked her face.

A bright white flash filled her field of vision, and when it cleared, the meadow was engulfed in flames, and the spot where Lily and the beaver had danced was a just crater in the charred and broken ground.

Joe bolted upright in the dark, unfamiliar room. His heart hammered in his chest. The metal taste of fear filled his mouth.

Aroostine was screaming. An anguished, high-pitched wordless scream.

He fumbled for the bedside light, terrified of what he'd find once he managed to force his trembling fingers to switch it on.

A soft yellow circle of light illuminated the bed, and he steeled himself.

Beside him, his wife continued to scream, open mouthed and drenched in sweat. She thrashed from side to side.

She was sound asleep.

He grabbed her shoulders and pulled her up from the pillow, pressing her shaking body into his chest.

"Wake up! Roo, you're having a nightmare. Baby, wake up!"

He held her struggling shape as tightly as he could and just kept repeating the words in her ear, over and over. Still, she screamed.

He leaned back and held her at arm's length. He shook her firmly.

"Aroostine! Snap out of it."

Should he slap her? Throw cold water on her face? His brain raced as fast as his pulse.

Then, all of a sudden, she stopped screaming and slumped forward and began to sob softly.

"Roo?"

She opened her eyes and looked up at him, hot tears streaming down her face.

"I . . . I had a vision . . ."

She was panting, struggling to bring herself under control.

He stroked her hair.

"Shhh, it's okay."

He felt her heartbeat begin to slow.

And then a fist began to pound on the door outside. Urgent and loud.

Her eyes widened with fear, and she grabbed his T-shirt with both hands, fisting the material tightly.

"You stay here," he said, as he gently extricated his shirt from her clammy grip. His kissed the top of her head then eased the covers off and rose from the bed.

He padded through the dark, unfamiliar halls and flicked on the dim light over the stove as he passed the galley kitchen. The urgent knocking resumed. The sound echoed, hollow and loud, in the still night. He grabbed a knife out of the chef's block on the counter and gripped it near his thigh.

When he reached the door, he hesitated with one hand on the deadbolt, wishing for a peephole.

He wet his lips and called, "Who's there?"

"It's Boom Cowslip."

The sound was muffled through the thick wood door, but Joe recognized the voice as belonging to the man he'd met on the trail. He inhaled deeply and then exhaled slowly before pushing back the deadbolt and flinging open the door.

Boom regarded him with concern, then his eyes dropped to the eight-inch knife in his hand, and the concern morphed into real worry.

"What's going on in here? I heard a woman screaming."

Joe followed his eyes to the knife. "Oh, Aroostine had a night terror. The knife was just . . . a precaution. You heard her screaming?"

Boom nodded gravely. "Yes. May I?" He gestured toward the living room.

"Oh, jeez, sorry. Of course, come in."

He ushered the older man into the house, closed the door, and rebolted it. Boom lowered himself into a chair while Joe returned the knife to its slot in the wooden block.

"Night terrors, eh?" Boom called from his seat.

Joe was turning around to answer when he saw Aroostine in the doorway leading from the bedroom, with a blanket wrapped around her shoulders.

"It was a vision, actually," she said in a hoarse, shaky voice.

Boom peered at her from the chair for a moment. Then he rose and walked over to the doorway.

"A vision?"

She nodded mutely.

"Did your spirit guide make an appearance?" Boom asked in a knowing tone.

"Yes."

Joe stood awkwardly in the kitchen, feeling very white.

"Aroostine, this is Boom Cowslip, the man I told you about. Why don't you go sit down with him and I'll put on the kettle for tea? I'm pretty sure Lee said there's tea around here somewhere."

She gave him a shaky smile as she trailed the older man to the seating arrangement. "Tea would be great if you can find some."

He busied himself at the stove and listened with half an ear as Aroostine recounted her vision, which sounded like a fairly standard horrible and terrifying nightmare with the addition of one large beaver. By the time he'd brewed a pot of chamomile tea, she'd finished and was cocooned in the sage green blanket, staring blankly at the wall. He placed saucers and cups down in front of both Aroostine and Boom then put down a third for himself.

As he poured the steaming hot liquid into each cup, Boom broke the silence.

"It's interesting that your beaver would alert you to the drones that fly overhead. Or did you already know about the testing facility?"

Joe watched as Aroostine opened her mouth and then clamped it shut, remembering her promise not to tell anyone that Ruby had told her.

"I already knew," she said simply. Her tone didn't invite any further questions on the topic.

Boom narrowed his eyes and regarded her for a long moment.

"I think your guide believes there's something amiss with the drones. Do you think it's tied to Isaac's death? Or perhaps this young girl you described?"

She lifted her shoulders in a shrug but Boom shook his head, rejecting the gesture.

"It's your vision. What do you think the message is?"

His words hung, solemn and searching, in the air while Aroostine sipped her tea. At last she balanced the saucer in her lap and said, "I don't know. I . . . I'm pretty removed from the culture, Boom. My visions usually aren't crystal clear; they're more like watching a staticky TV program without cable. The only ones that are vivid are portends of danger. I know that much."

"You need to sit with it, daughter. The message will reveal itself."

Joe was tempted to roll his eyes at the hokey shaman talk, but judging by Aroostine's grave expression and wide eyes, she was taking it seriously. She'd mentioned her spirit animal to him a few times, and she claimed it had helped her find him last year when he'd been kidnapped, but she generally avoided talking about anything mystical or native with him. Now, listening to her conversation with Boom, he felt extraneous, almost invisible. Outside.

"I will," Aroostine promised the old man.

Boom gave a somber little nod of the head and then set his tea on the side table.

"I'm glad no one was hurt. I'll leave you folks to get back to sleep. The sun won't rise for a few more hours. You should rest."

Joe let Boom out and bolted the door, then joined Aroostine on the couch. She was staring at the wall. He didn't know what to say, so he rubbed her shoulders. After several minutes, she leaned into him.

"Let's go back to bed. I don't think I'll be able to sleep but maybe you can get some rest," she whispered into his chest.

He didn't answer. Instead, he scooped her into his arms and carried her into the bedroom like a child, the blanket trailing along the floor.

CHAPTER NINE

Aroostine was sure she wouldn't be able to go back to sleep. And she was half-certain she didn't *want* to, not if it meant she might have another vision. But Joe insisted she try.

"I don't want to have another vision," she finally whispered.

He'd always put more stock into her visions than she had. In fact, she had kept the whole spirit animal guide thing a secret when they'd been dating and well into the first few years of their marriage. Because, by then, she couldn't quite figure out how to say, "Honey, I've been keeping this secret from you."

But when she finally screwed up the courage to tell him, he hadn't laughed or asked a bunch of ignorant questions. He'd just nodded, sat with the news for a while, and then asked one question: "Does it have a name?" And when she told him no, it was an unnamed beaver, he'd tilted his head and painted her with a look. "If it were my spirit guide, I'd at least name it."

Now he nodded, "I bet. But you have to sleep. Just relax, Roo. I'm right here." He cradled her like a child and stroked her hair.

After a moment or two, his reassuring words melted into a wordless song. He was humming something—a lullaby, maybe. His mouth brushed her ear. She closed her eyes.

She didn't know how long he'd soothed her like that, it could have been minutes or hours. She just knew that at some point he succeeded in lulling her to sleep. She knew this because now she was tucked under Joe's right arm struggling to open her heavy eyelids in response to a hammering noise.

Joe stirred beside her. He raised himself on one elbow and cocked his head to listen to the sound while she blinked herself awake, taking note of the sunlight streaming through the curtains.

She'd slept past sunrise? Her body must have been utterly drained for her not to have risen with the first rays.

She pushed herself upright, too. The pounding grew louder.

"That's the door," she said.

"I'll get it." He was already on his feet, pale and grim-faced.

She bet he'd stayed awake all night to watch over her. That was the sort of thing Joe did.

"Do you think it's Boom again?"

"It better not be. I mean, c'mon. Surely he has a telephone." He stomped toward the front of the house.

Aroostine raked her fingers through her tangled hair in an effort to achieve a semblance of presentability and then raced across the cold floor on tiptoes, following him to the door.

He unlocked the door and yanked it, not bothering to hide his annoyance.

Ruby Smith pushed her way past him and into the house. Her fists were clenched, tendons bulged in her neck, and her jaw jutted out.

"Who'd you tell?" she shouted at Aroostine, leaning in and putting her face close to Aroostine's.

Aroostine took a reflexive half step back.

"Whoa, hey. Who are you?" Joe demanded, moving to step between the two of them.

"Hang on. This is Ruby Smith. Close the door, honey." Aroostine spoke in the softest, calmest voice she could manage. A voice geared to soothing a wounded animal or calming a lost child. Miraculously, it seemed to also work on enraged cocktail waitresses—or, at least, it worked on the one who mattered.

Joe shut the front door, and Ruby just sort of deflated. All the anger leaked out of her like air out of a balloon, and she sagged. Aroostine reached out a hand, ready to catch the woman if she fell. But she steadied herself and turned her face to Aroostine with fat tears shining in her eyes.

"Who did you tell?" she asked again in a tight voice.

Aroostine led her by the elbow to the couch and piloted her to a seated position. Then she lowered herself to the spot beside her and took both the woman's hands in hers. They were ice cold. And shaking.

"I didn't tell anyone what you told me last night, Ruby. Only Joe, my husband. And he hasn't said a word." She cut her eyes toward Joe and gave him a meaningful look.

He hurried over to join them, crouching in front of the distraught woman.

"That's right," he said, giving his words the weight of a promise.

Ruby hung her head. Tears fell to the floor.

"What happened?" Aroostine asked.

The woman cried silently for a long moment before she raised her head to answer. "Someone broke into my house."

Aroostine's heart skipped.

"When?"

"I walked Lily to the bus stop this morning. I usually let her go herself. It's just two streets away. But I figured better safe than sorry—what with Isaac and all. So I walked her up to the stop around seven o'clock and put her on the school bus. I didn't come straight back. A few parents were gossiping about the murder, so I stuck around to see what they were saying—"

"What are people saying?" Aroostine interrupted to ask.

Ruby tossed her hair. It was an irritated gesture, as if Ruby couldn't believe the stories that were flying around the reservation.

"Mainly, folks are saying he had a drug problem and white dealers from the city killed him because he owed money. There's no truth to that. None. I don't know where that story's coming from, but I kept my mouth shut."

Lee Buckmount.

Joe's eyes met Aroostine's over Ruby's head. He was thinking the same thing.

She turned back to Ruby. "Okay, so what happened next?"

Ruby exhaled shakily. "Well, I walked back home and stuck my key in the lock to open the door, but it was already unlocked. It swung open as soon as I touched it. It's a piece of plywood crap, not like this one." She jerked her head toward the solid oak door.

"You're sure you locked it?" Aroostine knew the question would set Ruby off, but she had to ask it.

As anticipated, Ruby stiffened and her eyes blazed.

"Yes, I'm sure." She spat out the words from between clenched teeth.

"Does anyone else have a key?" Joe asked.

Ruby leaned forward as if she were going to explode again but stopped herself.

"I don't know," she admitted, her voice soft and uncertain.

Aroostine arched a brow. She didn't know?

Ruby went on. "I didn't give a key to anyone else—except Isaac."

The room felt cold suddenly.

"So, anyone might have his key." Joe finally put words to the chilling thought that they all shared.

Ruby nodded wordlessly. Her hands began to shake again.

"Okay," Aroostine soothed. "We'll worry about that in a minute. What happened when you opened the door?"

"I was scared. I knew I locked it before I left. I thought maybe I shouldn't go in—in case someone was in there. But I'd left my purse and phone on the counter. And I could see them from the doorway. The house was quiet, so I figured I'd just run in, grab my stuff, then leave and call the police."

"So that's what you did?"

"No. I forced myself inside and got my purse and phone, but then I ran back outside. I didn't call the police."

"Why not?"

Ruby dropped Aroostine's hand and reached into the leather shoulder bag she'd dropped at her feet when she'd sunk into the love seat. She rifled through it with trembling hands and came out with a sheet of lined paper that had been ripped out of a notebook. She pushed it into Aroostine's hands.

"Because of this. It was on the counter next to my purse."

Someone had scrawled the words with a black marker:

If you want your daughter to live, keep your whore mouth shut.

Aroostine paced in a fast circuit around the bedroom listening to the Criminal Division's recorded hold message exhorting her to report any suspicious behavior she happened on when she was out and about. Sid's secretary came back on the line.

"Are you still there?"

"I'm here, Polly." She tamped down her irritation at being put on hold. She needed to stay on Polly's good side.

"Sorry, Aroostine. He's finishing up a meeting. He asked if you wanted to hold another minute or two or if he should call you back?"

She walked to the door and pushed it ajar. Joe was leaning against the kitchen counter, talking to Ruby, who was not in her line of sight. Judging by the big gestures he was making, he was continuing to reassure Ruby that they wouldn't let anything happen to Lily.

"I'll wait," she said into the phone.

"Good. That'll give me an excuse to buzz his office again in another minute to hurry him along. Poor Mitch Swope's been in there for darn near an hour now. I don't know what Sid's raking him over the coals about, but I'm sure he'd welcome the interruption."

Aroostine nearly laughed despite her anxiety. Sid was a stern taskmaster. But all of the AUSAs who worked for him knew what they'd signed up for—and Mitch, more so than most, welcomed Sid's probing analyses and (sometimes constructive) criticisms.

"Okay, hon, I'm putting you back on hold now. Sorry about the PSA. I can't turn it off."

"No worries, Polly. You better believe if I see something, I'll say something."

They shared a chuckle at the dated slogan. And then the earnest prerecorded voice resumed its spiel, midword. Aroostine returned to her pacing and tuned out the voice.

"Higgins." Sid's voice jolted her back to attention.

"Hi, Sid."

"What's the status?"

"The status is this thing is spiraling out of control. Joe met some old guy in the woods who pointed the finger at the casino's CFO. The CFO, a man named Lee Buckmount, is going around the reservation insinuating that Palmer was killed by drug dealers from the city, and a . . . casino employee says Palmer told her the embezzlement might be tied to some missing military drones. Are there military drones *missing*?!" She realized belatedly that she was shouting. "Sorry. On top of all of that, someone broke into my source's home and left a message threatening her little girl. This is . . . I think you need to turn this over to the FBI, Sid."

He was silent for what seemed like a long time. When he spoke it was slowly, in a deliberate tone.

"Get a hold of yourself, Higgins. Now, take a deep breath." He paused. "Did you take a deep breath?"

She inhaled then released her breath in a loud *whoosh*.

"Yes."

"Good. Now, let's try this again. Where are you, back at your resort?"

"No. We stayed on the reservation last night—it's a long story."

"Well, what would you tell a witness, Higgins?"

"Start at the beginning."

"So start at the beginning. You found the body, called the local authorities, and then hung around to see how they responded, right?"

"Right. Officer Hunt interviewed me. The only way to describe the interview is cursory. He was clearly just checking boxes."

"You're sure about that?"

"Yes, I'm sure. I told him I found the corpse of a large, adult jackrabbit with a bullet hole through the center of its head, just like Isaac Palmer, in the field directly across from Palmer's house. He blew it off."

Unflappable Sid momentarily lost his composure. "That's valuable forensic evidence, for crying out loud! Tell me it's not just lying in the grass decomposing. Do I need to send out a team from Eugene?"

"Take it easy, Sid," Aroostine said, relishing the turned tables. "I pointed it out to the police chief when he finally roused himself to come to the scene."

She waited while he mumbled a few of his favorite curses under his breath.

"The police chief comped us dinner at the casino—"

"Us?"

"I called Joe to come meet me, Sid."

"I realize this is some sort of recapture-the-romance trip, but I trust you're keeping your husband at arm's length from the investigation."

She bit her lip and swallowed the response that came to mind. Instead she said, "Of course. As I was saying, we had dinner at the casino—in part, because it had been a long day and, surprisingly, I was hungry and in part, because I wanted to get a better sense of the place. That's where the purported embezzlement is taking place, after all."

"And?"

"And it seemed to be a well-run establishment. The parking lot was mostly full, the casino floor was bustling, and the food was passable."

"Anything else?"

"The decor was sort of over-the-top with the clichéd Indian motif."

"That's not what I had in mind."

"Oh, well, if you mean did I see anyone walk by with a big burlap sack marked 'pilfered funds,' the answer is no."

"Point taken. So what happened after dinner?"

There was no way she was recounting the argument for Sid. She glossed over the reason for the stop along the side of the road and said, "Joe was taking a walk when he ran into a man on the tribe's cultural board, a guy by the name of Cowslip—Matthew Cowslip, but he goes by Boom. He mentioned to Joe that he thought Buckmount had something to do with Palmer's murder. He seemed to think the local authorities were unlikely to look into the issue with any real vigor."

Sid harrumphed in bitter agreement. Then he said, "He's no doubt correct about that—especially if Buckmount is involved."

"What do we have on Buckmount?"

Silence.

"Sid?"

"Not much. That's part of the problem. These Indian—er, Native American—casinos are pretty much black boxes. They're not subject to the same level of scrutiny and oversight as regular casinos. In fact, we have some concerns that organized crime is moving its focus away from Las Vegas and Atlantic City and trying to make inroads with the reservation casinos for that very reason."

"You think there's a mob connection at White Springs?"

"I don't know, but according to our friends in the Bureau, that's a good possibility."

"So Isaac's death could be a professional hit."

"Could be."

An image of Lily flashed in her mind.

"Well that's a real problem, because there's a seven-year-old girl in danger."

"Tell me about the girl."

"She lives next door to Palmer. Her mother's a cocktail waitress at the casino. Mom claims Isaac had a crush on her and told her about the missing money to impress her."

"Great. Wonder who else he blabbed to?"

"According to her, no one. She told him he was playing with fire and, apparently, scared him. That's probably why he went dark on us and stopped cooperating."

"Hmm, maybe. He tell her anything else?"

"Yeah, he told her he thought the missing money was somehow tied up with some drones that disappeared from the testing facility on the reservation. Do you know anything about that?"

"Missing drones? No. But I'll poke around." Sid's tone was infuriatingly unconcerned.

"Do more than poke around, Sid. If there's even one unmanned military drone floating around out—"

"Simmer down, White Springs is a *civilian* testing facility. The drones aren't armed. They're just annoying."

"You knew about the drone testing?" she asked incredulously.

"What are you, some kind of Luddite? Drones, civilian drones, are big business. Especially in Oregon. There've got to be eighty private companies working on civilian drones out there—maybe more. But the programs are completely safe and walled off from weaponized drones, Higgins. Get a grip."

"Wrong. Apparently, through the magic of budget cuts, the Department of Defense decided to cost share with the Federal Aviation Authority. They may not practice detonations over White Springs, but they're flying military drones out of the facility. And, apparently, some have gone missing."

After a long, heavy silence, Sid let loose a string of invective that made Aroostine's ears burn. She could picture him, stomping around his office with his stupid wireless headset firmly in place, his face getting redder by the second. She waited.

"That's not . . . are you sure?"

"No, I'm not sure. It's an unsubstantiated rumor. But, someone broke into the cocktail waitress's house this morning and left a message threatening her daughter if she doesn't keep her mouth shut. So, whether it's true or not, someone's worried about the word getting around."

"Crap."

"Exactly. I need protection for the mom and girl, Sid. And I need someone to look into Buckmount, fast. I think it's time to call in the guys with the guns. This isn't a lawyer problem at this point."

Sid exhaled. "See, here's the thing . . ." he trailed off.

"Oh, good, there's a thing."

"It's politically delicate. The G-men can't just muscle their way onto a federally recognized Native American reservation. There are protocols."

For a wild moment she considered telling him about her vision— as if that might impel the bureaucratic machinery into action. But she dismissed the thought almost immediately. Even if, by some miracle, it worked, she'd lose credibility with Sid forever. Messages from psychic beavers weren't going to help her get her job back.

"Missing weapons, a dead guy, and a child in danger should move the needle."

"Probably, eventually—but it's going to take time."

"Who's going to take care of this kid until all the right butts get kissed?"

His answer was both what she expected and what she dreaded. "You are."

Joe drummed his fingers on the side table and smiled blankly at Ruby. She clearly wasn't in the mood for small talk, but they couldn't just sit there and stare at each other while Aroostine conducted her whispered conversation with Sid in the back room.

He cleared his throat. "So tell me about Lily."

Ruby looked up from examining her chipped nail polish. "Why?"

"Because she must be a special kid. After Aroostine met her, she insisted we needed to help bring Isaac's killer to justice. She made an impression on my wife, so I'm curious about her."

The hint of a reluctant smile crossed Ruby's face.

"She is a special kid. Always has been. I got pregnant with her when I was a senior in high school. Her dad took off, just vanished from the reservation one day. Even his folks couldn't find him.

Anyway, I finished up school. She was supposed to be born in August, but Lily had a different plan. She came in June—six weeks early."

Ruby paused and shook her head at a private memory then continued, "Man, was she a fighter, though. They sent us home even though she wasn't even five pounds. Tiny but fierce, the doctors said. And that's the way she's always been. She's a tough kid and smart as the dickens. Creative, independent. She deserves better than this dump, that's for sure. That's one reason I liked her being around Isaac, you know? Show her there's more to the world."

She fell silent again. He could tell she was thinking about the threat that had been left on her kitchen counter. He couldn't blame her. He tried to imagine being a parent and knowing his child was in danger. Just the thought of it chilled his blood. Part of him wondered why Ruby stayed on the reservation at all if she found it so depressing. But that was a thought for another time. They had to focus on protecting her daughter now.

"We won't let anything happen to her."

Her dark eyes narrowed, and she pinned him with a shrewd, searching look. "Is that a promise you can keep? Who are you guys, anyway?"

"I'm a carpenter."

She blinked. "Like, with wood?"

"Yeah, like that." He was technically a master woodworker, but he doubted Ruby would be impressed by the distinction.

"Um . . ."

"Aroostine's a lawyer with the Department of Justice," he rushed to assure her.

"Yeah, that's what she said. But I mean, *who* are you? You're white, obviously. She's native, right? I mean, she looks like it, but she sure doesn't act like she grew up on a res. I figure with a name like Aroostine, though . . ." Ruby trailed off, whether from embarrassment at her stereotyping or just because she really couldn't place Aroostine, he couldn't tell.

"She's a member of the Lenape Nation. But she was adopted by a white family when she was about Lily's age." As he said the sentence, something clicked into place in his brain. Aroostine had been about Lily's age when her grandfather had died and she'd been whisked away from her heritage. Her fierce need to help the girl was starting to make more sense—to him, at least. He wondered if Aroostine had pieced it together.

"Oh." Ruby fell silent again, processing the information.

He resumed his drumming on the side table. They sat like that until Aroostine emerged from the bedroom.

"Well?" he asked.

"Sid's working on getting protection for Lily and Ruby."

Ruby's head snapped up. "What kind of *protection*?"

"It'll depend. How would you feel about a vacation, somewhere back East? Could you get off work?"

"Probably. I'd have to pull Lily out of school, but, shoot, she'd learn more on a trip off the reservation than she will sitting at a desk for the next fifty years." At the notion of getting away for a while, Ruby's face softened and her shoulders relaxed.

Aroostine nodded her agreement at the sentiment.

"Okay, it'll take a few days to arrange. In the meantime, we'll stick around and help keep an eye on Lily while you're at work."

Joe felt his eyebrows shoot up his forehead. They would? There went their getaway.

Aroostine painted him with a look like she knew exactly what he was thinking and thought he needed to get over it.

He twisted his mouth into a knot and gave her a look right back. They weren't qualified to act as bodyguards for the girl.

Her black eyes flashed. *Later, not in front of Ruby.* The message came across so clearly it was as if she'd spoken the words aloud.

He nodded; there was no point in trying to argue now. Aroostine on a mission was an unstoppable force.

"Sure, right. So now what?" he asked.

She rewarded him with a warm smile and turned back to Ruby. "What time does Lily get home from school?"

"Um, the bus drops her off at quarter to four. I have to leave for work at six tonight."

"Great. You catch a nap. Joe and I are going to get our stuff and check out of our hotel. We have a few errands to run, too, but we should be back well before Lily gets home. Just in case, though, we'll stop by Boom's and ask him to keep an eye out, too. Is that okay?"

Ruby nodded slowly. "Yeah. Boom's an odd duck—stuck in the past. But most folks respect him. I don't think anyone will mess with us if it's clear he's got our back."

"Perfect." Aroostine crossed the room and took the woman's hands in hers. "We aren't going to let anything happen to you and your daughter. You have my word."

For his part, Joe sincerely hoped that was a promise they could keep.

CHAPTER TEN

They walked Ruby home and confirmed that her house was empty. She locked herself in with a promise to rest. She sure looked as if she needed it—her eyes and skin were dull and tired and she was pale with worry. But if she showed up for her shift looking so much like the anxious mother she was, she'd never get any tips. The heaviness of Ruby's responsibilities was weighing on Aroostine. She had to wonder how the woman—younger than she was by a few years—was coping so well.

She walked in silence toward Boom's house, lost in her thoughts. Beside her, Joe kicked up dust with his feet. He cleared his throat once, and then a second time. Belatedly, she realized he was trying to get her attention.

"Sorry. Do you want to say something?" she asked.

He stopped in the middle of the path. His blue eyes flashed with a rare glint of steel. *Uh-oh.* She held her breath and waited.

"For the record, I'm not going to try to talk you out of this."

She exhaled.

"Duly noted, for the record." She smiled at him, but he wasn't mollified.

"The reason I'm not going to argue about this is I know it'd be a waste of my breath. That doesn't mean I think this little scheme is a good idea. It isn't. It's a *terrible* idea."

She regarded him for a moment. Then she nodded. "Yeah, it is. As far as ideas go, this one sucks. Unfortunately, Joe, I don't see a better alternative. Do you? If you do, spit it out and we can go back to the previously scheduled program of five-star meals, overstuffed beds, and soaks in the private hot tub on the balcony outside our room."

He huffed and then reluctantly said, "No. I don't."

She nodded. "Then let's get on with it, okay?"

A half smile sprung to life on his lips, and he leaned in to kiss her by her ear. "Yes, ma'am."

They lapsed back into silence, but she reached over and interlocked her fingers with his as they continued along the path.

Her shoulders felt lighter somehow.

They reached the front of Boom's worn but tidy home, and she hesitated. He seemed to sense the reason.

"How much are you going to tell him?"

"I don't know. As much as we have to."

Ruby thought it was okay to trust the old man. And Aroostine's gut wasn't telling her otherwise, but she didn't know Boom from Adam.

"He seems okay," Joe offered.

She shrugged. "It's not like we really have any choices. We need to get our stuff, and I want to stop by a library. Someone's got to keep an eye on Ruby and Lily for us."

"A library? You looking for some light reading?"

"I want to look at articles about the drone facility. And, yes, I realize I can search them from my phone—or laptop. But I don't want anyone to be able to trace it, and I think we both know—"

"Nothing's private in the electronic age."

They'd learned that one the hard way. But it wasn't a lesson either of them would forget any time soon: you never knew who might be monitoring your every move from some remote location.

"Yeah."

Joe looked at her for a full thirty seconds, his face serious. "Okay. You talk to Boom. I'll call the hotel and just let them know we're coming. Don't worry, I'll keep it short and sweet." He stepped a few feet away from the house and pulled out his cell phone.

She stepped up to the door and gave it a solid rap with her knuckles. While she waited, she took note of the feathered dream catcher hanging in the front window. She wondered if Boom really cared about the old Ojibwe custom or if the decoration was for the benefit of tourists. Her grandfather used to shake his head at old ladies hawking dream catchers at flea markets and roadside stands. He said they were as bad as the yuppies who bought them, if not worse. *Selling off our heritage one trinket at a time, until there's nothing left.* At the time, she hadn't understood. Couldn't they always make more dream catchers? Now, of course, she realized he was objecting to his people participating in their own cultural appropriation—a subject that she didn't truly understand, having left the traditional ways behind.

The childhood memory was interrupted when Boom's front door swung open. He stood on the other side, completely unsurprised to see her.

"Aroostine. Good morning, daughter." He beamed at her.

The term of endearment tripped her up, coming on the heels of her memory of her grandfather. Her grandfather may not have ever hung a woven, feathered web in his front window to filter out his bad dreams, but Boom shared his quiet gravitas. It unsettled her.

"Uh, good morning."

"I trust you were able to rest after I left?"

After the vision.

"I did; I really didn't think I'd go back to sleep, but that tea must have held some magic." She was just making small talk, but he nodded gravely as if to say, yes, there was magic in the tea.

Get a hold of yourself, Higgins, she ordered internally in her best Sid impression.

"Would you like to come in?" He stepped aside to give her a path.

"Thank you, but no. Joe and I have to run some errands, but I'm here to ask you a favor."

His hooded eyes sparked with interest, and a small smile played across his lined face.

"Yes."

"Yes what?"

"Yes, I will help you."

"Don't you want to know what I need?"

"No. It doesn't matter, daughter. You are helping our people, so I shall help you."

She blinked at that and glanced behind her. Joe was ending his call and putting his phone back in his pocket.

"Oh, okay. That's great. What I need is for you to keep an eye on Ruby and Lily Smith, just until I get back."

It was his turn to blink.

"Ruby? You don't—surely, she's not involved in this mess?"

"No, nothing like that. She was friendly with Isaac. It seems someone believes she knows something, and they're trying to convince her to keep it to herself."

His face clouded. "Ruby's been threatened?"

"And her daughter."

"Your spirit guide was trying to warn you."

"Maybe." She didn't want to think about the vision. "Right now, though, we need to worry about whoever wrote the note, and not an imaginary beaver."

"Buckmount," he spat, storms gathering in his black eyes.

She took a half step back. "Maybe. He does seem to have spread the story about Isaac being mixed up with white drug dealers. But don't assume it's him. That would be dangerous. It could be anyone."

"It could be, but it isn't. Yes, I will do what I can to keep Ruby Smith and her daughter safe. But I cannot protect Ruby while she's at work. Sadly, Lee and his armed security guards will have complete access to her at the casino."

She swallowed around the lump in her throat. "I know. We'll try to be back before her shift starts. Joe can go to the gaming floor and play the role of drunk white man while he watches out for her."

Joe approached as she explained her idea. Even though she'd just come up with it on the fly, he nodded like it was a well-considered plan.

"Yup."

Boom nodded as well. "That could work. Lily should be safe as long as she's at school. But to be sure, I'll stop by. I teach a session on our traditional ways each semester. My presence there won't draw any interest or surprise."

"Does your seminar include dream catchers?" Aroostine asked the question before she could stop herself. It was rude, but the dream catcher seemed so out of place, she really wanted to know.

His eyes shifted to the feathered decoration hanging in his window. "Eh, that. It's nothing—you know, before you were born, that was a symbol of pan-Indian unity, Aroostine. A way for the tribes to reach across our differences. But now? It's just tourist crap. Hanging it there was Lee's bright idea. He treats me like some curiosity to display to his investors, but he also funds my cultural board generously, so I choose my battles."

"Oh." She felt a sudden wave of sympathy for the old man. She waited a beat and then continued, "Speaking of the cultural board, is it okay if we stay in the cottage for a few more nights? We'd be happy to make a donation to the board," she asked.

"Nonsense. You'll stay as long as you like, as our guests."

"Thank you."

Behind her, Joe shuffled his feet in the dust. "We should get going, Roo, if you want to be back before six."

Joe was right. They had a good distance to cover.

"Thank you, Boom." She turned to leave.

"No, thank you, daughter. And Aroostine—?"

"Yes?"

She turned back, and he pierced her with a meaningful look. "Be open to your spirit guide. You may get another message. Trust it."

She nodded, trying to shake the feeling that Boom was himself trying to give her a message, and fell into step next to Joe. They headed toward the Jeep. She glanced over her shoulder. Boom stood watching them from his doorway.

CHAPTER ELEVEN

Joe unlocked the passenger door for her and held it open. Then, as he did every time they'd gotten in a car since college, he leaned over and kissed her. It was part of their routine, as natural as breathing after all these years. She smiled, her lips parting against his warm mouth, and leaned in close to him.

Then she sniffed the air twice and pulled back.

"Jeez. I'll grab a shower at the hotel," he said in mock indignation.

She shook her head. "No. Do you smell that?"

He turned his nose toward the front of the car and inhaled. "What?"

"Cleaning supplies." She wrinkled her nose. "Or maybe pool chemicals?"

He took another deep sniff.

"Nope, sorry. It's probably just rental car detailing." He dismissed it with a shrug.

"I guess."

She slid into the passenger seat, but unease had lodged itself in the pit of her stomach. Joe walked around the front of the Jeep. The sunlight glinted off his blond hair turning it gold.

He settled into the seat beside her and put the key in the ignition. She sniffed again. The smell seemed even stronger. Her eyes were watering.

"Wait—you really don't smell that?"

He gave her a careful look. "I really don't. What are you thinking?"

Her mind flashed to Lee Buckmount standing beside the vehicle when they'd walked back from their stargazing in the meadow.

"What if somebody tampered with the car?"

His blue eyes darkened. He removed the key from the ignition without another word and popped the hood release.

He stepped out of the car and she followed. He lifted the hood and stared down at the engine and at—whatever the other parts were. As a nondriver, she wasn't sure what they were looking for, but she trusted Joe would notice if anything seemed out of the ordinary. He stuck his head into the engine compartment and poked around with both hands for a few seconds. He straightened to standing and slammed the lid shut with a solid *thunk*.

"Everything seems fine, babe."

She forced a smile.

"That's good. I guess I'm just spooked."

"Understandably." He gave her shoulders a quick squeeze and then returned to the Jeep. He started the ignition and let it idle, waiting for her to join him. Apparently, the door-holding/kissing ritual applied once per trip. She grinned at that notion and started back to the passenger seat.

As she reopened the door, the smell of chlorine wafted over her, unmistakable this time.

"Wait," she shouted into the front compartment of the Jeep.

She squatted beside the vehicle and twisted her neck to examine the undercarriage. It was oily and streaked with black dirt. She grabbed hold of the side with some reluctance. Her hands were going to be filthy. But she pulled herself underneath and scanned the length of the vehicle.

There it was. Right under the gas tank, a filmy white plastic soda bottle was affixed to the underside of the Jeep with electrical tape. She reached for it, unthinkingly, and then stopped herself. Her hands began to shake uncontrollably, while her brain processed what her eyes saw.

Plastic soda bottle. Chlorine. Improvised incendiary device.

The words scrolled across her mind. Jumping out at her from a national security bulletin that Homeland Security had shared with the Department of Justice about a year earlier. Apparently, terrorists had learned that filling a soda bottle with swimming pool tablets and rubbing alcohol wasn't just a juvenile delinquent prank. Add some nails, strap the bottle to the bottom of a car, and you have yourself a reasonably serviceable weapon.

She scrabbled out from the under the car, screaming Joe's name. "Get out! Hurry!"

He swiveled his head toward the sound of her voice. The wild look on her face must have put off any thought of asking questions. He jerked the car door open and dove out. She grabbed his hand, and they half stumbled, half ran toward the meadow, the Jeep still running.

As they cleared the fallen log, the Jeep exploded in a ball of flame and twisted metal. The heat of the blast hit their backs. Aroostine glanced over her shoulder as she ran, but all she saw was a cloud of black smoke undulating through the waves of the flames. She ran harder.

They ran until they couldn't run any further, then they collapsed, their legs shaking and spent, their lungs burning. Aroostine surveyed the wide open plain and the empty sky. They were miles away from any signs of civilization, unlikely to be spotted by a farmer or hiker. But that wouldn't matter if a drone flew overhead. They needed to rest, but they had to stay out of sight. She gestured toward a canopy of low-hanging tree branches, just a few yards away.

"Under there."

She trudged toward the trees. Joe trailed her. Once she reached the copse, she ducked under some branches and slid down to rest against a tangle of trunk and roots. Joe sat across from her, his long legs stretched out toward hers so that the soles of their feet touched.

She wiped the sweat from her forehead with a grimy hand and took a long look at her husband by the light filtering through the leaves. His face was gray, his eyes clouded, and his mouth set in a hard line.

"You okay?"

He nodded. "That was close."

Joe Jackman, master of understatement.

"Yeah."

"Thank God you have the nose of a bloodhound."

She managed a wan smile, unwilling to imagine what would have happened if they'd pulled out and started to drive away with the chlorine bomb unnoticed under the gas tank.

He tried to smile back, but his lips tugged down into a sudden frown. "Our phones were in the car."

She nodded. Another habit. As soon as they'd entered the Jeep, they'd both plugged in their smartphones to charge.

Panic flooded his eyes.

"It's better, anyway," she told him. "We need to stay off the grid." She tried to keep her tone casual, but her stomach was jumping and jerking like a colt on unsteady legs.

"What? Like hide?"

"Run and hide." As she said the words, their rightness resonated. Someone on the reservation wanted them dead. Sid was thousands of miles away and limited by rules, regulations, and committee oversight in how much help he could provide. They had to stay alive—and keep Ruby and Lily alive. The way to do that was to disappear.

"You think it's Buckmount, don't you?"

She shrugged. "It doesn't much matter at the moment. Whoever set that bomb wants us out of the picture. By now, I'm sure the EMTs have responded to the scene and ascertained that there are no bodies. Someone's going to be looking for us—whether it's Buckmount, drug dealers from Eugene, or someone else, we have to lay low. But, yeah, I think it's someone from the reservation. Don't you?"

He chewed on his lower lip and answered with a question of his own. "What about Ruby?"

What about Ruby? And Lily? Their names had run through her brain like a mantra as she and Joe had hauled themselves through the fields. She'd made a promise to Ruby. But their going back to the reservation with targets painted on their backs wasn't going to help either mother or daughter.

She wet her dry lips. "We'll have to count on Boom to take care of them until we can get our feet under us again. We need to neutralize the threat against them, and we can't do that if we're dead. We have to disappear at least until Sid comes through with plane tickets for them."

"You have a plan, don't you?"

Her heart ached at his optimistic tone. She evaded the question, unwilling to destroy his hope.

"Right now, the plan is to find us some drinking water. Maybe some edible plants, berries if we're lucky. We'll stay here just long enough to rest and then push on until nightfall, find a spot where we can make a fire and get some sleep."

"Ahh, water. That sounds amazing."

"Okay, water's easy. You want to stay and rest or come with me?"

She pushed herself to her feet, crouching to avoid the branches overhead.

He groaned but hoisted himself to standing. "I'm not letting you out of my sight."

Despite her aching body and parched throat, a warm tingle started in her chest and spread through her entire body at his words. She smiled. "Good. Come on."

He laced his fingers through hers and let her lead him out from under the trees.

CHAPTER TWELVE

Aroostine thrashed through the tall weeds as if she had a destination in mind. Joe knew that was impossible, though, because they didn't have the faintest idea where they were.

Or at least he didn't.

He picked up his pace, trotting a little to catch up to her.

"Where are you heading? Not back to the reservation?"

"Definitely not," she muttered, her head down as she scanned the ground below her feet.

He tried to picture the GPS map he'd followed from their resort to the reservation. The closest town to White Springs was Boylestown, but that had to be a good forty-five miles to the west of the western edge of the reservation.

"You don't think we can walk to Boylestown, do you?"

She stopped and turned to face him. "Right now, we're heading for the nearest stream. Have you noticed we've been walking uphill?"

"Yeah. So?"

"So, the safest drinking water we're likely to find will be a fast-running stream at a high elevation. I'm following these tracks—probably an opossum—through this wet, marshy grass because it's going to lead us to a stream." She peered more closely at the tracks. "Maybe a skunk."

Her tone was gentle, but he felt useless and stupid just the same. Here he'd been trying to remember a GPS map, and she'd been observing their environment—something actually helpful to them in their circumstances.

"Oh."

"We don't have anything to carry water in, though. So we're going to drink up and then follow the stream as far as we can, keeping it nearby. Okay?"

"Okay. Sure, of course."

She leaned in and kissed him, slightly off-center, her lips grazing the side of his mouth.

"Trust me on this part. We'll be fine. It's not going to be the height of luxury or anything, but I won't let you die of thirst, starvation, or exposure. Deal?"

Her serious brown eyes painted him with a long look.

He nodded slowly. "Deal. This isn't exactly what I meant when I proposed a romantic getaway, but we can make the best of it."

Her eyes danced with sudden humor. "I think you'll find the not dying of exposure part kind of enjoyable."

He raised a brow into a question mark. "Really?"

"We'll have to think of a way to conserve body heat while we sleep."

She scrunched her face up and winked. He laughed harder than he thought he was capable of under the circumstances. She waited until his smile had faded and then cracked the whip.

"Come on, we're getting close."

Spurred on by the promise of fresh, cold drinking water he started forward beside her.

He heard the stream before it came into view.

He'd always thought "babbling brook" was just a saying. After all, the creek behind their place back home sounded like tinkling water, if that. But as they walked on, he heard something that sounded like the high-pitched chatter of a couple children.

"What's the noise?"

"Rushing water." Aroostine pushed ahead, excited, and he raced to keep up. They followed a bend in the earth, and there it was: a ribbon of white water, streaming and foaming over the rocks.

"This is perfect. Fast moving means it's probably clean."

"Probably?"

She shrugged. "I can't make any guarantees. But high elevation, quick-moving water, animal tracks that show the local wildlife drinks from it—it's pretty much the best we can do, unless we boil it, but we don't have a pan or anything."

She knelt and cupped her hands, scooping the water into her mouth. He hesitated. As he stood there focusing on how thirsty he was, his throat seemed to constrict and fill with dust. The more he thought about it, the drier it felt.

He sent a quick prayer heavenward and crouched beside his wife. The cool water flowed over his hands for a few seconds, then he formed his palms into a bowl and slurped the water. It tasted like a crisp fall day, fresh and clear. He dipped his hands into the stream again and again, and drank greedily.

She laughed at his transformation and plopped down on the bank, legs outstretched, supporting herself with her elbows. He joined her in the grass.

"What if you hadn't found this stream? Or if it had been polluted? What would we have done?" He asked mainly to satisfy his curiosity. She was such a different person out in the woods—calm, decisive, completely sure of herself.

"There's lots of ways to get water. If we hadn't found a clean source, we could get water from plants or rocks. Or even by waiting until morning and gathering the dew."

She said it in a casual tone, as if harvesting dew drops for hydration was the most natural activity in the world.

He smiled down at her, taking in her upturned face, high, slanted cheekbones, the curved hollow of her neck. Memorizing her in this moment.

"What?"

"I was thinking it might be time to conserve some body heat."

She laughed and smacked his arm.

"Oh, please. First we find something to eat and then push on until it gets closer to sunset. We need to cover as much ground as we can before dark if we want to get to Boylestown by tomorrow evening."

"*Tomorrow* evening?" His light-hearted innuendo dissipated as reality set in.

"Yeah, tomorrow. It's not like there's a straight path between here and there. Not to mention, I'm not exactly sure where *there* is. I have a general sense, but we should plan on twenty miles a day, minimum. And we have to stay off the main roads."

Her eyes clouded, and he knew she was thinking about the car bomb. Someone was willing to kill them to keep them from uncovering whatever was going on at White Springs. And they both knew that whoever wanted them dead wasn't going to give up after the first attempt failed. Someone—or maybe a team—was probably out there, somewhere between the shadow of the distant mountain and the dusty roads of the reservation coming through the fields, stopping at every gas station and roadside stand, searching for them. By now, they'd probably set up a sentry at their hotel to attack them if they ever made it back to their suite.

His heart thumped in his chest. "This is insane. Suicidal even."

"We're going to be okay, Joe. I promise. No one's going to find us out here. I just hope tomorrow night isn't too late for Lily and Ruby."

The drummer in his chest sped up, double time. Cut off from everyone, with no way to contact Ruby or Sid, they had no way to know what was happening on the reservation.

"Boom will take care of them."

"I hope so."

They sat in mutual, brooding silence for several long seconds. He stared out at the water as it tumbled past them down the hill, mesmerized for the moment by its rolling motion over the rocks. Then he shook himself back to action and rose to his feet.

"Come on. I believe I was promised a gourmet meal of berries and weeds." He bent and extended a hand. She grabbed it and pulled herself up.

"Chef Aroostine's special of the day, coming right up."

Aroostine cradled the mound of fat, gem-like currants and the two large fistfuls of salsify leaves in the bottom of her shirt and hiked back to the spot where she'd left Joe. He looked up at the sound of her footsteps.

"Lunch is served." She plopped down next to him and displayed the fruit and weeds, like a shopgirl showing her wares.

"Um. What is it?"

She plucked a currant from the pile and held it between her thumb and forefinger, turning it so the sun filled its translucent shape with light.

"This baby is a golden currant, like the jam. Even though some are yellow and the rest are red and black, they're all ripe golden currants. The plants are meadow salsify. I just brought the leaves because the stalks are kind of tough and bitter. This is enough to make a decent salad."

He still looked uncertain, so she popped the globe of fruit in her mouth and bit into an explosion of sweet, honey-like fruit. It was much less tart than she'd expected, which was good—Joe liked sugary fruits.

"Mmm, try it."

She offered him a berry. He eyed it suspiciously but took it. As he chewed it, his face relaxed.

"Not bad," he admitted.

"Good. You might want to wrap the leaves around some berries and eat them together, because—I'm not gonna lie—the leaves aren't quite as tasty. But they're filling, so eat them, okay? Fill your belly and then we'll get another drink of water and push on." She squinted at the sky. "We have maybe five more hours before we have to stop and make camp for the night."

"Then what? What's our ultimate goal?"

He reached for a leaf and the fattest remaining berry. She dropped a currant into a leaf of her own and ate it as she considered his question.

"I'm hoping Boylestown will have a semiprofessional police presence. We'll report the car bombing and ask the police to call Sid so we can get an update on what's going on at the reservation. Then we'll call the hotel, get the driver to come fetch us and enjoy some indoor plumbing and soft beds while we figure out what to do. How's that sound for a plan?"

His eyes crinkled as he grinned. "It sounds great, except for one little snag."

She furrowed her brow. *What had she missed?*

"I give up. What's the snag?"

He shoveled another berry/leaf bite into his mouth and shook his head. "I love that you're still so trusting, but really? Think about it. If Lee Buckmount did kill Isaac Palmer to cover up the embezzlement and tried to kill us, what do you think he's doing now?"

"Swimming in a bathtub of gold ducats like Scrooge McDuck?"

"Uh, no. If he's smart, he's concocted a story that paints us as mixed up with Isaac and drug dealers. If I were him, it would go something like this: We met with Isaac to sell him drugs, and it went bad. We killed him and you called it in, pretending to be some prosecutor from back East. The drug lords are angry that we brought attention to them, so they tried to kill us with the car bomb. He's probably working the phones as we speak, putting the word out to every small town between here and Eugene. I'm sure there's someone sitting outside our hotel room right now."

He sat back, obviously pleased with the narrative he'd spun. She stared at him wordlessly.

"What?" he demanded.

"What? Really? That's demented. It makes no sense. He'd have to be—"

"Evil? Arrogant? Powerful enough to believe he could get away with it?"

She faltered. "Well . . . yeah."

"And which of those descriptions doesn't apply to him? Let's at least be realistic. There's no honor among thieves, Roo. You of all people should know that, you're a freaking *prosecutor*."

Her stomach cramped, and a sour metallic tang filled her mouth. He was right, of course. And yet it hadn't crossed her mind—the notion that Buckmount might have painted an even bigger target on their backs. A sort of "shoot first, ask questions later" kind of target aimed at law enforcement personnel.

"Well, I would hope that when Sid can't get in touch with me today, he'll put out some feelers of his own."

Her words rang weak and hollow even to her. But Joe gave a brisk nod of his head, as if it sounded convincing to him. Then, in an obvious effort to change the subject, he leaned forward and snaked the last berry out of the hem of her shirt.

"Open up!" he ordered and dropped it in her mouth.

She shook off the worry that had dropped over her like a cloud and ate the currant.

"Thanks."

"Any time."

She leaned into him and gave him a long, tight hug. Reflexively, she glanced up, scanning the bright blue sky for drones. She didn't really think that anyone would unleash a drone attack against unarmed civilians in Central Oregon. *Did she?* Over Joe's shoulder, up on the ridge line, she spotted the silhouette of a tall, sleek animal with silver eyes. She blinked, and when she reopened her eyes, the beaver was gone.

CHAPTER THIRTEEN

The clock on Boom's mantel chimed four o'clock. He walked to the front window and stood, shaded by the fluttering curtain, and watched the tribal police walking around the chalk marks that they'd placed around what was left of the rental Jeep while he waited for Ruby and Lily to appear at the corner. Officer Hunt scratched his chin and scribbled something on his notepad before pulling a tape measure from his pocket and hunching over the debris.

Boom was sufficiently curious that he almost stepped out the front door and asked the man what he was doing, but then two thin figures rounding the corner caught his eyes. One small, one tall. He snagged his keys from the table and hurried outside, pausing to lock the house up tight even though he was only going to be two doors away. As a rule, Boom left his front door unlocked—an open invitation to his people to visit any time they felt moved to do so. But in light of Isaac's murder and Aroostine and Joe's exploding car, no one could fault a man for taking all reasonable precautions—especially a man who lived in this particular corner of the reservation.

"Officers." He nodded toward Hunt and his colleagues as he trotted past them on a diagonal, beelining toward the girl and her mother.

As he crossed the road, his shoes fell heavily in the dry dirt, drawing Ruby's attention. She met his eyes over her daughter's head. Her cocktail waitress warpaint was in place—bright red lips, flushed cheeks, and blue eyelids—but all that makeup couldn't hide her drawn, tight expression or the worry that clouded her eyes.

Although she couldn't know exactly what he planned to say to her, her look blazed a warning: *Not in front of Lily.* He nodded once, almost imperceptibly, just enough movement to assure her he understood.

"Ruby, Lily, how are my two favorite ladies today?" He smiled down at the girl as he fell into step beside the pair.

Lily giggled for a second but then grew serious. She contemplated him, wide-eyed. "Did you know that some kids don't go to school year-round like we do? Becky Proudfoot told me her cousins in New Jersey don't have school *all summer.*"

He considered everything he knew about Ruby Smith's precocious daughter. Then he nodded. "Those poor kids."

"I *know.*"

Beside her, Ruby indulged in a proud maternal smile. Then the girl switched gears and pointed to the twisted wreckage across the street. To his eye, it wasn't recognizable as a Jeep, but somehow she knew.

"What happened to Aroostine's car? Is she okay?"

Lily's eye flew to her mother's face, seeking reassurance. Ruby cleared her throat. Before she could speak, Boom crouched beside the girl, meeting her on her eye level. Her luminous eyes were already filling with tears.

"Lily, listen carefully. Aroostine's car blew up but, this is important, she wasn't inside when it happened. I saw her with my own two eyes, run clear of the car before it exploded. She and her husband didn't die."

Ruby's eyebrows shot so far up her forehead they seemed to meet her hairline.

"Do you promise?" Lily asked.

"I promise."

"Where is she? Is she hurt? Can I see her?"

Boom answered her questions in order and honestly. Childless himself, he knew that some people would frown on telling a girl Lily's age the truth. Bunkum, that was what he thought of that. Children, after all, are people living in this imperfect world. It wasn't his place to shield her from reality. But he took pains to explain it on a level she could understand.

"I don't know where she is. She ran away, so I don't think she's badly hurt or she wouldn't have gotten far. And since we don't know where she is, we can't see her."

"But I want to see her."

"I'd like to, too."

She chewed on her lower lip and considered the information he'd given her.

"Will she come back?"

"I don't know."

"Did someone try to hurt her?"

"Maybe. I don't think the police have decided yet if the explosion was an accident or on purpose."

Ruby pulled a face at that. He shrugged at her. Everyone with two brain cells to keep one another company was well aware that the car bombing was intentional. But Chief Johnson hadn't yet made the official call. So his answer was technically true.

The girl dropped her eyes to the ground but asked no more questions. He suspected she was thinking about her neighbor, murdered just one day earlier, but he respected her right to her private thoughts and said nothing.

Ruby cleared her throat again. "Listen, Lil, let's get you home, and you can get started on your homework. I'm going to ask Mr. Cowslip to stay with you tonight while I'm at work. Would you like that?"

Lily's head snapped up. Her worried eyes now shone with excitement. "Really? Will you, Mr. Cowslip? After I do my homework will you tell me about the Dream Daughter?" Her eyes darted from her mother's face to Boom's.

He smiled. For all their infatuation with technology and the world off the reservation, the children of White Springs loved nothing better than to gather in a tight circle around Boom and hear him tell stories of their people and the old ways of living.

"I'd be honored. On one condition."

"Okay?" the girl breathed.

"Stop calling me Mr. Cowslip. Call me Boom—or Grandfather."

She smiled up into his face, and it was as if the sun itself had slipped from its anchor in the sky and beamed out from the girl's soul.

Ruby placed the mug of steaming tea on the scratched but polished table and handed him a honey dipper and pot of honey.

"Local?" he asked.

"From Mary's bees."

He swirled the viscous, golden liquid into his hot drink. She glanced at the closed door to Lily's bedroom, where she'd set up the girl with a glass of water, a plate of apple slices, and her school books.

"You've done a good job with her, Ruby."

She flushed with pleasure and pride at the compliment and let her long eyelashes flutter down to her cheekbones.

"Thank you, Boom. I'm trying so hard. She's a special girl."

"Yes. She is." He sipped his tea.

"Is everything you said true—about Aroostine and her husband?" She asked the question in a low, husky voice, barely above a whisper.

"Of course it's true. They'd just left my home—they'd come to ask me to help keep watch over you and your daughter."

Ruby made a small sound, a little mew. He paused to let her speak, but she said nothing.

He continued, "I was watching from my doorway. They got into the vehicle and immediately got back out. Joe checked the engine, seemed satisfied that everything was in order, then started the engine. Aroostine started to get into the passenger side, but something must have seemed wrong to her. She crawled beneath the car and emerged a moment later, screaming Joe's name. They ran toward the field and seconds later . . . the Jeep was in flames."

He stopped here, and the two of them sat in silence. He was picturing the scene. He wondered what images were running through her mind's eye.

Finally, she spoke. "Why did they run? I mean, once they were free of the fire. Why didn't they come back and ask you for help?"

That question had been running through his thoughts for hours.

"I don't know. I'm not sure we'll ever see them again, Ruby. They may not be sure who they can trust here. Or they may just be too frightened. Or . . ."

"Or what?"

He could tell from her tone that she knew what he didn't want to say. He sighed. "Or they may be regretting their promise to help you. They don't have any real connection to us, to our people. They may have decided you and Lily aren't worth getting mixed up in our bloody battles, Ruby."

Her chin jutted out. "They wouldn't do that."

Boom placed his palms flat on the table and pierced her with a look.

"We don't know them. And they don't know us. I hope I'm wrong. But if I'm right, you have my word that I will take care of you and Lily. Now, it's time for you to kiss your daughter good night and get up to the casino for your shift. You don't want to give Lee any reason to be suspicious of you."

She blanched at the reminder that she was about to totter into the lion's den on four-inch heels for an eight-hour shift of slinging drinks at drunk white tourists.

"Give me strength," she muttered.

"Ruby Smith, if there's one thing you have in spades, it's strength." He flashed her a comforting grin and was gratified to see a small smile bloom on her tense lips.

CHAPTER FOURTEEN

When the sun threatened to dip behind the distant purple mountains, Aroostine stopped walking and turned to face Joe, who'd been lagging about a half step behind. He jerked to a halt.

"Is something wrong?"

"It'll get dark fast out here once the sun sets. We should find a good spot to stop for the night, set up our shelter, and get some dinner."

"Dinner as in a burger and fries or dinner as in another handful of grass and berries?"

She gave him a wistful smile.

"Sorry."

Then she narrowed her eyes in thought. She had planned to skip making a fire. She was confident they'd be able to stay warm for one night without one. Plus it would be a hassle to start one without the benefit of matches, and smoke would be a telltale sign, liable to lead bad guys right to them. But . . . a fire would give them more options for food. And there was something comforting about sitting in front of a fire on a dark night. The heat, the light, the dancing flames.

She scanned the horizon. Nobody was going to find them, not out here. Not tonight.

"What?"

"Do you think you could catch a fish or two with your bare hands?"

"Maybe. Probably. Why?"

"Let's find a shelter then you go down to the stream and catch us some dinner while I get a fire going."

"You've got yourself a deal."

His bravado couldn't hide the fact that he wasn't at all certain he could catch a fish without a rod. She didn't have the heart to tell him that she'd given him the easier of the two jobs.

"Great."

She turned and surveyed their immediate surroundings. For just one night, there was no point in constructing a shelter. It made more sense to find a natural shelter. Her grandfather's voice sounded in her mind:

Location first. High and dry ground—uphill from the stream. Southern exposure to take advantage of the sun's heat and light. Facing east to capture the sun's early rays for warmth.

She identified the general vicinity that would satisfy all of her grandfather's requirements just over the next ridge. Before she headed toward it, she turned to Joe and pointed. "I'm going to head up that way and get a fire started. Good luck."

He blew her a kiss and headed down toward the stream. She hoped it took him a good long while to either catch a fish or give up because it had been about two decades since she'd started a fire without a man-made fire starter.

It's like riding a bike, she told herself, even though it was nothing at all like riding a bike. She trudged up the hill. Shelter first. Then the fire. She scouted and rejected a handful of options—a fallen log, a tangle of boughs. Then, in the foothills of the mountain, she spotted a rock outcropping that checked all the requisite boxes.

Home sweet home.

She sidled into the space between the rock walls and pounded on them with her hands. No loose stones or debris came crashing down on her. She swept the ground clear of twigs and pebbles with her feet. The sleeping arrangements would be adequate once she lined the ground with leaves for bedding.

Time to tackle the fire.

She worked quickly, gathering rocks to create a low, semicircular wall and digging out a shallow bowl of the dirt within the space. Then she loaded her arms with dry, dead tree branches and carried them to her fire pit. Each time she brought back an armload of sticks, she scanned the brilliant, cloudless sky overhead.

Uneasiness had been building in her veins ever since she'd spied the beaver watching them on the ridge. She couldn't shake the idea that her spirit guide was portending danger. A snippet of a documentary on unmanned drones that she must have seen months earlier kept spooling through her mind. A scrawny boy, no more than six, maybe younger, was pointing to the cloudy gray sky overhead and explaining to the filmmaker in halting English that the parents in his village no longer let the children play outside when the sky was blue. The clearer the day, the more likely a drone attack. Everyone knew, he said, that the bombs didn't fall when the sky was dark and cloudy.

A low-flying hawk swooped by, and its shadow blocked the sun for a second. Aroostine's entire body tensed and she froze, waiting for the light and blast that would mean the end. Then the bird circled away and the sun returned. She exhaled and dropped the pile of kindling to the ground with the rest.

She knelt on the hard earth beside it and worked to regulate her breathing. As her heart rate slowed, her fear and anxiety began to turn to hot anger. Anger at whomever was out there, wishing her dead. Anger at the penny-pinching desk jockey who'd approved the use of a civilian site to test armed drones. And anger at the scientists and military strategists who'd created a weapon that could destroy a life without conscience.

That same documentary had included a piece about the distant operators of the drones. Young men, mostly, barely out of their teens, who remote controlled the bombs from thousands of miles away. Watching the action on a screen, as if they were playing video games. And the distance seemed to make the destruction as unreal to those boys as a video game. They didn't have to lock eyes with the target, didn't have to hear the screams, see the hot blood and disintegrating body parts.

They simply jerked their joysticks, pressed their buttons, and watched the distant, grainy explosions as their bombs hit their targets. "Bug splats" they called the dead; evidence—according to a psychologist who'd been interviewed—that they were so far removed from the battle they didn't even regard their victims as human. The psychologist had warned that this sort of warfare—detached, clean, mechanical—was unlike any that had come before it and would likely take an eventual toll on the bomb operators that no one would be prepared to address.

At the moment, Aroostine's concern was not for the emotional distress that might someday befall those video game playing boys, but for her and Joe, alone on the run under an endless sky.

Joe. She wondered how he was faring. Whether he was successful or not, he'd likely be returning from the stream soon. The light was fading quickly now. She roused herself to action.

She stood and walked to a thicket of long grasses and shrubs to the left of the fire pit. She plucked several long cattails and weeds for tinder and fluffed them in her hands until the material formed a loose cloud. She wove in some long grass and scraps of bark she'd picked up along with the kindling then placed the little nest of material in the center of the hollowed-out pit. She separated the kindling sticks into the thin slivers she would use to start the fire and the thicker branches she would add once she had a blaze started. Remembering her grandfather's long-ago caution to use slow, sure movements, she piled the sticks around the ball of tinder, propping the sticks against each other so they formed a tent over the tinder. She worked out from the center, adding the larger, heavier branches in a constant, careful rhythm.

She rarely thought about her adoptive parents when she was in the woods—they weren't outdoorsy people—but the process of building the fire reminded her of building houses of cards with her father when she was home sick from school with strep throat. She'd been bored, tired of being stuck in bed, but had been too drained to do much else. He'd shown up in her room with a deck of playing cards and proceeded to teach her how to carefully place the cards so as to construct ever taller and more sturdy houses. She could see his long, steady fingers placing each card with precision and then hovering, still, for a moment while she held her breath to see if it would stay or if the entire structure would go tumbling down.

Now her hands were suspended, just as his had been, over the teepee shape she'd built around the tinder. She waited. Waited. The sticks held. She exhaled slowly and went off in search of two stones and Joe, holding thoughts of her grandfather and her adoptive father in the same space in her mind. It felt right, surprisingly.

Joe heard footsteps approaching from behind. He craned his neck and saw Aroostine making her way down the steeply sloped bank.

"Hey." He gestured toward the three rainbow trout still flipping intermittently on the ground beside him.

"Hey, yourself. Wow, I'm impressed."

He grinned. He was, too, to tell the truth. He hadn't had much confidence in his ability to catch a single fish with his hands, let alone three, but it hadn't taken long. The front of his shirt was sopping wet but he'd managed to snag—and, more importantly, hang on to—three medium-sized trout.

"Yeah, although I think that's all she wrote. I haven't seen another fish in several minutes."

"Three's plenty."

"That's kind of what I figured." He glanced down at the fish, which appeared to have taken their last gasping breaths. "So, now what?"

She flashed him an apologetic smile. "Well, first I need to find two rocks to serve as my flint and steel. While I'm doing that, can you look for a really sharp rock on the bottom of the stream, something we can use to take their heads off?"

"Sure."

"And a big flat one that we can use as a pan."

He nodded then pushed his already wet sleeves up farther and started feeling around on the stream bed. Aroostine moved slightly downstream and squatted near the water's edge. She stuck her hands in the water and pulled up two clumps of rocks then began to sift through them, discarding those she deemed unsuitable in a pile to her left.

"You're really going to start a fire by banging two rocks together?"

"I really am."

Joe had learned not to doubt his wife when it came to matters of nature, but the idea sounded so far-fetched, like something out of a bad movie, that he felt his mouth twist into a knot of disbelief.

She caught his look and laughed. Her breath rustled her long bangs, pushing them away from her face.

"There's no magic to it. Flint is pretty much any one of a couple different hard quartz rocks. Some people call it chert." She sifted through several large rocks in her hand. "Out here, it looks like jasper is pretty common."

She pulled an irregular quadrilateral of mottled red and green from the pile and held it out for him to see. The fading sun glinted off it and gave it a glow.

"It's pretty."

"It is. But I'm not sure it's sharp enough." She tested the jagged edge on her finger and scrunched up her nose. "I guess it'll do if I don't find something better."

He sorted through her cache of rejected rocks and found a dark gray stone shaped almost like an arrowhead. "This looks like a good fish knife."

She glanced up. "Do want me to help you clean them?"

Yes.

"No. I'll figure it out."

"You sure?"

He grinned at her, hoping he projected a confidence he didn't feel. "I'm sure. I mean, I doubt they'll pass muster in a fancy restaurant, but I'll get the scales off and the guts out. How's that sound?"

"Perfect." He started to walk away but she snagged the elbow of his shirt and pulled him back. "Can I borrow your watch?"

He unclasped the bracelet and handed the heavy stainless-steel watch to her.

"Here you go."

"Thanks. I'll try not to break it."

He turned back. "Break it? What are you going to do with it?"

She pushed her hair out of her eyes with the back of her free hand. "I'm not seeing much pyrite, just little slivers inside larger rocks. Jasper is a sufficient flint—well, chert, but close enough—but I need a steel. Your watch is perfect." She hefted it, obviously satisfied by its weight in her hand.

He hesitated. She'd given him that watch just six weeks ago on their anniversary. He loved it because it was waterproof and uncomplicated, sleek and dependable. And because every time he checked the time, he thought of her.

"Joe. It's just a thing."

He could have guessed that she'd say something like that. She was as unsentimental as she was honest and generous.

"I know."

She must have heard the petulant tone that crept into his voice because she paused in her rock hunting and took a moment to do nothing but look into his eyes.

Finally, she said, "I'll be as careful as I can. And if I give it back to you with a dent or a ding, well, then you'll have a new memory to carry around." She smiled gently.

He felt his own mouth twitch and allowed the grin to take hold. "Okay."

He strode over and lifted the fish from the ground. She took the jasper and his watch and headed back up the embankment.

"Good luck," she called over her shoulder as he contemplated the trout's head, with his sharp rock in hand.

Aroostine sighed and scooted closer to Joe. The sigh was one of pure contentment.

A good-sized fire blazed in the pit, the flames reflecting off the wall of the rock outcropping that would serve as their bedroom and warming her face. The smoky fish flaked apart in her fingers and tasted like heaven. With her belly full, a safe place to sleep, her husband beside her, and a starry sky overhead, she smiled out into the black, still woods. The wilderness felt like a pair of protective arms rather than an ominous danger, comforting rather than frightening.

Joe shoveled a hunk of fish into his mouth and gave her a curious sidelong glance as he chewed it.

"What are you thinking?"

"If I didn't know better, I'd swear you're happier out here than you were in Central Oregon's swankiest resort."

She considered her response for a moment before answering.

"I am."

He leaned toward her, and the firelight highlighted his face.

"You mean that, don't you?"

"Yes, I do. I'm not perfectly happy because I'm worried about Ruby, about Lily, about those blasted drones that may or may not have gone missing, but you're right. There's something about being outside, away from civilization, that just feels *right*, deep in my bones." It was her turn to look at him questioningly. "But, you know that. It's not exactly a secret."

"It's not a secret that you like to hike or just sit out under a tree or whatever, sure. Or even go camping. But this . . . this is some primitive camping, Roo. We're using our fingers to eat fish that I caught with my hands and you cooked on a rock. I mean, think about that?"

She smiled. "Not only that. We're about to go to sleep on a bed of long grass and weeds covered with leaves."

"Yeah, exactly my point. That's a far cry from a pillowtop mattress and Egyptian cotton sheets."

"Agreed. But it'll be just you, me, and the crickets under this big sky. Doesn't that sound romantic?"

A smile played across his face. "Depends on what you have in mind."

"We'll let this fire die down, and then I'll show you exactly what I'm thinking," she said, her voice thick with promise.

She drove thoughts of the reservation, Sid, the drones, the dead man—all of it—from her mind. Tonight she wanted to couple with

Joe in the heart of Mother Earth, the way her ancestors had since the beginning of time, the way a man and woman were meant to.

"You've got yourself a deal." His voice sounded as husky as hers, full of longing.

He snugged an arm around her and pulled her closer. She closed her eyes, leaned into the warmth of his chest, and inhaled deeply, filling her lungs with the crisp night air.

If her spirit animal was lurking around somewhere out in the shadows, watching them with its liquid silver eyes, she fervently hoped it would leave her alone until morning.

CHAPTER FIFTEEN

The sound of Ruby's temperamental old car wheezing its way down the road broke the silence of the overnight hours. Boom blinked himself awake on the couch and tucked his shirttails back into place. By the time Ruby knocked softly on her front door, he had his shoes on and his hair smoothed down. Even in the middle of the night, it was important to appear presentable, respectable.

He slid the chain and unlocked the newly installed deadbolt. He pulled the door inward and stepped aside to let her pass.

"How was she?" she whispered.

"She had a snack around eight, brushed her teeth, and settled into bed. I told her the story of Thunderbird, the creation tale, and she was snoring before I reached the part where I explained why we must always slit the salmon down their backs."

Ruby graced him with a tired smile.

"Thank you, Boom."

He put a fatherly hand on her shoulder. "You don't need to thank me, Ruby. Part of living within the circle means you don't need to do everything alone. Remember that."

She nodded and stifled a yawn. Then she reached out a hand to steady herself against the wall while she eased her feet out of her stilettos.

"I left some stew warming on your stove in case you're hungry. I'll come over the same time tomorrow?" he asked as he headed toward the door.

"I'll let you know."

He turned, his hand on the door. "Oh?"

She rubbed her eyes with her knuckles, smearing her eyeliner.

"Yeah. I can't do this much longer. I was a nervous wreck at work, worrying that Lee was going to turn up and tell me he needed to talk to me. Every time I saw one of his security goons, my hands started to shake. If I keep spilling drinks like I did tonight, I'm not going to have a job."

"What's your plan?"

"I'm going to call the Department of Justice in the morning."

He cocked his head but didn't speak.

"Even if Aroostine's gone for good, she already reached out to her boss—Sid Somebody or Other. He said he'd help us, so I'm going to hold him to it."

Boom noted the fire that sprang to life in her eyes and held his tongue. It wouldn't do to argue with Ruby when she had her mind set on something.

"All the same," he said mildly. "Even the Justice Department can't work miracles. I'll plan to watch Lily tomorrow unless I hear otherwise from you."

Once she realized he didn't plan to try to dissuade her, her jaw relaxed and she nodded. "I appreciate that. And you're probably right—I doubt the government will move that quickly."

He opened the door. "They rarely do, daughter. Unless they're taking something from us—in that case, they spring faster than a cheetah. Lock this behind me."

"Good night."

He walked out into the dark and took in the starry sky above. He stepped off the porch and wondered if Aroostine was looking up at the same sky. Behind him, he heard Ruby slide the lock into place with a click.

CHAPTER SIXTEEN

Aroostine woke, chilled but rested, when the first early rays of light streamed into the shelter.

She'd slept soundly, a dreamless sleep that had also been free of visions or nightmares. She lay there for several minutes, listening to the birds chattering in the trees and Joe's even, deep breathing just beside her ear.

Only when the call of nature became too urgent to ignore did she ease herself out from under his thigh, which was resting heavily across hers. She slowly lifted his arm from around her waist and laid it gently on the ground before rising to her feet and slipping soundlessly out of the nook.

The morning dew dotted the grass like tears. But the sun was already gaining in strength, hinting a warm, cloudless day. She took a moment to wish for gray cloud cover before continuing down to the stream to wash up.

When she returned to the campsite, Joe was awake, pulling on his shoes.

"I woke up and you were gone," he said in a voice that couldn't hide his panic.

"I had to pee."

His worried frown turned to a sheepish smile. "Oh."

She crossed the small space and kissed him.

"I didn't mean to scare you," she murmured, her lips brushing his. "Good morning."

"Good morning." He whispered back, his breath tickling her.

"How'd you sleep?"

He tucked a strand of her hair behind her ear as he answered. "Surprisingly well. Of course, you did wear me out pretty thoroughly . . ."

She felt her cheeks grow warm. Before he could laugh at her, she pulled back and searched his face.

"I hate to be the buzzkill, but we need to move out."

The humor faded from his eyes, and he nodded. He raked his fingers through his hair, shaking out small dry leaves.

"Okay. Let's do it."

"You should go to the stream and get some water first. Make sure you drink up, because we're going to veer away from it and cut a diagonal toward Boylestown."

"I thought you wanted to follow the stream?"

She had. Tracing the path of the snaking stream would ensure they had access to drinking water, but it would be faster to leave the ribbon behind. And all of a sudden she felt convinced that speed was paramount. The longer they were out of contact with Sid, the more vulnerable Ruby—and Lily—became.

"I think we need to get to town as early in the day as we can. Get to a phone and get Sid to send us some backup, some transportation, maybe some cash to get food."

"Are you saying you didn't like my hillbilly hand fishing?"

She grinned at the crack but grew serious again right away. "No, I'm feeling exposed out here. Another bright blue sky is another chance for someone to fly a drone over our heads."

"You don't really think anyone's stupid enough to bomb two US citizens out of existence in the middle of Oregon." He paused a beat. "Do you?"

She pinned him with a look. "I have no idea. But I do know, for a certainty, that if it were to happen, the Department of Defense, Department of Justice, and Homeland Security would be out here so fast to cover it up that no one, *no one*, would ever know what happened to us."

"What, they'll send out the Men in Black?"

"Look around, Joe. Do you see anyone whose memory will need to be erased? We'll be reported as hikers who got lost and disoriented and then starved to death or something."

She waited while he made a slow survey of the expanse of wilderness that lay ahead of them. Then he swallowed hard.

"Okay. Give me three minutes."

His large watch, which she'd strapped around her own wrist after she'd used it to ignite the tinder, banged against her hand.

"Wait. Here. I forgot to give this back to you last night. It's just got a little dent in the one side." She unclasped it and handed it to him before he walked down to the stream. He rubbed his fingers over the indentation and smiled.

They crossed the rise and headed west toward the town side by side in silence, conserving their breath and maintaining a good clip. Every minute to ninety seconds, Aroostine glanced up, scanning the sky for a dark shadow. The lack of a drone flying overhead did nothing to alleviate her concern. If anything, the quiet served to ratchet up her anxiety.

"We should head toward the highway," she said, her panic overtaking her plan to stay out of view.

"Someone might see us."

"That's kind of the point. Maybe we could hitch a ride to Boylestown."

Joe coughed. "You look lovely, don't get me wrong. But I look like a man who slept in the woods. Would *you* pick us up?"

She inspected him closely and imagined what she might look like despite his flattery.

"Probably not."

"Besides, the risk that someone who works for Buckmount is going to drive by and see us is too great. That road's the main thoroughfare to the casino."

He was right, but she couldn't shake the feeling that they had to get to town. Fast.

He eyed her.

"Did you have another vision?"

"No."

And the truth was at this point—for the first time in her life—she would have welcomed one. She felt adrift, unsure of how to help the mother and child who counted on her. She increased her pace, almost jogging now, as though she could outrun her worry.

"Hey. Roo, look at me."

She stopped and turned to face Joe, who'd fallen behind and was now lagging by several paces. But before he could launch into whatever inspirational pep talk he had planned, her eyes slid over him and locked on a set of deep ruts that had been carved into the soft earth.

"Joe, look."

A wave of irritation rolled across his face, but he followed her gaze and craned his neck to look over his shoulder and off to the left.

"Tire tracks?" He crouched and traced the indent with a finger. "Looks like an ATV. Must have been carrying a heavy load."

A spark of excitement raced up her spine.

"Maybe we can get a ride, if the driver's still around."

"What makes you think they're still around?"

"Only one set of tracks," she pointed out. "So, whoever it was didn't come back this way. We should follow them and see where they go."

He hesitated.

"Come on," she urged.

"Wait. A minute ago you were all hopped up to get to the highway and catch a lift to town. Now you want to go off on what's likely to be a wild goose chase and a huge waste of time? Do you have a plan or not?" his voice shook with anger and betrayal.

She stiffened and prepared to fire back defensively when a flash in the distance caught her eye. As if she'd summoned it, her spirit animal stood on its hind legs about fifty yards away, its feet planted smack in the middle of the tracks. A sign. An unmistakable sign. The only clearer sign would have been if it had worn a placard around its neck with the words "GO THIS WAY" displayed in flashing neon lights. She had to follow it, not because it made logical sense, but because it didn't. She simply had to trust her guide.

She looked back at Joe. Now to explain that she was taking instructions from an imaginary semiaquatic rodent.

"I had a sign."

"Like a vision?"

"Sort of."

She glanced back toward the beaver, but was not surprised to see that it had vanished. Joe was watching her face.

He cleared his throat. "Well, that settles that. Let's go."

He started off along the tracks. She blinked at the ease with which he put his faith in a pretend beaver that he couldn't even see and that she still had never bothered naming and followed him.

Joe figured they'd followed the ATV tracks for about a quarter mile before the ground sloped up and the sporadic trees that had lined their path grew denser and taller. Another couple hundred yards and they were in a densely wooded area. The temperature fell by several degrees as the canopy of leaves overhead blocked the heat of the sun. He had to squint a little to make out the tracks in the filtered sunlight.

The ground itself was drier and rockier now, making the tracks less pronounced. Twice they veered off course without realizing it. Both times, Aroostine realized it first and retraced their steps back to the tracks. If her beaver was giving her any more clues, she kept them to herself, but he didn't think the beaver was leading her. This was all her.

Joe tried to keep his eyes on the tracks, but he kept scanning the dirt on either side as well. He had no idea what kind of snakes were indigenous to this part of Oregon, but this shady, hard-scrabbled area seemed like the sort of environment a snake would love.

He was raising his head to call ahead to Aroostine and ask about the reptile situation when he bumped right into her back. She'd come to a stop and was standing frozen in path, staring at a natural cave just ahead.

"What the . . ."

"Only one way to find out." She stepped forward and walked into the mouth of the cave.

He glanced from side to side. Forget snakes, if he were a bad guy, he'd probably consider an isolated cave hidden deep in the woods to be an excellent place to get rid of a nosy federal prosecutor and her dashing husband.

His pulse pounded and his shoulders tensed as he looked around, expecting Buckmount to be lying in wait behind the nearest tree, but he saw no signs of human life. Just a startled bird, which left the tree where it had been perched with a furious flapping and squawking.

He exhaled and followed Aroostine into the cave. He stood just inside the entrance and blinked several times, waiting for his eyes to adjust to the dim light.

The space was cavernous, at least twenty-five feet across and twice as deep. The walls were rough and gray, much rockier than the sides of the outcropping where they'd slept the night before.

Aroostine was just a dark, shadowy shape, barely visible in the gloom. She was standing over beside the far right wall, about three yards into the space.

She turned and called over her shoulder, "You have to see this."

He crossed the uneven floor of the cave, taking care with each step. He proceeded in an exaggeratedly slow tiptoe, which he was sure looked ridiculous. But that was fine with him; he imagined tripping and getting a chin full of the jagged ground would hurt like hell. And whatever she wanted him to see probably wasn't going anywhere—assuming it wasn't alive, of course.

Oh, dear Lord, please don't let it be a snake.

At last, he reached the spot where she stood. He stared at the shape in front of her, and his breath caught in his throat.

"Is that a drone?"

A sleek, brushed-silver-looking, bullet-shaped *thing* sat on a pallet. The nose of whatever it was faced them. And the tail extended another twenty feet back into the recesses of the cave. He reached out a hand and touched it gingerly, as if it might be hot to the touch. The metal was cool under his fingers. A chill ran down his back. If anyone would've ever told him that one day he'd look at an inanimate machine and feel the presence of evil, he would have said that person read too much Stephen King.

And yet, confronted by the silent, motionless drone, he couldn't shake the feeling that it was a bringer of death.

"Has to be," Aroostine whispered. She moved around to the side of the machine, giving it a wide berth as if she too sensed destruction. She bent and peered at the tail and then walked back to the front to stand beside him, her shoulder brushing his. "It doesn't look armed."

Thank God for small mercies, he thought.

Then her eyes met his, gleaming in the near-dark. "There's another one behind it, nose to tail."

"Did Ruby say how many were missing?" He choked the words out despite the rising nausea in his throat.

Aroostine shook her head. "No. We never got any details out of her. When she showed up with that note, I went into crisis management mode. I was so focused on the threat to Lily and getting Sid to do something, I didn't press her on the specifics."

"Don't."

"Don't what?"

"Don't do that thing where you start beating yourself up for some perceived failure. For one thing, you did the right thing—of course Lily's safety takes priority. For another thing, we don't have time for you to self-flagellate."

She gave him a sheepish smile. "Self-flagellate, huh? You been brushing up on your fifty-cent words?"

He smiled back. "Something like that." He'd read a history of the Roman Catholic Church, mainly to pass the long evening hours during her last jury trial. Some of it apparently had stuck.

"We need to do something. Fast. Before the person who stashed these here comes back for them."

He swallowed around the lump in his throat. He'd pay good money for a bottle of water right about now.

"Any ideas?"

She set her mouth in that determined line he knew so well. "Yes. You stay here. I'm going to run to the highway and flag down the first car that comes this way."

"What if it's Buckmount or one of his lackeys?"

"We don't have time to worry about that. I'll take care of myself."

"Why don't you stay here? I'll go."

"No. I'm faster than you are. Besides, you have a watch. If I'm not back in two hours, go for help."

She turned to go. He grabbed her elbow and pulled her close.

"Hurry. And remember, Roo. I love you."

She didn't answer. Instead, she covered his mouth with hers and laced her hands together behind his neck in a long kiss.

He stared at her face, memorizing the curve of her cheek, just in case he never saw her again. Her eyes were fierce, like a warrior's. He could almost see the ancient heritage running through her.

She locked eyes with him for an eternal moment. Then she smiled sadly, dropped her arms, and jogged out of the cave without a word.

He listened to his heartbeat pound in his ears while he set the timer on his watch. Then he crossed to the opposite side of the cave—as far away from the drone as he could get—and slid down the wall to the ground to wait for his wife to return with the cavalry.

CHAPTER SEVENTEEN

Boom parked Isaac's red car in the first empty spot in the elementary school's small parking lot. He felt vaguely guilty about using the car without seeking permission from Isaac's mother, but he reasoned that Cathy Palmer had enough on her plate trying to get a handle on her son's affairs and—not to be cruel—Isaac had no use for the vehicle anymore.

He killed the engine and slipped the key into his pocket. As he locked the door, he noticed that he was parked askew—the back end of the Tercel was over the line, encroaching into the next spot. He considered trying to straighten it out, but he was enough of a realist to know he was unlikely to improve the situation. It had been well over a decade since he'd had occasion to get behind the wheel of a car. He was a cautious and reluctant driver but a terrible parker. That had been true even when he used to drive regularly; he thought it unlikely his parking skills would have improved with disuse.

He put the car out of mind and focused on what he was about to say and do. Walk into the school building and tell Kelly in the office that he needed to fetch Lily Smith. Everyone at the school knew and trusted him; they all loved his storytelling sessions with the kids. Once they'd called Lily out of class, he'd get her to the car and off the reservation before Lee or anyone else knew what had happened. He hoped Ruby had told the school that he was authorized to pick up the girl, but he didn't think it really mattered one way or the other.

He mounted the wide, cracked steps slowly, holding firmly to the metal railing splitting them down the middle. Inside, he paused for a moment in the silent hallway and thought of all the trusting, young souls sitting in quiet circles and uneven rows in the rooms that lined the hall. Then he smiled and pushed open the door to the office to greet Kelly.

Four minutes later, he walked back out of Mary Proudfoot Elementary School with Lily by his side.

"I don't understand. Why does my mom want me to leave early?" Lily asked as she adjusted the wide, padded straps of her backpack, stooping a little under the weight of her school books. "And why didn't she come get me herself? She doesn't work until tonight."

Boom waited until they reached the parking lot to answer. He turned and faced the girl squarely.

"Lily, I'm going to treat you like an adult, okay?"

"Okay." Her small voice quavered.

"I was reading a book by my living room window when I heard a car door slam. I looked up and saw Lee Buckmount getting out of a car in front of your house. He knocked on your front door. A moment later, he and your mom got in the car, and he drove off."

Lily scrunched up her face in confusion. "Mr. Buckmount picked up my mom? Where did they go?"

Boom spread his hands wide. "I don't know, little one. But it seemed to me that I should come and get you now. That is what my heart told me to do."

Lily shook her head, still puzzled. Then her eyes fell on the red car. "You're driving Isaac's car?"

Boom unlocked the passenger side door and held it open for the girl.

"Just borrowing it."

He shut the door and walked around to the driver's side, scanning the road in front of the school as he did so. He saw no signs of casino security, tribal police, or anyone for that matter. *So far, so good.*

He lowered himself into the seat and contemplated the steering wheel like it was a wild horse. Then he inserted the key and exhaled a long, slow breath before starting the car.

CHAPTER EIGHTEEN

Aroostine ran.

She ticked off all the tips on form that Rosie had drummed into her head during their grueling lunchtime runs when she'd been working at Main Justice. Rosie had been training for a marathon. Aroostine had been running to forget her failing marriage, so she hadn't really cared if she was breathing efficiently or putting too much strain on her shins. But listening to Rosie's enthusiastic advice had helped pass the long, excruciating minutes. If she'd known she'd be putting the wisdom to the test under such dire circumstances, she might have paid closer attention.

She dug in and increased her speed as she crested the hill. Whenever her energy flagged, she flashed back to the ominous metal beasts crouched in the cave and found a new burst of power.

Finally, the asphalt ribbon of gray highway appeared in the distance. She poured it on and sprinted flat out toward the road. She reached the berm and bent, hands on knees, panting.

Keep moving when you cross the finish line; stay loose.

She groaned a curse at the little voice of Rosie Montoya that had taken up residence in her brain, but did as it said. She walked, taking big strides, with her arms raised overhead and gulped down the clean air as if it were cold water.

She walked on, following the curve of the road. All that running seemed to have depleted the oxygen from her brain nearly as much as it had taxed her muscles. Her ears were popping as if she were in an airplane, and the only way to describe her thinking was fuzzy.

She didn't recall Rosie mentioning a decrease in IQ points with each completed race. She laughed aloud at the thought then stumbled, tripping over her shoelace. She caught herself at the last second and bent to tie the loose lace.

As she was crouched near the ground, a black Lincoln Navigator blew past her so fast the wind ruffled her loose hair.

"No, no. No!" she staggered to her feet and raised her arms overhead, waving them as if she were flagging down a rescue helicopter.

Hot salty tears spilled from her eyes as the SUV grew smaller.

Failure. Blown opportunity. Disaster.

She was glad Joe wasn't around to comment on her self-talk. She wiped the sweat from her forehead and piled her thick, long hair on top of her head, twisting it into a loose bun, to cool her hot neck.

The Navigator screeched to a halt. Her pulse skyrocketed.

Thank you, Universe. She raised her face to the sky, joy pulsing through her veins. She began to jog toward the vehicle, a smile of gratitude on her face.

And then the driver's door opened. A man in a business suit emerged from the car and stormed around to the passenger side. He reached inside and dragged out a person—a woman. She was screaming at him. Aroostine couldn't make out the words from a distance but the way the woman struggled against the man's grasp was unmistakable: she was afraid.

Aroostine's heart sank and landed somewhere in the vicinity of her knees.

She did not have time for this Good Samaritan business. And yet she couldn't pretend not to see—even if it ended up that she'd stumbled onto a garden-variety lovers' quarrel, she couldn't ignore the woman's plight. She slowed to a cautious walk as she approached the couple.

Meanwhile the man half pulled, half dragged the woman across the shoulder of the road and down a small hill. Out of sight of anyone who might drive by.

Aroostine's adrenaline rose another notch. She began to scan the side of the road for something, anything that might be a serviceable weapon. Orgeon's geological formations came to her rescue once again. She bent and hefted a large gray rock—more of a small boulder, really. She conservatively estimated its weight as twelve pounds or so. The woman's shouting carried to her on the wind. She recognized that raw voice—a mixture of fear and anger. *Ruby.*

She sped up and reached the top of the hill, hoping she was wrong. No, she was right. Ruby twisted, screaming and trying to wrench herself free of Lee Buckmount. Buckmount stood with his back to Aroostine and the road. He had both hands clamped on Ruby's shoulders and was shaking her violently.

"Damn you, tell me what else he told you and who you told!" Lee raged at her.

"I told you, Lee! I swear, I told you everything." Tears streamed down Ruby's face.

Aroostine took another step closer. The movement must have caught Ruby's eye because her gaze traveled over Lee's shoulder. Her eyes widened when she spotted Aroostine, but she managed to keep her expression smooth. Aroostine put one finger to her lips and raised the boulder, pantomiming bringing it down on someone's head.

Ruby blinked once. An instant later, she did something that probably saved her life. Lee dropped his hands from her shoulders and pulled a handgun from inside his jacket. Ruby swooned and pretended to faint. She let her legs buckle under her and crumpled to the ground.

Aroostine crept behind Buckmount as he bent over Ruby, holding the gun down by his side. She inhaled deeply as she raised the rock, two-handed, over her head. Then she exhaled and smashed it into the back of his skull with a sickening crunch. The impact of rock meeting bone jarred her arms, but she clenched tighter.

The force carried her forward, and she fell on his back as he rocketed toward the ground. Ruby rolled to her left and managed to dodge them. Lee collapsed in a pool of blood, moaning. Aroostine pushed herself off him, faintly nauseous at the sight and coppery smell of so much blood. She scrabbled for his gun, but Ruby already had it. She held it with shaking hands, her foot pressed firmly against Lee's wrist, pinning him to the ground.

"I don't think he's going anywhere any time soon," Aroostine told her.

She gently pried the gun from Ruby's hands, peeling her fingers back one by one. Once the weapon was out of her hand, Ruby began to sob wildly.

"You saved my life. I thought you were never coming back," she muttered.

Aroostine figured the other woman was either in shock or about to go into a shock state.

"Listen, Ruby, this is important. Call Boom and tell him to meet us here."

"Shouldn't I call the police?"

"Yes. But, Boom first, okay? I want him to be here when the tribal police get here. I don't want to try to navigate the politics without his help."

It was true, as far as it went. But it was also true that Aroostine just wanted Boom there for comfort and support. The way a young girl might want her grandfather, she realized. The realization startled her, and she told herself she'd give it due consideration sometime when she wasn't quite so busy apprehending a criminal.

At the mention of the authorities, Buckmount began to writhe and groan. She pushed aside the emotions that threatened to overtake her and crouched beside him. She intended to whisper in his ear, but the drying blood that covered the side of his head turned her stomach, so she averted her head and said, "Don't even think about trying to get up. I'll hit you like I mean it if I have to hit you again. Or maybe I'll just shoot you with your own gun. Wonder if this'll be a ballistics match for the gun used to kill Isaac?"

He went limp and silent.

She turned back to Ruby, but Ruby already had the phone to her ear. Excellent. She mentally ticked off the phone calls they would make.

First Boom. Then Sid. Then the tribal police.

Hang tight, Joe. I'm coming.

CHAPTER NINETEEN

The red car that had been parked outside Isaac Palmer's house screeched to a halt at an angle behind Buckmount's Navigator. Aroostine waved from the top of the hill and then pointed down to the far side. Once Boom exited the car and waved to indicate he understood, she jogged back to join Ruby.

She was no longer afraid that Ruby would slip into shock, but she did have some concerns about leaving her alone with Buckmount for too long—Ruby was mad enough to kill the man. And Buckmount wasn't doing himself any favors. Once he regained his power of speech, he'd indulged in a running diatribe directed primarily at Ruby.

Aroostine was tempted to whack him on the head with the rock again to knock him out and spare them all. Instead she settled for removing the bullets from the gun and telling Ruby to hit him with it if necessary.

She skidded to a stop at the bottom of the hill.

"Boom's here."

"Good." Ruby answered without taking her eyes off Buckmount.

Aroostine was reasonably confident he wouldn't try anything. His eyes were glazed, and he seemed to be having trouble focusing. He also had to have one heckuva headache. All the same, she was glad Boom had arrived—more than glad, to be honest.

She heard loose rocks tumbling down the hill and turned to see Boom sliding down the embankment sideways, as if he were snowboarding. Lily ran behind him, a pink-and-green backpack banging against her shoulders as she bounded toward her mother.

"Mom!" she shouted, racing past Boom.

Ruby shoved the gun into Aroostine's hands. Lily jumped into her mother's arms and wrapped her legs around her waist. Ruby hugged her daughter close, stroking her hair.

"What were you thinking, bringing her here?" Ruby asked over the top of the girl's head.

"It's after two o'clock, Ruby. We're unlikely to be back home before school lets out." Boom seemed chastened by the scolding, shuffling his feet in the dirt.

"Oh. Right. Of course." Ruby dropped the subject.

Lily lifted her cheek from her mother's shoulder. "Boom said he saw Mr. Buckmount taking you away from the house, Mom."

"You did?" Ruby asked.

"I wasn't sure what was going on. But something felt wrong to me. So I borrowed Isaac's car and headed toward school to pick up Lily. I'm glad I did. We got here a lot faster than we would have otherwise."

At the mention of Buckmount, Boom turned and looked at the man. As instructed, he was lying flat on his stomach with his hands crossed behind his back. He strained his neck, forcing his head up to meet Boom's gaze with a defiant expression.

"You old fool." Boom spat in the dirt near Buckmount's head.

"You're one to talk."

"Here—" Aroostine handed the gun to Boom, butt first. "I took out the bullets." She dropped them into his palm. "I need to get back to Joe. Can you stay here with Ruby until the tribal police come? She already called them and asked them to send two units and requested that Chief Johnson come to the scene, too."

Boom dangled the gun from two fingers as if he were reluctant to touch it. She knew the feeling.

"Why two units?"

Aroostine stared hard at Buckmount and answered in a low voice so Lily wouldn't hear. "Because we found two drones that need to be secured."

Buckmount's face remained impassive. No reaction.

"I'm not sure the tribal police are the right people for the job," Boom said.

"I'm sure they aren't. But they'll do until the Department of Defense and Homeland Security work out who's sending a team. I called Washington already. They're probably in the middle of a heated round of Rock, Paper, Scissors as we speak."

He didn't laugh.

"That last part was supposed to be a joke."

"This is a very grave matter, daughter. The government will vilify us."

She shook her head. "I don't think so, Boom. They're going to want to sweep this little event under the rug as quickly as they can. Public perception and whatnot."

"I hope so."

She gave him a smile meant to reassure him, but her mind was back at the cave.

"I really have to go. I'm afraid Buckmount's goons are already on the way to the cave."

"Cave?"

"Yeah, the drones are in a large cave back near the foothills of a mountain—"

Boom interrupted as she tried to describe the location. "I know the cave. Go. I'll bring Atlas and his officers and meet you there."

"Thank you," she said. Then she walked over to Ruby, who was still clutching her daughter to her chest.

"I have to go. You're okay now. He can't hurt either of you."

Ruby nodded.

Aroostine reached out and patted Lily on her narrow back. The girl turned and beamed up at her. Aroostine's throat threatened to close.

She inhaled deeply and started to run, up the hill, over the valley, and back to the dark cave where her husband sat, guarding two sophisticated pieces of military equipment armed only with a dented wristwatch. She dug the toes of her shoes into the earth and ran faster than she thought possible.

CHAPTER TWENTY

Forty-nine more minutes.

It had been an hour and eleven minutes since Aroostine left. She'd said if she wasn't back in two hours to go for help. One hundred and twenty minutes of not knowing if she was okay. If she'd been picked up by a helpful motorist or Isaac's murderer. If she had tripped over a root and snapped an ankle and was lying, writhing in pain, in the dirt. Or—if he was being honest, the nightmare scenario that had been running through his head in a loop—if she'd felt a dark shadow pass overhead and then been annihilated, pulverized into dust in a flash of heat and light.

Joe eyeballed the drone as if it might tell him something about his wife's fate. Unsurprisingly, it sat silent and still, like an animal waiting to spring.

Stop it.

He stood and walked to the mouth of the cave, telling himself he was just keeping his muscles loose. He wasn't afraid of a machine.

He made windmills with his arms. Jogged in place. Did some halfhearted jumping jacks. Checked the watch again.

Forty-seven more minutes.

He was going to go crazy in this cave before he managed to hit the two-hour mark. He scrubbed his hands over his face. Maybe some fresh air would help. It couldn't possibly hurt.

He strode out of the cave—four big steps—and breathed in deeply. The breeze ruffled his hair. A bird chattered nearby. The woods were shady now that the sun had begun its afternoon descent. But the light that did manage to stream through the trees was a welcome change from the funereal gloom inside the cavern.

Forty-four minutes.

He turned his face up to the sky and closed his eyes for a long moment.

The sound of twigs snapping and grass rustling filled the quiet. He popped his eyelids open and swiveled his head, looking for the source of the noise. He saw nothing. But now his heart was banging so loudly in his chest that he also couldn't hear anything other than the sound of it thudding.

"Hello?" he called. He scanned the ground for a thick stick or other suitable weapon.

"Joe?" came the reply.

Aroostine. His shoulders relaxed, and his breath whooshed out in an enormous sigh of relief. The drumming of his heart slowed and quieted to normal.

A moment later his wife emerged from the woods. She ducked under a bough and stepped onto the path. A frisson of joy shot through him at the sight of her. But no one followed her out of the trees. She was alone. His joy evaporated—or, more acurately, burst suddenly as if someone had stuck a pin in it.

"No help?"

"On its way."

She joined him in front of the cave and wrapped her arms around him. She clung to him so tightly that he couldn't draw a breath, but he didn't complain. Instead he pressed his nose into her hair and clung right back. They stood that way for a long time, he didn't know how long, because checking his watch was the farthest thing from his mind. Instead, he held his wife wordlessly and breathed in her scent—she smelled like sunshine and, after a night sleeping on the ground, a hint of earth.

After a while, she relaxed her grip and stepped back a half step.

"Am I glad to see you."

"Evidently."

Her mouth curved into a bow. "Sorry. I just . . . I was so worried."

"Never apologize for a hug like that," he told her. "So, how'd you get to town and back so quickly?"

"I didn't."

She leaned against the outer wall of the cave and began to tell him the entire story—how she'd run across Lee Buckmount threatening to kill Ruby, how she'd bashed his skull in, and how she and Ruby had restrained him until Boom arrived.

"Do you really think Buckmount would have killed her?" he asked when she paused to take a breath.

"I really do. He was so angry. He knew she knew *something*, but he didn't know what. He was never going to accept that Isaac hadn't shared any specifics with her." She shuddered.

He moved closer and wrapped an arm around her shoulder. "Cold?"

"No, I got a chill."

He realized that, despite her dispassionate delivery, the encounter with Buckmount had rattled her—maybe even more than had the discovery of the drones.

"You're okay."

"I know. I just . . . I think I held the gun that took Isaac Palmer's life, Joe." She stared down at her hand.

He gave her a moment then asked, "What did Sid say about the drones?"

She looked up with a miserable expression, as if the topic pained her.

"The government's putting together an ad hoc, cross-agency team to come out and handle the mess. All they want the tribal police to do is secure the darned things until they get here—and to do it without anyone noticing."

"Where are they going to store two monstrously large aircraft on the down low? Do the tribal police have an airplane hangar?"

She made a disgusted noise. "They want the chief to station two men here. The plan is to leave them in the cave until the Defense Department can arrange transport back to Pendleton."

"Here?"

"That's what they want."

"What did Chief Johnson say about taking two officers away from the reservation for an unspecified period of time?"

"Nothing yet—Sid wants me to be the bearer of that happy news."

"Ouch."

"Oh, there's more. Justice doesn't want tribal police to question Buckmount. They want me to interview him."

"You mean about the drones?"

"About all of it—the drones, Isaac's murder, Ruby's abduction and attempted murder, the embezzlement at the casino."

The mask of disgust didn't slip from her face, but he sensed a hint of excitement in her voice.

"That's great, though!" He said it with as much enthusiasm as he could muster.

She painted him with a bemused look. "You think so?"

"This is your break, Roo. Your ticket back to the fast track."

"Hmm. I thought you weren't such a fan of the fast track."

Boom's admonition about clipped birds echoed in his ears. He took his time answering but when he did, he spoke from a place of truth.

"I'm not. But I'm a huge fan of yours. And I want you to do what fulfills you. Will that fulfill you—getting back into Sid's good graces and another shot at being a superstar prosecutor?"

She leaned her head on his shoulder. "I'm not sure, to be completely honest. I thought it's what I wanted."

"But?"

"But I feel like something is shifting inside me. It's hard to explain. Being on the reservation. Seeing Lily growing up here. I think . . . I don't know what I think." The raw emotion running through her voice caught him off-guard.

He searched for a response. But the sound of loud motorized vehicles shattered the stillness of the woods. Car doors slammed, and loud voices shouted to one another.

"Here comes the cavalry," he said.

She straightened her shoulders and took a centering breath. "One thing I do know is this part isn't going to be fun—telling Chief Johnson he's been relegated to chief babysitter isn't going to go over well."

CHAPTER TWENTY-ONE

As a rule, Aroostine hated to be proved wrong. But in this case, she could make an exception to that policy.

Chief Johnson had just about melted into a puddle of relief to hear that she was taking over what had to be the biggest case to come out of the White Springs Reservation since, well, ever. He assured her he'd provide whatever resources and support she needed and practically ran back to his car to radio for a second officer to come out and join Officer Hunt on caveman duty.

Judging by the resigned slump of his shoulders, Hunt was somewhat less enthusiastic about the turn of events than his boss.

"Seems like you sure manage to get yourself into trouble, don't ya'?" the police officer observed.

"Mmm. Seems as though there's an awful lot of trouble to get into around here."

He narrowed his eyes and gave her a frown but didn't respond. Joe coughed into his hand to cover a laugh.

"So, who handles security at the testing facility? Is that in your department's jurisdiction?"

She asked the question casually and without judgment, but Hunt answered stiffly.

"The facility is on our land, yes, but the Tribal Board voted to contract that work out to a private firm."

"Outsiders?"

Hunt sucked air through his teeth, considering the question.

"No. Matter of fact, the board awarded the contract to Buckmount Security Services, Inc."

"As in Lee Buckmount?"

"One and the same. He operates a bunch of companies. This one provides security for the casino and resort—and now the drone testing facility."

"Isn't Buckmount on the Tribal Board?"

"Yup."

"I assume he recused himself from the vote in light of the obvious conflict of interest?"

Hunt laughed. "Good one."

Chief Johnson trudged out of the woods and onto the path. Officer Hunt stood a little straighter and wiped the traces of amusement off his face.

"Okay, we're all set. Stan Hartman'll be along shortly, Hunt. You two are on until shift change. Don't let anyone near that cave."

"Yes, sir."

Chief Johnson turned to Aroostine and Joe. "Do you folks mind helping me out by driving Isaac's car back to the reservation? We had an officer drive Ruby and Lily Smith and Boom home in Lee's vehicle. Another officer took Lee to Doctor Scott's office to check out that bump on his head. Officer Hunt drove Isaac Palmer's car here from the scene, but he'll catch a ride back with Hartman after their shift ends. I'm short a driver."

Aroostine shifted her gaze to Joe. He shrugged.

"Sure, no problem."

"Actually, could we borrow it to run an errand first?" she asked.

The police chief and Joe gave her matching quizzical looks.

"I suppose so," Chief Johnson said. "The car isn't evidence in Isaac's murder, and it'll just be sitting around. But what am I supposed to do with Lee while you're off running around?"

"After he gets his head bandaged, let him cool his heels in a holding cell. He can wait."

She smiled coolly at Chief Johnson. He tossed Joe the keys to the Tercel and pointed through the trees.

"Fine by me. Car's down there."

They started toward the path.

"Hang on. How did Boom get the keys?" she asked.

"Says Isaac kept a spare in a magnetic case affixed above his rear right tire. He told Boom in case he ever needed to borrow it—Boom doesn't have a car of his own, you know. Isaac was being neighborly."

Aroostine nodded. She wondered if Isaac's neighborliness extended to leaving a spare house key lying around, too, or if Buckmount had simply knocked on the door and Isaac let him in. She'd know soon enough—as long as Buckmount didn't lawyer up.

Joe leaned against the car and waited while she crawled around the undercarriage to satisfy herself that the thing wasn't going to blow up when he started the engine. She stood and dusted the knees of her pants with her hands.

"All set?"

"Yeah."

He held open the passenger door and gestured her inside. She leaned up for her kiss and then settled into the seat. He walked around to the driver's side, slid behind the wheel, and stuck the key in the ignition.

"Well, my lady, where to?"

She grinned. "We're going to the hotel to take hot showers and change our clothes." On a hunch, she popped open Isaac's glove compartment. A twenty, neatly folded into thirds, was tucked in the corner behind a tire pressure gauge. She pulled it out and waved it triumphantly. "But first, we eat."

"Now you're talking."

He put the car in reverse and bumped it down the rocky ground until they reached the meadow, then shifted into gear and crossed the meadow, wheels spinning through the long grass, and headed for the road.

Aroostine rifled through Isaac's tidy, organized glove compartment: service records stacked and rubber banded together; the owner's manual; registration and insurance cards; a log in which he appeared to have recorded his gas mileage; a packet of tissues; a small first aid kit; and a state map.

Joe glanced over at the pile in her lap.

"Anything interesting?"

"No. Isaac Palmer was either the embodiment of the reasonably prudent person or someone sanitized his stuff."

"The reasonably prudent person?"

"It's a legal standard—to determine if someone acted negligently, you ask what would the reasonably prudent person have done? If your defendant didn't do that, then he was probably negligent. Only problem is the reasonably prudent person doesn't exist. Nobody keeps their tire pressure exactly at the manufacturer's recommendation, drives precisely three car lengths behind the car in front of them, changes the air filter in their furnace at ninety-day intervals, never off by a day. The reasonably prudent person would never use a shoe as a hammer or stand on a wheeled desk chair to change a lightbulb. But, judging him by the contents of his glove box, maybe Isaac Palmer was that mythical guy. Although I guess even he wasn't prudent enough, seeing as how he got his head blown off."

Joe gave her another sidelong look.

"What?" she demanded.

"Two things."

"Go ahead." She shoved the papers back into the small box.

"One, you're one to talk. You do all those reasonably prudent things."

"I do not!"

"Most of them."

She frowned. "I'm not that regimented."

"When does Rufus need his next heartworm pill?"

"On the twenty-sixth," she answered instantly.

"What temperature is our hot water tank set to?"

"One hundred forty degrees Fahrenheit to best avoid pathogens. But if we had small children or elderly relatives living with us, one hundred and twenty degrees would be preferred to minimize the risk of scalding."

"Why did you check the glove compartment for money?"

"Come on, you know why."

"Answer the question, Counselor."

She sighed. "Because I keep an emergency twenty in your glove box."

"I rest my case."

"Shut up."

He laughed.

"Whatever, Joe. What's the second thing?"

His tone changed from teasing to serious. "What would *you* have done if you were Isaac Palmer? You have information that's serious enough to get you killed. What do you do with it?"

She was silent for a moment, thinking.

"I make a copy of it. And I give it to someone I trust—no, that's not right. I wouldn't do that. It would expose someone else to danger—someone I care about, presumably." She chewed her lower lip. "No, I make a copy and hide it somewhere safe."

He nodded. "That's what I'm thinking."

"Where would he have hid it?"

"How should I know? You're the reasonable prude or whatever—you tell me."

"Reasonably prudent person." She pushed his shoulder.

"Close enough. Hey, look!"

Twenty feet ahead an exit ramp led to a commercial strip off the highway. It had no signage to indicate the name of the town or what businesses were located there, but the view was clear. The road made a bugle just off the ramp. On the side of the road, just at the point where it straightened out again, sat a gleaming aluminum structure with distinctive red stripes. A tall sign in the parking lot read "Barkley Diner—Homemade Pies. Breakfast Served All Day."

He swerved right and took the exit. Aroostine's stomach growled in anticipation as he pulled into a spot next to a blue pickup truck. She tucked Isaac's emergency twenty into her pocket and practically ran to the door. A hand-lettered signed read "Open Twenty-One Hours A Day."

"Wonder which three they're closed?"

"Who cares. As long as they're open now." Joe pushed open the door and held it for her.

Walking inside she felt as if she were a time traveler. The Barkley Diner wasn't retro. It was the original—evidently unchanged since circa 1960. A long aluminum counter anchored the space and ran most of the length of the narrow room. Red vinyl barstools lined the counter every couple feet, evenly spaced on the black-and-white checkerboard floor. On each end of the building, two sets of vinyl booths were wedged in the corners, providing eight tables for patrons who didn't want to sit at the counter. All of the booths were unoccupied. Two stools were taken, each with an empty stool on either side.

A young waitress with bright blond hair and cat-eye glasses raised her head at the tinkle of the bell over the door.

"Hi there, folks. Go ahead and sit where you like. I'll be over in a minute with some menus."

The old guy closest to the door didn't look up from his paperback and plate of steak and eggs, but the younger man, two stools away, turned and raised his ceramic mug in silent greeting.

"You go pick a table. I want to wash up real quick," Aroostine whispered to Joe.

"What do you want to drink?"

"Just water. Lots of water."

She scanned the room. There was only one logical location for the restrooms, so she walked to the right, went down a short corridor, and squeezed through the doorway that separated the corner booths from the counter and the kitchen behind it. The bathroom was tiny and dimly lit but clean. She let the water run until it was as hot as she could stand, then pushed up her sleeves, and scrubbed her hands—from her fingernails to up past her wrists—as though she were prepping to perform surgery. Then she wet a coarse paper towel, wrung out the excess water, and wiped the grime from her face. She grimaced at her reflection in the warped mirror. She'd done what repairs she could—her efforts would have to suffice until she got back to the hotel. The thought of a very long, very hot shower—or better yet, a bath—was almost more appealing than food. Almost. She tossed the towel in the wastebasket and headed back to the front of the restaurant.

Joe had settled on the booth tucked into the far left corner. He stood when she neared the table.

"My turn." He turned sideways and shimmied past her in the narrow aisle.

She hesitated. If she took the seat across from where Joe had been sitting, she'd have her back to the door—inadvisable, considering someone was trying to kill them. Sitting side by side would be cozy, she decided. She scooted across the booth and situated herself in the corner. Then she looked around. The wall to her left was one long mirror. The opposite wall was a floor-to-ceiling window that ran all the way to the diner's door. Even worse, though, right behind her head was another floor-to-ceiling window that ran across the entire side of the building. They were eating lunch in a fishbowl.

No one's going to kill you in broad daylight in a diner in Barkley, Oregon—mostly, because nobody knows you're here, she told herself.

Joe returned. He raised a brow at her seating choice but slid in next to her. He raised his hips off the booth, dug Isaac's keyring out of his front pants pocket, and tossed the keys on the table. The stainless cylinder dangling from the ring thudded against the Formica table.

"Look at you two lovebirds. You folks ever been here before?" said the waitress with a wide smile as she slapped two laminated menus down in front of them.

"Nope. We're tourists." Joe grinned at her.

"You're lost then. Nothing worth touring out here," she informed him. "But the silver lining is you wandered into the home of Elle's fabulous homemade pies."

"We're going to have to try some then," Aroostine said. "But I think I need a meal first."

"Let me get your drink order in and you can take a look at the menu."

Aroostine asked for a glass of water, and Joe ordered an iced tea. The waitress, whose name tag identified her as Donna, left them to consider their lunch choices.

Joe studied the menu while Aroostine stared out the window at the mostly empty parking lot. She craned her neck to look out the window behind them and then scanned the front of the lot. She felt someone watching her and looked at the counter. The younger of the two men sitting on the stools gave her a curious look.

She flashed him a forced smile then picked up her menu.

"What are you getting?" she asked Joe, turning the pages absently.

"A reuben and fries. You?"

"Scrambled eggs and toast. Want my bacon?"

"What do you think?" he asked, elbowing her in the ribs.

She smiled and absently spun the keyring in a circle. The weight of the cylinder made it turn more quickly than she anticipated. It flew sideways and skittered to a stop against the mirror.

"Oops."

Donna returned with two pebbled plastic tumblers.

"Here you go." She placed the drinks in front of them and flipped open her order pad. "What'll it be?"

They ordered their meals, and she rattled them back to confirm she had them right. As she headed back to the kitchen, the younger man from the counter stood and headed their way.

The waitress turned to eyeball the guy's back as he passed her. Aroostine's stomach tightened. Beside her Joe stiffened. She grabbed the keys and held them in her fist with the key sticking out between her index and middle fingers, ready to jab the guy in the eyes. Under the tabletop, Joe gripped her thigh—whether in warning or to calm her she couldn't tell.

The guy stopped about three feet away from the table and cocked his head. He was an unremarkable-looking white guy some-where between five feet, ten inches and six feet tall, somewhere between twenty-five and thirty-five years old.

"Can I help you, buddy?" Joe asked, not rudely, but with no invitation in his voice.

"Just wondering where you got the car out front." His tone was flat, nasal but not menacing.

"It's a loaner. Why?"

The guy narrowed his eyes. "Looks a lot like a car a friend of mine used to drive."

"Oh? Who's your friend?" Aroostine asked brightly, hoping he couldn't hear her heart pounding from where he stood.

"Nobody. Just a guy I know."

They looked at the man, and he looked back at them for a moment in silent détente.

"Do you work at the casino up at White Springs?" she pressed.

His face closed. Gave no clues. He just turned and walked back to his stool.

"Weirdo," Joe mumbled under his breath. He loosened his grip on her leg.

She exhaled and relaxed her hand, letting the key slip to the table.

"Yeah. Just some freak. We need to chill out." She kept her voice calm to reassure him, but her heart was knocking against her chest.

"A hot bath and some rest will go a long way to rebalancing us," he agreed.

A hot bath. She let herself drift into a daydream about bubbles and a nearly endless supply of water.

When Donna came back balancing their food on a round tray, Aroostine asked if she knew the guy at the counter.

Donna wheeled around and looked at the counter. "Who? Old Christian over there reading his Harlequin Romance folded inside a military biography?"

"No, the other guy—" Aroostine pointed to where the man had been sitting but the stool was empty. He was gone—he'd slipped out without her noticing.

CHAPTER TWENTY-TWO

Joe followed the circle through the parking lot to the guest drop-off at the resort. A valet ran out from under the canopy, his collar turned up against the light misty rain that had been falling ever since they'd gotten back on the road.

"Park it for you, sir?"

Aroostine shook her head. "No. We're going to self park. He's just letting me out."

She was too jumpy to let someone else have access to their vehicle—especially after their run-in with the man at the diner. She'd choked down her eggs and found she'd lost her appetite for Elle's homemade pie. They'd eaten in a hurry, spooked by the stranger, and left the twenty on the table for Donna. When they walked out into the diner's parking lot, she was glad she'd passed on the dessert. She almost lost her breakfast at the sight of a piece of paper stuck under the Tercel's windshield wipers, fluttering in the wind.

Joe had taken a deep breath and plucked it with two fingers, glanced down at it, then handed it to her still folded in half. Her full name was scribbled on the front. Inside was a telephone number with a local area code. After she'd spent a good ten minutes crawling around underneath the car, they'd driven in silence to the resort—Joe split his attention between the road ahead and the rearview mirror, as if he expected to see someone chasing them; she stared down at the telephone number on the scrap of paper in her lap.

Joe cleared his throat. "Go ahead, Roo. I'll park it and be in in a minute."

She jolted back to the present. "Right. Sorry."

She hopped out of the car and smiled at the valet, who seemed to have no hard feelings about the loss of the tip and was already holding the door open for her. She crossed the gleaming marble floor and stood in front of the rosewood front desk.

The willowy Asian woman clacking softly on the keys of a computer smiled up at her.

"Oh, Ms. Higgins, good afternoon. I have a package for you."

She glided to a credenza behind the desk and scooped up a large brown envelope. She handed it to Aroostine with a graceful gesture. Her every movement was precise and beautiful, as if she were some modern-day geisha performing a complicated tea ritual.

"Thank you." Aroostine glanced down at the package. The computer-generated label showed the Eugene Department of Justice field office as the return address. *Good work, Sid.*

"Certainly. Is there anything else, Ms. Higgins?" the desk clerk asked.

"Actually there is. I'm afraid I've lost my room key." She smiled apologetically.

"No trouble at all," the woman assured her. She swiped a key card through a reader in a fluid motion and handed it to Aroostine. "Will there be anything else?"

"Nope. All set. Thanks so much."

Aroostine turned away from the desk just in time to watch Joe jog into the lobby, shaking the rain out of his hair like a dog.

"What do you have there?" He nodded toward the package in her hands.

"Care package from Sid. Come on, we'll open it in the room."

They made their way to the elevator bank and boarded the waiting elevator car. As the door closed, Aroostine turned to Joe. "I call the bath."

His blue eyes darkened with desire. "I thought maybe we could share. You know, conserve resources."

Her pulse fluttered—but for the first time all day, it wasn't from fear.

Aroostine melted back into the pile of overstuffed pillows that covered the bed and closed her eyes, her wet hair fanned out behind her. She sighed contentedly.

"Feeling okay?" Joe asked.

She opened one eye. "Are you kidding me? 'Okay' doesn't begin to do my current state justice. I'm clean, sated, and spent."

"Then I suppose my work here is done."

He pounded his bare chest in faux machismo and tightened the towel around his waist. She rolled her eyes and pushed herself off the bed, wrapping the sheet around her and tucking one end into the top as if she were wearing a very long sarong. She picked up the package from the Department of Justice and ripped it open. She shook out the contents onto the bed: two new passports; Pennsylvania driver's licenses; a thick wad of rubber-banded cash, two smartphones with chargers; and a replacement credit card. She nodded her approval.

"Thanks, Uncle Sid," Joe said behind her.

She scanned the short memo authorizing her to lead the investigation into the various recent criminal incidents on the White Springs Reservation, noted that it was signed by both Sid and the director of the Office of Tribal Affairs, and set it aside.

"Looks like we're back in business."

"Tell me you mean in the morning."

"Get dressed, Tarzan," she instructed. "I've got some calls to make."

She started with the easiest one but Sid didn't answer. She left a short message thanking him and letting him know she'd received the package. Then she waffled, trying to decide who to call next. She settled on Chief Johnson.

The dispatch operator put her through immediately.

"Lee Buckmount's got himself a hotshot criminal defense attorney all the way from the city. He's stinking up my station with his expensive cologne. Are you coming back tonight or what?"

"Hello to you, too, chief."

"I'm serious, Ms. Higgins. Boom insists we can't do anything without your say-so. So get yourself back here and say something."

"Is Boom there?" she asked, ignoring the grumping.

"I think so. Last I saw, he was trying to con Lee's big-city lawyer into a game of poker. Hang on."

A loud clunk sounded in her ear. Apparently, Chief Johnson put callers on hold by dropping his phone receiver on his desk. While she waited, Aroostine cradled the phone between her ear and shoulder and rifled through her suitcase for a pair of yoga pants and her softest long-sleeved T-shirt.

"Yeah, he's here," Chief Johnson said, slightly out of breath. "Hang on."

She stepped into the pants and pulled the shirt over her head before Boom got on the line. Out of the corner of her eye, she saw that, despite his complaining, Joe was also getting dressed.

"Hello? Aroostine?"

"Hi. What's Buckmount's lawyer's name?"

"Gordon Lane. Do you know him?"

"No. Should I?"

"He's the go-to guy for professional athletes and rich businessmen who get themselves into trouble. Usually prostitution scandals, as far as I know. Though he did represent a member of the judiciary who tried to run over a fellow judge over a dispute about a parking space."

"Sounds distinguished."

"Lane or the judge?"

"Both."

Boom chuckled. "Do you want to speak to him?"

"Nope. Let him cool his heels a while longer. I'll be back in a couple hours. I wanted to talk to you, though."

"You are talking to me."

"Right." She pushed past the awkwardness she felt at the position she was putting both of them in and said, "Listen, Washington wants me to take the lead on investigating what's going on there. Chief Johnson seems more than happy to hand the mess off to me. But he's focused on career preservation. I don't know that anyone's worried about what the tribe wants. I know you can't speak for the entire tribe, but you're on the cultural board—"

"Actually, Lee's been relieved of his responsibilities as the head of the Tribal Board, pending the outcome of this . . . mess. I've been appointed to fill his seat in the meantime. So, I *am* authorized to speak for the tribe on this matter. And not only do we support your federal investigation, we'd like to ask you to handle the prosecution before the Tribal Court."

"But—"

He anticipated her concern and cut in. "There's a procedure for authorizing a member of a sister tribe to fill that role. Akin to deputizing someone. We're prepared to accept you, if you'll take the job.

We can pay you a stipend and provide you and Joe with housing, transportation, and a meal allowance for the duration."

"Um . . . I'm flattered, but I need to talk to Joe. And my boss. I can't take an appointment that will conflict with my duties as an assistant US attorney." She wanted more than anything to say yes—but whether that was from a longing to belong to a tribe or from the career challenge, she wasn't sure.

"You should talk to Joe, of course, but we've already received word from the Department of Justice that the Criminal Division has agreed to loan you out. You should get official approval soon."

"Oh—okay." If that had been the intent behind the memo from Sid and his counterpart at the Office of Tribal Affairs, the point had been obscured by the bureaucratic language. Her mind was racing.

"I'm not asking you for an answer right now, of course. Think. Talk it over. Perhaps you could sleep on it and see if your spirit guide weighs in."

The quiet gravitas of his voice acted as a balm. Her worries about how she'd be perceived by the members of the tribe dissolved in its wake. Being asked to help the tribe felt like a great honor. It felt like something she should approach with due deliberation and consideration, but it also felt like a warm invitation.

"That sounds like a plan. I should let you get back to jawing at Mr. Lane."

She ended the call to the sound of his laughter.

Two down, one to go.

"Why don't you pack us an overnight bag? Let's keep this as our base of operations but plan on sleeping at the cottage on the reservation tonight."

"Works for me. You want anything in particular?"

"Nope."

He started to gather toiletries and clothes in a neat pile while she pawed through the heap of dirty clothes they had discarded on the bathroom floor. She dug out the telephone number that had been under the windshield wiper. She grabbed the hotel-branded notepad and pen from the desk and tapped out the number.

While the phone rang, Joe finished dressing and sat down across from her with open curiosity on his face.

"Want me to put it on speaker?"

"Kind of."

She shrugged as if to say "why not" and pressed the speakerphone button.

Another ring. Then a wary male voice answered.

"Hello?"

"This is Aroostine Higgins."

The sound of a shaky breath being exhaled filled the room through the tinny speaker.

"Thank you for calling."

"Don't thank me yet. Who are you, and how do you know who I am?"

"My name isn't really important, but I think I'm probably the last person who spoke to Isaac Palmer before he was killed."

Joe's eyes widened. He mouthed, "I thought that was you."

"So did I," she mouthed back.

The man continued, "Which is how I know who you are. Or, at least, who I thought you were when I saw you at the diner."

"How so?"

"Isaac called me two days ago. Said some federal lawyer, name of Aroostine Higgins, was coming to see him. Said she was an Indian chick from back East. When I saw you two pull into the diner in his car I figured you were the lady he was talking about."

Good use of context clues, she thought. Joe must have been thinking the same thing, judging by the way he nodded his head.

"You thought right."

"Figured it was worth taking a chance to get you to contact me."

"You've got me. So . . ." she trailed off, leaving the rest unsaid.

"So. I work at the drone testing facility."

A tingle of excitement ran up her spine.

"Oh?" She struggled to keep her voice casual.

"He thought you might be interested in some drones that disappeared."

"I might be," she agreed.

"I'm going to need some assurances before I talk to you about that."

"What kind of assurances?"

"The kind where you promise me I'm not going to end up like Isaac." His voice hitched on the dead man's name.

She bit the inside of her cheek and made a clicking noise with her tongue.

"I can't do that. I wish I could. But I'm not going to lie to you. I'm not sure *I'm* not going to end up like Isaac."

It was a true statement and not a revelation, but saying it aloud chilled her. Joe's face tightened, and his skin paled a shade.

The man breathed a heavy sigh as he digested her words.

"Fair enough. But I need to think about this some more."

"I understand. Why don't I give you a call tomorrow?"

"No. I'll get in touch with you." He ended the call without further comment.

She stared down at the silent phone in frustration.

Joe zipped the duffel bag closed and came to stand beside her. He massaged her shoulders with strong, warm fingers, working tight knots out of her upper back.

"Buckmount's locked in a cell, babe. You're not going to end up like Isaac. He can't hurt you."

She suspected that even from behind bars, Lee Buckmount had enough reach and power to make her life miserable, if not downright dangerous. He no doubt had associates through the gaming world whose motives and backgrounds ranged from slightly shady to pure black. But voicing her fears served no purpose.

"I hope you're right. Let's go find out." She scooped up Isaac's car keys from the desk and tossed them at Joe. Then she took one last longing look at the inviting bed and headed for the door.

CHAPTER TWENTY-THREE

Pink and orange bands stretched across the sky as the sun set behind the mountains. Joe marveled at how different the approaching twilight felt from inside the Tercel than it had when they were tromping through the foothills of the mountains racing to find shelter and food before dark.

"It's really beautiful country out here, isn't it?" Aroostine said beside him.

"It is."

They lapsed into silence. After several miles, Joe cleared his throat. "Are you going to tell me what Boom asked you?"

He peeked over at her. Her brow was furrowed. She stared straight ahead at the long ribbon of highway in front of them while she answered.

"The tribes at White Springs have asked the Department of Justice to loan me out to help them with their investigation into Lee Buckmount's various crimes."

He tried to pinpoint the source of the anxiety he heard in her voice but couldn't.

"Well doesn't that kind of make sense? You're going to lead the charge for the feds anyway—isn't it really just a matter of efficiency?"

"Maybe," she allowed. "But it would mean spending more time out here than we'd planned."

He heard the unasked question and answered it slowly.

"We could make it work. I don't have a ton of custom orders pending. My parents would be happy to dog sit Rufus as long as we want."

"You'd stay out here with me?"

He glanced at her face again, but she maintained her laser-like focus on the windshield.

"If you want me to—yeah, I would."

If she was thinking about her ill-fated move to Washington, DC, when he said he'd go with her and then hadn't, she gave no indication. But the memory stung him.

"So, leave aside the logistics—do you *want* to do it?" he continued.

"I'm not sure."

He waited.

She turned toward him. "On the one hand, yes, sure. It'd be a feather in my cap. Justice and the Office of Tribal Affairs will be thrilled to be able to point to their inter-department cooperation and sharing of resources. Boom and the Tribal Board will be happy to have someone they kind of already trust running interference with the feds. And it's not like it's totally outside my skill set."

"What's the issue, then? Why are you hesitating?"

She wrapped a strand of hair around her finger and answered in a halting, unsure voice—so soft he had to strain to hear her.

"On the other hand, I'm not sure that career advancement is really what's motivating me. I think I'm drawn to the idea of spending time on the reservation, surrounded by the people. I know they aren't my people, but it feels . . . right."

"So? How is that a bad thing?"

A hint of irritation snuck into her voice. "Come on, Joe. You know, I've never been big on exploring my roots or embracing my nativeness. Why would I start now—thousands of miles away from home?"

No, you've spent your whole life distancing yourself from your history and pretending to have no roots, he thought. He stopped himself from saying it and, instead, made a gentle suggestion. "Maybe it feels safer for you to open up to that side of yourself here just because it is so far from home?"

"Hmm. Maybe."

Encouraged, he braced himself and soldiered on. "Maybe Boom reminds you of your grandfather a little bit, too."

Too far. Her face closed off, blank and expressionless, and she resumed her staring out the window.

After the dashboard clock showed five solid minutes of uninterrupted silence, he reached for the radio button. But when he started to turn the knob in search of a station, she closed her hand over his.

"Wait." He focused on the road but listened hard. "I think you're right . . . about all of it. White Springs is different enough from where I lived before—before the Higginses came for me. It doesn't remind me of my parents. But it does feel vaguely familiar. And, yes, Boom makes me think of Grandfather."

The words poured from Aroostine in a rush, as if they were a confession she had to make quickly, before she lost her nerve. Then she removed her hand from his, settled back against the headrest, and closed her eyes.

Joe started to speak, to suggest that working through her grief over the loss of her grandfather was long overdue, thought better of it, started again, then finally decided to leave Aroostine to her thoughts. He turned on the radio and settled on the first station that was more music than static.

⎯⎯⎯⎯⎯⎯⎯⎯⎯⎯

Aroostine closed her eyes mainly to forestall any further attempts from Joe to probe her psyche. But as soon as she rested her head, exhaustion overcame her in a wave. Rather than fight it, she let her body relax into the seat. *Just a catnap,* she thought.

The vast mountains shimmered, dissolved, and re-formed. Oregon's fields of wildflowers morphed into woods she knew well—the woods behind her grandfather's house. The rows of tall oaks covered with red, orange, and yellow leaves, stretching toward the sun, the dirt path leading past the creek and through the field of long, swishy grass. She watched from the path as a small girl with a long, dark braid swinging against her back skipped through the grass.

She knew that girl and exactly where she was headed. She *was* that girl. She was watching five-year-old Aroostine doing the thing she loved the most. She would make her way up the hillside to the old horse barn where her grandfather was waiting with the archery target he'd set up for her.

In the dream, Aroostine followed her girl-self at a distance. She watched the child whoop with delight when her grandfather turned and scooped her up, twirled her in a wild, high circle, and then returned her to the ground. She collapsed in a heap of giggles. Her grandfather waited until she was calm and then helped her to her feet.

"Are you ready, granddaughter?" he asked with a gentle smile.

"Oh, yes!"

"Very good."

He bent to the ground and lifted a small child-sized bow, which he placed in her outstretched hands. He adjusted a quiver of arrows on her back then knelt beside her and turned her to face the barn's wide west wall, where he'd painstakingly painted a perfectly round, red target. Then he knelt beside her.

The girl gripped her bow. She stared at the barn, concentrating. The tip of her tongue poked out of her mouth. She squinted, all business, and nocked an arrow. Her grandfather rested on one knee beside her and watched as the arrow flew fast and straight, heading for the dead center of the target.

A gust of wind kicked it high and slightly left of the center circle. It hit the barn and stuck in the wall. The girl's face crumpled in disappointment but, at her elbow, her grandfather beamed.

"Very nice, child. Very close to the center."

"But I missed."

He nodded. "This is true. Do you know why?"

"The wind began to blow?"

"This is partially true, yes. What else happened, though?"

She wrinkled her nose and thought. "I didn't test the wind before I aimed."

"That's right."

She set her mouth, determined, and readied another arrow. Then she licked a finger and held it in the air. After a moment, she nodded and repositioned herself slightly. Then she let fly another arrow. It wobbled in the wind but curved as it arced toward the barn and landed smack in the middle of the target.

"Yes!" the girl pumped her fist excitedly.

On the path, Aroostine mirrored the movement. "Yes," she whispered.

Her grandfather smiled and ran a hand over the girl's hair.

Aroostine suddenly felt like an outsider, spying on them from the woods. She was about to walk away when her grandfather turned and stared over his shoulder in her direction. For a moment, she thought he'd spotted her, but he wasn't looking at her. Instead he seemed to be looking through her.

She craned her neck and scanned the woods behind her. In the spot where he had fixed his gaze, the silver-eyed beaver had appeared. Its nose twitched in the wind; and like her grandfather, it seemed to be looking past her, at him.

After a moment of silent communication, her grandfather turned back to the girl Aroostine, took her hand, and led her to a grassy hillside and sat beside her. Aroostine listened as he told her a traditional Lenape story about a pretty maiden who was too proud for her own good—the girl rejected the beaver as a suitor because she thought it was ugly. In the end, she drowned because the beaver refused to save her when she fell in the river.

The archery lesson had happened in real life. The morality tale had not.

Aroostine started awake.

"You okay?"

She shook her head to clear it of the dream, or vision, or whatever it was.

"I'm fine. I just had a weird dream."

He gave her a close look but didn't press her.

"We're almost there anyway. Do you want me to take you straight to the police station or do you want to freshen up at the guest house first?"

She looked down at her athletic wear. Ordinarily, she'd want to make herself look more presentable, but the dream was gnawing at her, making her uneasy and unsettled. Boom had told her to look for a message from her spirit guide. Instead, she'd had a dream about her grandfather warning her that she rejected her spirit guide at her peril. She had no idea what any of it meant, but she suddenly felt that it was important to talk to Boom sooner rather than later and formally agree to handle the prosecution for the tribe.

"Let's go straight there. I promise I won't be too long."

CHAPTER TWENTY-FOUR

Boom was making a cup of tea in the worn kitchenette behind the chief's office when Aroostine breezed into the station. He breathed a sigh of sheer relief at the sight of her—her confident stride, the dark hair streaming behind her as she hurriedly explained to the desk officer who she was and why she was there. He mixed some milk and honey into the mug and then rushed out to the lobby to meet her.

"Aroostine."

She turned away from the desk at the sound of his voice. He waved, noting that she seemed distracted, pale, maybe a bit jittery.

"Boom, hi." She walked around the half-moon desk and came to greet him. "How's Ruby? And Lily?"

"They're fine, both fine. In fact, Ruby is roasting a chicken and some vegetables for you and Joe. She was planning to leave dinner in the guest house for you as her thanks, modest though it is, for your saving her life. We all owe you a great deal more than a chicken dinner."

Her cheeks burned red at the praise.

"That's kind of her—unnecessary but appreciated. I'm so glad you're still here. I'd like to talk to Buckmount and his lawyer—if Lee's talking—or just the lawyer if he isn't. But first I wanted to officially accept the role of prosecutor in the Tribal Court proceeding, with the caveat that I know exactly zero about tribal law or legal procedure."

He beamed. "Understood. We'll get you a set of law books and a manual and have them sent over to the cottage. I'm glad you decided so quickly." He searched her drawn face. "Vision?"

She hesitated. "Sort of. Not really."

"I hope some day you will feel comfortable enough to trust me with your messages. I'd be honored to help you interpret them."

"Please don't misunderstand. It's not a matter of trust—it's . . . complicated. And you helped me a great deal that night I had that horrible dream." She shuddered at the memory and placed a hand on his forearm. "But I mean no disrespect. I'm just, I guess you could say, private about the whole spirit guide thing." Her voice dropped to a whisper.

"Oh, I take no offense. I'm just offering my services in case you decide you'd like to forge a solid relationship with your spirit animal. In any case, you're doing the Chinook people an important service. This terrible event can serve as a turning point for the tribe. From the ashes of this scandal, we can emerge stronger, more centered, with a renewed commitment to our heritage. Having a native daughter handle the case for us will help ensure the federal agencies respect our ways. That will be the focus of my leadership in all areas—a deeper understanding of the old ways."

She smiled politely, but her face was closed off. He laughed at himself.

"Ah, please forgive the ramblings of an old man. I know you are quite busy and eager to talk to Lee."

"Don't apologize, please. Your vision and plans to return to tradition remind me so much of my grandfather. I think it's great."

"That's very kind of you to say."

They stood in shared silence for a moment. She felt awkward and unsure of herself, like she was eighteen again and Joe Jackman had just walked into her Art History class and taken the seat next to hers.

"Uhm—"

He snapped out of his daze and placed a light hand on the small of her back to pilot her down the hallway.

"If you follow me, I'll show you where Mr. Lane and Lee are waiting."

Boom ushered her into the small, windowless room where Buckmount and his lawyer were waiting. She wasn't sure what she expected from a high-profile criminal defense attorney named Gordon Lane, but whatever she had imagined was far splashier and sleazier than the somber, silver-haired gentleman who stood to greet her.

"Ms. Higgins, it's a pleasure," he intoned after Boom introduced her and scooted out of the claustrophobically crowded room.

His handshake was firm but not bone crushing, his tone self-assured but not arrogant.

"The pleasure's mine, Mr. Lane. Please excuse my appearance." She gestured at her yoga pants and long-sleeved T-shirt, but her voice held an undercurrent of "of course, I might look more pulled together had I not just spent two days running for my life from your client and then rescuing a woman from him at gunpoint."

Lane either missed the unspoken jab or was too professional to let it rattle him, but his client reacted. Buckmount had rose from his metal chair and waved his handcuffed wrists at her. "Where have you been? I've been sitting in this blasted box for hours waiting—"

Lane turned his head almost imperceptibly toward Buckmount and arched one eyebrow by a fraction of an inch. Buckmount instantly clamped his mouth shut, fire blazing from his eyes. The attorney returned his focus to Aroostine.

"I understand today's been trying for many people—including my client. He did receive some basic medical attention before the officers brought him here, which is appreciated. But I'm sure you agree that given his age, his ties to the reservation, and his reputation as a businessman, it would be most appropriate for you to arrange a time to interview Mr. Buckmount at your mutual convenience some time during the next few days, and let an old man go home to his bed."

Lane's tone suggested that his request was the most logical, reasonable way to handle a man who was suspected of embezzlement, murder, attempted murder, and theft of military weapons and who also had access to almost limitless cash, to release him on his own recognizance to minimize the disruption to his life. She tilted her head and regarded the criminal defense attorney. He either had the drollest sense of humor or was devoid of shame.

Unable to determine which was the case, she said simply, "No."

Lane shrugged. "You don't ask, you don't get."

Oh, shameless. Got it.

"I do need to determine what capacity the tribal police have for housing Mr. Buckmount, though. I don't know what the facilities—"

"There are no 'facilities,' girl. Atlas Johnson and his team are the equivalent of a rural police force. This isn't going to be like your federal government with all its crime labs and bottomless budgets. As CFO of the reservation, I can tell you the police have a budget of ninety-six thousand dollars a year. That covers everything—salaries and benefits, vehicles, equipment, training. Do you know how much it costs to house and feed prisoners awaiting trial, Ms. Higgins?"

Buckmount's tone see-sawed between a rant and a lecture. It gave her an unpleasant flashback to first-year law school and her Torts professor.

She ignored the question. Only a rank amateur would let her advisory frame the argument.

"A five-figure police budget?" She raised an eyebrow. "That hardly seems sufficient for a population this size. Not to mention all the crime the casino undoubtedly brings to the reservation. It almost makes a person wonder if the CFO might have deliberately underfunded law enforcement for reasons of his own. I'd be curious to know the value of the various contracts the tribe entered into with Buckmount Security Services."

The veins in Buckmount's neck bulged, and his face turned a purple-red color, darker than the blood that stained the large bandage on his head. He began to sputter. But one sharp look from Gordon Lane and he fell silent.

"Perhaps we can cut through some of the positioning. My client is prepared to accept responsibility for his actions."

"He'll plead?" Aroostine struggled to hide her surprise, but her terrible poker face was working against her.

Buckmount's rage simmered. Aggression rolled off him like waves. But Lane's tone was congenial and even.

"For an attractive deal, Mr. Buckmount would be willing to enter a plea of guilty in regard to charges stemming from Mr. Palmer's accidental shooting death."

"He *accidentally* nailed Isaac Palmer in the middle of the forehead?"

Lane spread his hands wide and raised his shoulders.

"Did he *accidentally* embezzle funds from the casino, *accidentally* steal at least two weapons of mass destruction from the United States military, *accidentally* break into Ruby Smith's home and threaten her daughter, *accidentally* plant a car bomb on my vehicle, and *accidentally* abduct Ruby and take her to a remote location where he *accidentally* battered her and threatened her life at gunpoint?" She didn't even bother to pretend she wasn't outraged. She shook with anger.

"Now, you listen here—" Buckmount shot to his feet and yelled.

"Lee. Sit down." Lane spoke to him as if he were an errant child.

"I will not. I will not sit down and listen to this web of fantastic lies." He banged his handcuffed wrists against the table with a metallic thunk.

"Sit. Down."

Buckmount glared at his lawyer but lowered himself into the chair. Lane turned to Aroostine.

"It seems my word choice was counterproductive. We can work out the details of a plea after everyone's had a good night's sleep. But the general idea I was aiming at is that Mr. Buckmount would be willing to plead to a homicide charge that didn't include any sort of enhancements. There's no real mystery here. After the ballistics reports come back, the gun the police seized today will prove to be a match for the one that killed Isaac Palmer. My client's a pragmatic man, Ms. Higgins. He's under no delusions. But he does have his own version of the events that precipitated both Mr. Palmer's death and the altercation with Ms. Smith. He also has a talented and experienced attorney, if I do say so myself. You should consider what you will be able to prove in court and at what cost before you decide whether a plea is in order and what the appropriate charges might be."

He was right. She knew it. He knew it. As Sid was fond of reminding his AUSAs in one of his famously mixed metaphors, a half a loaf was better than a tick in the loss column.

"Hypothetically, am I to understand that Mr. Buckmount is willing to enter a guilty plea for the acts related to Mr. Palmer's death and Ms. Smith's kidnapping, but none of the other criminal acts?"

"I'm not copping to something I didn't do," Buckmount exploded from the table.

"Lee," his lawyer warned him before addressing Aroostine. "He maintains he had nothing to do with any other events."

"Gordon—may I call you Gordon?"

"Please."

"Thanks. With all due respect, come on. Isaac Palmer was killed to keep him from talking to us about the alleged embezzlement. I personally heard your client demanding to know who Ruby told about that same alleged embezzlement. Maybe you should take the night to consider whether you want to go to court with a client who can't control his temper and claim that, what, he killed Palmer for kicks?"

He raised a hand like a school crossing guard to forestall Buckmount's brewing outburst and nodded his agreement. "It seems we each have some thinking to do tonight. On that note, it's getting late."

She glanced at the metal wall clock. It was nearly eight o'clock. And Ruby's chicken was waiting for her. She examined Buckmount's face. He wasn't a young man. And he looked drained, spent. An idea was forming, but she hesitated. Sid would never go for it. *Sid doesn't get a vote,* she reminded herself.

"I'd be willing to place Mr. Buckmount under house arrest with the following conditions: he surrenders his passport; he turns over day-to-day control of the casino and the security force to the Tribal Board; and he pays the wages for a tribal police officer to be stationed outside his home."

Gordon was already nodding halfway through the proposition.

"That sounds eminently fair and workable. Lee, what do you say?"

"I say go to hell. I'll sleep in this chair before I agree to that."

"Suit yourself, Mr. Buckmount. I'll let the officer on duty know. May I walk you out, Gordon?"

The lawyer started to make an appeal to his client to be reasonable, but then stopped himself, shaking his head sadly. "I'll see you tomorrow, Lee." He clasped the man's shoulder for a moment and then turned to leave.

"Good night, Mr. Buckmount." Aroostine pulled the door shut and gestured for Officer Hunt, who'd been posted just outside the door. She filled him in on the plan for the evening and then stepped out in the cool night air beside Gordon Lane.

"That was a decent gesture," he said as he blinked up at the night sky.

"The offer stands if you can get him to change his mind. Think you can?"

He sighed deeply and then lifted his shoulders. "Who knows? The practice of law is . . . one problem after another. And then it gets dark." He stared out into the black fields ahead for a long, unblinking moment before turning to her. "Good night, Ms. Higgins."

He trudged away, heading toward the gleaming BMW she'd pegged as his. Joe sat behind it in Isaac's car, the engine idling.

She stood there for a moment, perfectly still, and the lawyer's words echoed in the quiet:

One problem after another. And then it gets dark.

CHAPTER TWENTY-FIVE

"What are you doing today?" Aroostine asked Joe as he pulled into a spot near the tribal police station, killed the engine, and pocketed the keys.

Apparently, Cathy Palmer had offered them the use of her dead son's car for the duration of their time in Oregon. Aroostine wanted to meet her—both to convey her condolences and to get a better sense of the kind of loss Isaac's death had caused before she went to trial. It was her practice to get the clearest, most fully formed picture of the victim. But in this case, she was going to be scrambling to ready a basic case.

Her morning wake-up call had been from Boom telling her that the Tribal Board wanted to put the "Buckmount incident" behind them by the end of the week if at all possible because the tribe was participating in some cultural powwow over the weekend and didn't want to have a cloud over their name. That news had woken her up more effectively than an ice-cold shower. She'd gone into great detail with Boom about why a rushed criminal trial was a terrible idea, but she got the distinct impression he hadn't been listening. In fact, she had a niggling suspicion he might have put the phone down and walked away while she yammered to no one.

"I'm meeting Boom here, actually. He needs my help with some top secret woodworking project." Joe shoved his hands in his jean's pockets and winced.

"Who has top secret woodworking projects?"

He shrugged and dug the keys out of his pocket. "Boom, I guess. Hey, can you throw these in your purse until I get back? This is the world's worst keychain. It weighs a ton and it's so bulky."

She tossed them into her bag. They landed with a thud.

"Sure. You don't need the car?"

"Whatever we're doing, Boom said it's just down the street."

She swiveled her neck and looked both directions. The street where the police station was located wasn't exactly densely populated. To the left, there was nothing at all. To the right, about two football fields away, there was a small ramshackle building that may have been a double-wide trailer up on blocks—it wasn't clear from that distance. It was, however, clear that the street followed the general aesthetic rule she'd noticed on the reservation: the closer something was to the casino and resort, the more likely it was to be presentable.

The grounds and buildings that made up the sprawling casino complex, for instance, were as well manicured and ostentatious as anything she'd seen in Las Vegas; areas in the immediate vicinity of the casino were also impeccable and well cared for. But as they'd ventured farther and farther away from the casino, it seemed almost as though the casino's gravitational pull weakened. The standards slipped little by little until, within a mile and a half of the casino's gold-leaf etchings and indoor tropical garden, the men and women who worked there lived in relative squalor. Beyond their creaky, run-down homes, their neighbors who weren't lucky enough to have a guaranteed paycheck and benefits lived in abject poverty. Dirt floors, trash bags over broken windows, cracked sidewalks sprouting weeds taller than Aroostine littered the portions of the reservation where white tourists would never wander.

It was the way of a capitalist society, no different than any other resort destination that catered to those who had income to dispose of. She remembered when she was in college and her adoptive parents took a thirtieth anniversary trip to Maui. They'd returned from Hawaii struck by both the expansive beauty of the island and the harsh economic inequity. They'd explained that the islanders who worked at the oceanside resorts lining the white-sand beaches couldn't afford to live in paradise, so they commuted two, three, four hours from the rainy mountains, where they lived in shacks and huts hidden from sight on the road to Hana. But the isolated poverty of the Chinook who called White Springs home struck her as starker and crueler, somehow. The giant money-making machine at the heart of their home was run by their own blood, ostensibly for their benefit.

Lost in her musing, she didn't notice that Boom had materialized on the sidewalk next to them until he spoke.

"Good morning. Did you both sleep well?"

The question jarred her back to everyday life.

"Fine, thanks. I hear you're borrowing my husband this morning?"

"Yes, he's graciously agreed to help me with a project over at the cultural board's offices." Boom pointed toward the dilapidated house off to the right.

"Those are your offices?"

His face clouded for a moment, but the shadow passed quickly. "For now, but not for long. Before he broke ground on construction, Lee had promised us space in the administrative wing of the casino, but somehow he never got around to dedicating a spot for us. I've already begun making arrangements to move the office up there after the powwow. It's a much more fitting space, in any event. I don't know if you happened to see the permanent exhibit of Chinook artifacts and historical documents on display in the main hall when you had dinner?"

"I'm afraid we missed it."

"Well, we curate that. And we could do so much more—educational programs, tours, performances—if we were located up there. This will be a good step for us."

It sounded like a positive development, but his mention of the powwow reminded her about their earlier conversation.

"On a tangential note, Boom, I want to make sure you understood what I was saying this morning. There's really no way to try Lee Buckmount before the weekend. It's just not doable."

"Oh but it is doable, as you say. I spoke today to the chief judge, Carole Orr. She said she will hear your case on Friday."

"On *Friday?* As in tomorrow? That Friday; I mean *this* Friday?" Aroostine was sure she looked like a fish gasping for air.

Boom smiled. "Of course."

"Where is this Judge Orr? I need to talk to her."

Another implacable smile. "Indeed. She's inside. Gordon Lane is on his way. She'll see you both when he arrives. Come with me, Joe." Boom beckoned for Joe to follow him and began walking toward the cultural board's office.

Joe stopped long enough to shoot her a sympathetic, if bewildered, look. "You're a rockstar, Roo, you can handle this," he assured. He kissed the top of her head and traipsed after Boom.

She stood and watched them walk away, gasping as though someone had punched her in the gut. After several deep inhalations, she exhaled slowly, satisfied that she wasn't actually going to vomit. Then she mounted the rickety stairs to the police station and tried to ignore the sound of her blood pounding in her ears.

It was simply unreasonable to expect her to put together a case in one day. No, not unreasonable—impossible. This Judge Orr, whoever she was, couldn't be serious. Could she?

"Aroostine," a voice called from behind her.

She turned. Gordon Lane was trotting toward her. He aimed his key fob at his sedan without turning back and locked the doors. She stopped and waited for him.

Gordon would understand. Her breathing regulated. Of course. *She* wasn't going to have to convince Judge Orr of anything. Gordon would do it. He had the better argument—his client's constitutional right to a fair trial would be grossly impaired if he only had a single day to mount his defense.

"Good morning, Gordon. Does the practice of law look sunnier to you this morning?" she asked, remembering his morose words the night before.

He craned his neck and turned his face upward as though he were just noticing the sun for the first time. Then he met her eyes. "Not really. Shall we?" He pulled open the streaked glass door and ushered her inside ahead of him.

She waved a hello to the officer on desk duty.

"How'd your guest sleep last night?"

The young man rolled his eyes toward the ceiling.

"Mr. Buckmount was cold during the night. And he needed to use the facilities. He found the chair to be uncomfortable, so he moved to the floor. But the carpet was scratchy. He woke up crankier than my three-year-old and called my coffee 'swill.'"

"Sounds delightful."

"Ms. Higgins, whatever you do, please get him out of here before bedtime. I'm doing another split shift, and I don't think I can make it through another overnight with that prisoner."

She turned to Gordon. "The offer still stands. Do you think you can sell him on house arrest now?"

"Sounds like if I can't, I might want to give up this whole oral advocacy gig." He straightened his muted silk tie and squared his shoulders. "Let's go see him."

They followed the officer along the hallway. He unlocked the door to the conference room that had served as Buckmount's sleeping acommodation, and then scurried back to the front desk before his ill-tempered prisoner could accost him. She followed Gordon into the room.

Buckmount looked like a man who'd started the night sleeping in a chair and ended it sleeping on the floor. His hair was wild, his eyes were bloodshot, and his clothes were rumpled. He was a far cry from the polished, gun-toting businessman who'd been dragging Ruby around at the side of the highway.

"Lee," his lawyer said, imbuing the single syllable with empathy, concern, and just a hint of parental disapproval.

Buckmount glared up at him and then focused on Aroostine, who was hanging back to let Gordon take the lead with his client.

"I'll take it—house arrest. Get me out of this hellhole."

"All the conditions I outlined yesterday are still in play, Mr. Buckmount. An officer posted on your dime, surrendering your passport, the—".

"I remember the conditions. Just make it happen."

She arched a brow at Gordon as if to say, "rein in your client."

"Lee, Ms. Higgins is going to want to get this agreement papered. You can't just waltz out of here on a handshake. I understand you're in need of a decent cup of coffee. If you can just hang in there for another hour or two, I'll get you home and have my assistant meet us with Peet's."

She turned away. Gordon was doing what any good lawyer would do—making his client receptive to his advice, but the way he was coddling and indulging a killer turned her stomach. If she thought too long about Buckmount sipping a dark roast in the comfort of his home while Cathy Palmer was mourning the loss of her only child, her anger would bubble over.

"Fine."

Gordon turned to Aroostine with a triumphant grin. "We've got a deal."

"Great. I'll find a place to plug in my laptop and get an agreement drafted. I'll leave you gentlemen to talk, but before I do, may I have a word with you, Gordon?"

He patted Buckmount on the forearm and joined Aroostine near the door. They stood with their backs to Buckmount, and she spoke in a low voice.

"In case Judge Orr gets here while I am busy with the agreement, I wanted to give you a head's up on something," she said.

"Oh? She's coming here today?"

"Yes. Somehow, she seems to have gotten the notion that we can schedule a trial for tomorrow." She laughed. "I assure you, the idea didn't come from me. I wouldn't hamstring my opponent in that way. I'll be amenable to any postponement you suggest—within reason, of course."

She expected Gordon to join in her laughter. Instead, he scratched his chin, and his eyes turned contemplative, as if he were lost in thought, already planning his opening statement.

"Tomorrow, you say?"

Her earlier panic returned. *Is everyone in this town insane?* she screamed silently.

"Surely you can't be ready by then?" She managed to get the sentence out with only the barest tremor in her voice.

"Well, let's see now. Lee," he called across the room to his client, "do you want to go to trial tomorrow and put this mess behind you?"

Buckmount folded his upper lip under his lower lip and considered the request, shifting his head from side to side as he thought.

"Who's the judge?"

"Judge Orr."

"Sure. Why not? Better to get it over with, don't you think?" Buckmount said.

His lawyer nodded. "I do think so."

Aroostine felt her brow furrowing and smoothed her expression. As a little girl, she'd loved *Alice in Wonderland*, and now she finally knew what it felt like to go through the looking glass. She cleared her throat.

"Well, then, that's great news," she lied.

Gordon regarded her with faint amusement.

"I'm sure. I'll bet you'll be glad to get back East sooner rather than later."

"Definitely," Aroostine agreed.

She was about to excuse herself when a firm rap sounded on the door. It swung inward and Chief Johnson appeared in the doorway. He nodded in greeting to Aroostine and Gordon and ignored Buckmount.

"Excuse me, folks. Don't mean to interrupt, but Judge Orr's here. She'd like a word."

CHAPTER TWENTY-SIX

Chief Johnson led Aroostine, Gordon, and Buckmount through the building and out the back door to a small yard that was overrun with tall wildflowers. Bees hovered in the clover, and butterflies flitted through the long grass. In the corner, under a tree, sat a rough-hewn round table with two semi-circular benches.

Aroostine figured it was a popular lunch spot for the police and their office staff. At the moment, though, it was occupied. The woman seated at the table stood when they approached. Aroostine would have pegged her as a judge if she'd have met her on the street. She was very tall and slim—taller even than Aroostine—and had the most regal, erect bearing imaginable. Her shoulders were back, and her chin jutted forward. Her long silver hair flowed in waves down her back. Her face was a map of lines that hinted at hard-earned wisdom and strength. She wore soft blue jeans, a short-sleeved white shirt, boots, and a thick turquoise necklace.

"I'm Carole. And you must be Aroostine Higgins."

The judge extended a hand. Her skin was cool, almost papery, but her grip was strong and sure.

"I am. It's a pleasure to meet you."

The judge squinted. Her eyes were black and bird-like—they reminded Aroostine of a crow.

"Aroostine, eh? Sparkling Water?"

Aroostine blinked. "You speak Algonquian, Your Honor?" The language of the Lenape Nation was dying. As far as she knew, there were no fully fluent speakers still living. Her grandfather had been one of the last.

"Please, it's Carole. And, sadly, no. Chinook is a Penutian language. We have two very distinct linguistic lines, the Chinook and the Lenape. But I love languages. I try to learn a little bit everywhere I go. I was a foreign-language major many moons ago at Berkeley. I must have changed my concentration four times—ended up graduating with degrees in Portuguese and Thai." She smiled at the memory.

This lady is sharp.

The judge turned toward Gordon. "Mr. Lane, it's so nice to see you again. How is Aurelia? And your sons?"

"Everyone is well. The boys are off at college. Aurelia's enjoying the quiet. But I'm hurt that I don't rate a first name, judge."

Her laugh was raspy and deep. "Now, Gordon, you know I have to be just a touch more formal with the white folks. But if you'll call me Carole instead of 'judge,' we can be friends here."

Finally, she turned to Buckmount, who seemed to have shrunk into himself somehow, as if he were a turtle.

"Lee Buckmount," she said in a heavy tone, "what would your mama say if she could see this?"

Buckmount ducked his head and mumbled something inaudible.

The judge waved a hand at Chief Johnson. "Take those metal bracelets off him, Atlas."

Chief Johnson stammered, "Um . . . I don't know if that's such a good idea, Carole."

She cut her eyes back to Buckmount. "Lee, Atlas is going to remove your handcuffs at my request. If you do something stupid, it's on your soul. You hear me?"

He bobbed his head. The police chief gave Aroostine a sidelong glance as if inviting her to object but did as the judge asked. He dangled the handcuffs from one hand.

Aroostine wasn't stupid enough to take on a judge on her home turf, not even a judge as unconventional as Carole Orr—or maybe, especially not one as unconventional as her.

"Thank you, Atlas. You can go on along and get on with your day. I'll take this from here," Carole dismissed the police chief.

"Yes, ma'am."

He walked back to the building, turning to give Buckmount the hairy eyeball one last time before he went inside and shut the door. Buckmount rubbed his wrists. If the gesture was designed to garner the judge's sympathy, he miscalculated.

After a short silence, the judge shook her head. "Oh, Lee. What are we going to do about this?"

Aroostine was drowning in awkward uncertainty. She didn't know where to stand or what to say. When it became clear that Buckmount didn't have an answer for the judge's question, she cleared her throat.

"Your Hon—Carole, what is today's meeting? Is this a hearing or a conference or . . ." She trailed off, realizing she had no idea what the Tribal Court procedures were. The manual she'd been promised had never materialized. "Do the Rules of Evidence apply to this . . . conversation?"

Carole Orr threw back her head and had a hearty laugh at that. Even Gordon chuckled. Aroostine's cheeks burned.

Carole took pity on her. "I shouldn't laugh. You have it right. We're having a conversation—the four of us—to decide how to proceed with Lee's case. The federal rules don't apply. Procedure, evidence, chuck it all out the metaphorical window."

"Oh-kay?"

Gordon spoke up. "Forgive me if you already know this, but the various tribal courts are, well, all over the map as far as how they operate—*if* they even operate. There are some tribal courts that hew closely to the American justice system. This isn't one. I've had the privilege of working with Carole in the past, although not as often as I'd like. Most of my clients, even the ones who run into trouble on the local reservations—mainly in the casinos—aren't Native American, so the Tribal Court has no jurisdiction."

Carole was nodding along as he spoke.

He continued, "The White Springs Tribal Court, which consists solely of Carole, focuses on more traditional justice. I'd say it's more restorative justice."

"Restorative justice?" Aroostine echoed.

"That's right," the judge said. "Sit, everyone, sit." She spread her arms and gestured at the picnic bench.

Aroostine perched on the end next to Gordon. Buckmount took a seat at the far end. Carole smiled and launched into her spiel.

"I believe in peacemaking," she began. "In particular, the sentencing circle—or, as I like to think of it, the peacemaking circle." She saw the question forming on Aroostine's lips and raised a hand. "I'll explain. A sentencing circle is more concerned with setting things right for the victims than with meting out punishment to satisfy societal mores. Typically, I only accept defendants who've agreed to plead guilty. Then the victims and I will form a sentencing circle and work together with the defendant to restore the peace and heal the conflict."

Aroostine willed her expression to remain neutral. But her inability to bluff proved her undoing, and the judge leaned back and examined her face.

"You're skeptical."

It wasn't a question, but she answered it anyway. "Yes. In this instance, one of the victims is dead. Isaac Palmer can't join the kumbaya circle or whatever you want to call it. How's Lee Buckmount going to make things right for Isaac's mother? He can't bring back the dead. And what about the theft of the drones—that's not an issue you can resolve through a circle."

"No, Lee can't bring back the dead. And this process isn't about your federal laws." The judge paused for a moment then continued, "I know you've been living and working in the white man's world, Aroostine, but please leave your mind open to the possibility that Cathy Palmer doesn't want the white man's justice."

Aroostine opened her mouth to respond to that but closed it when she realized she didn't have anything to say to counter it. She didn't know what was in Mrs. Palmer's heart, although she suspected the judge did.

Carole confirmed that suspicion with her next sentence.

"I've talked to Cathy. She's willing to participate in a peacemaking circle with Lee. So are Ruby and Lily."

"Lily? She's just a kid."

"She's a child who was affected by Lee's actions. She's entitled to judge him."

Buckmount nodded glumly.

"That leaves you and your husband, as far as individual victims are concerned," the judge finished.

"Actually, Carole, Lee doesn't accept responsibility for the attempt on Aroostine's and Joe's lives."

"Oh?"

"No. Moving to the more white-collar-type crimes, he also denies that he was embezzling money from the casino and denies having anything to do with the stolen drones."

"Is that so, Lee?"

"Yes. I'll take my consequences for what I did. But I won't be held responsible for the actions of another."

The judge addressed Aroostine. "Well what are we going to do about this?"

"I can't prosecute him under federal law for trying to kill me. I think I'm probably conflicted out of representing the government in that case. But I can't just let the embezzlement and theft of weapons go unanswered for. Can you do your circle thing tomorrow and then preside over a more typical trial in another week or two, where I can introduce evidence and witnesses and all those goodies?"

She considered the request for what felt like a very long time. The sun warmed Aroostine's shoulders. A gray sagebrush sparrow perched nearby sang.

Carole waited until the bird fell silent. She spoke slowly. "I'm going to let you present your evidence of embezzlement and the drone theft at the circle on Friday."

Everyone—Aroostine, Gordon, and Lee—began to protest at once, speaking at the same time in a cacophony of objections. She held up a palm and waited until the noise ceased.

"Only birds chatter over one another. Now, I've made my decision. Lee, it doesn't take a master sleuth to determine that if you admit to killing Isaac and threatening Ruby, the logical motive is to cover up your alleged embezzlement. And if Aroostine believes the embezzlement is tied to the drones, well, then we'll let her try to prove it." Carole's face darkened at the mention of the drones. "Both of those crimes may lack single identifiable victims, but they victimize the entire tribe. Everyone who is a member of the tribe is affected. So we will invite the entire reservation to the judgment circle."

Gordon's eyebrows hit his hairline.

"The entire reservation?" he repeated.

"Correct."

"And this is still happening on Friday—tomorrow?" Aroostine asked.

"Two for two, you fine litigators."

"How? How am I supposed to get a case together and share any documents with Gordon before tomorrow?"

"I'm sure I don't know, dear. But do try to get any materials you plan to use into his hands by this evening, yes?"

"Yes, sure," Aroostine agreed numbly.

The only saving grace was that Gordon looked as shell-shocked as she felt. He fumbled through his wallet and pulled out a business card.

"My e-mail address is on there. Just send me what you have by the end of the day and I'll do the same, okay?"

She dug through her purse and found a card of her own. "Here's mine. And that's fine, but consider yourself forewarned: my day will probably be ending around midnight, so expect the documents to come over on the late side."

He met her gaze with a mournful smile. "Mine, too."

"One problem after another and then it gets dark, eh?"

"Always."

The judge watched the two of them commiserate. "I'm not heartless, you know. We won't start until late afternoon. Say, around four. Then we'll have a community dinner afterwards. A potluck. It will be very healing."

Aroostine narrowed her eyes. "A potluck? Don't tell me I'm also supposed to find time to make a casserole."

The judge laughed, a genuine full-throated laugh. "No, you and Gordon will be our guests. No need to contribute a dish. You just prepare your case and then go home and get some sleep."

That reminded her of her other task. "Carole, I was planning to draft an agreement with Mr. Buckmount, but perhaps the Court could issue an order from the . . . um, picnic bench."

"What do you have in mind?"

Aroostine started rattling off the conditions for Buckmount's house arrest. Carole waved her hand until she stopped talking.

"Did you hear all that, Lee? We're going to let you go home and sleep in your own bed. Don't do anything stupid. Make sure I have your passport and a check made out to the police force later today. Now, fly away, birdies." She winked at Aroostine. "That means 'court dismissed' in case it didn't translate."

Aroostine walked toward the police station slowly. Her head spun as if she'd been on an amusement park ride—something terrible that went in circles, like a Tilt-A-Whirl.

CHAPTER TWENTY-SEVEN

Aroostine's entire body was numb. Trial tomorrow. There was nothing to do but get started. She trudged out to the reception desk. An officer she'd never seen before was talking to Officer Hunt. They were arguing over the better way to prepare salmon—smoking or grilling.

"Excuse me."

They both turned their cop eyes on her, twin expressions of reserve. Like they were sizing her up. But neither said anything, so she plowed ahead.

"Is it okay if I use that conference room where Lee Buckmount slept last night?"

"You want to sleep there?" Hunt asked, puzzled.

"What? No. I want to use it as an office. Judge Orr set the trial—or judgment circle—or whatever it is for tomorrow."

That got a knowing laugh out of the other officer. Hunt rolled his eyes.

"Go ahead, use the room."

"Thanks. What's so funny about Judge Orr?"

Hunt answered, "She's a real do-gooder. Always trying to get victims and doers to reconcile. Big on tradition, restitution, and ritual. Not so big on, like, the law. Sometimes it seems like she's making it up as she goes along."

"Oh." It sounded like a judge's dream—no pesky procedural rules to follow or precedent to apply—and a lawyer's nightmare.

Hunt nodded at her. "Good luck. You're gonna nail Lee to the wall, right?"

It was funny how the tribal police had been uninterested in actually investigating Isaac's murder or apprehending the murderer, but now that she'd done their work for them, they sure were looking for a conviction.

"Hey, let me ask you something. If he's convicted, what happens to the casino? Who runs that?"

"Well, that's not just Lee. He's just the CFO. There's a whole board, so nothing much changes there. I imagine that some day-to-day changes will happen. Maybe Buckmount Security gets the boot, and we get to actually handle the biggest calls in our jurisdiction."

"I bet you'd also take over the security at the testing facility."

"Heck, yeah," the other officer piped up. "That's good money, too."

She thanked them for their time. They resumed their salmon debate before she even walked away.

Inside the conference room, she set up her laptop and pulled out her cell phone. Sid answered himself.

"Tell me you haven't blown up any more cars, Higgins."

She pulled a face at the greeting. Last she checked, *she* hadn't blown up any cars, ever.

"My vacation's going swell, Sid, thanks for asking."

He chuckled at that. "What's going on?"

"Well, this lunatic tribal court judge set the . . . uh . . . event for this Friday."

"Carole Orr is one of a kind, Aroostine. But she's smart and she's fair. And I think you're going to like her. She did a presentation on tribal issues for the department a few years back; she made quite an impression."

"Sid, I have a trial *tomorrow*. I don't like her."

"It's not a trial. It's a judgment circle."

"How did you already know that? Did she call you?"

"Fat chance of that. Judge Orr doesn't have much use for Main Justice or the Ninth Circuit, for that matter. As a matter of fact, I'm not sure she even feels particularly friendly toward the Supremes."

"So how'd you know about the judgment circle?"

"The Office of Tribal Affairs has had a few run-ins with the good judge over her judgment circles; she's infamous around there."

Great.

"Well, I'm sort of in a spot here. *You* agreed to loan me out to the Chinook, and apparently they want to do it this way. Any pointers?"

"Nope."

She'd say this much for Sid. He was an inveterate know-it-all when he knew something—to the point of being insufferable—but when he didn't know, he admitted it up front and moved on with his life.

"Thanks."

"Don't mention it."

He was not, however, funny.

"Good-bye, Sid."

"Good luck. You're gonna need it."

She blew her hair out of her eyes and examined her phone's display. The battery was low. Considering her makeshift workspace lacked a telephone, she couldn't risk having the battery run all the way down and die. She dug around in her bag in search of the charger. She tossed the car keys and her wallet onto the table. The paper that the man at the diner had stuck under the windshield wiper was peeking out of the wallet. She found the charger and plugged it into the wall outlet.

But instead of charging the phone, she pulled the scrap of paper from her wallet and dialed the number. She didn't know how she was going to convince the man to tell her what he knew about the drones, but she had to. The phone rang for what seemed like minutes.

Finally, he answered.

"Hello?"

"It's Aroostine Higgins. Please don't hang up."

He didn't speak, but he didn't hang up—she could hear him breathing.

"Please, I know you're afraid to talk to me. And I can't make any promises, but I will do everything I can to protect you if you talk to me."

"I don't know."

"Listen, Lee Buckmount is under house arrest for Isaac's murder. The police are watching his every move. And the judge has scheduled the trial for tomorrow. It seems as if Buckmount's going to plead guilty to the murder. All I need to do is connect him to the theft of the drones and the embezzlement."

"Well, if that's what you need, I can't help you anyway."

"Why not?"

"Because Isaac wasn't ever able to tie Buckmount to the drones. And he was the smartest guy I ever met. So, I don't think it can be done."

He was talking. She may not have liked what he was saying, but he was talking.

She grabbed a pen. "Let's back up. What's your name?"

"No. I'll talk to you off the record. I'm not testifying or giving a statement or anything like that."

She chewed on the pen. Ordinarily, she'd tell a source who wanted to remain anonymous to take a hike. The Department of Justice couldn't risk relying on information if they couldn't probe the source's credibility. She reminded herself she wasn't operating as an assistant US attorney at the moment—she was a lawyer bringing a case to the Tribal Court, which apparently had no rules.

"That's fine," she agreed. "Can you tell me how you knew Isaac Palmer?"

"Sure. We took accounting classes together at the community college in Redmond."

"You're an accountant, too?"

"Nah, I'm a bookkeeper. After we got our associate degrees, Isaac went on, got his CPA and everything. He loved numbers more than anybody I ever met. We used to study together back in the day and became friends. He could spot patterns and stuff real fast."

She had no idea what any of this had to do with military drones. But she scribbled it down anyway.

"Okay. So he told you about the embezzlement?"

"Yeah. He swore me to secrecy. He was worried about his girl-friend. She works at the casino, too, and he didn't want her to get into trouble for what he was doing."

The fact that Isaac had described Ruby as his girlfriend made Aroostine's heart ache.

"Sure."

"He said the siphoned funds were almost embarrassingly easy to spot. It was like whoever did it was so arrogant and confident, they didn't bother to really hide it. There's lots of ways to fudge numbers that would make it hard to detect, but according to Isaac, this was sloppy work."

That description squared with what she knew about Buckmount—arrogant and confident.

"And how'd the drones come into all this?"

"So, Isaac told me about the money transfers because he had heard from some guy that Buckmount had stolen some drones from the testing facility—not any drones, military drones. Isaac was worried that the money in the offshore account was going to be used to buy black market bombs to arm them."

"Why? I mean, there are lots of things Buckmount might have wanted to use the money for? Why did Isaac jump to bombs?"

"I'm not sure. Something the guy told him, maybe? Anyway, he asked me to look into it, on the down low."

"Why you?"

"My brother works at the testing facility."

"And?"

"So I told him I heard some drones had gone missing. He freaked out. He told me not to breathe a word to anyone about it because the military didn't know and Buckmount Security was going nuts trying to find them before news got out."

"Did you tell Isaac this?"

"Yeah. And I could tell it really bugged him. It didn't make sense for Buckmount to steal the drones and then send his security people out to beat the bushes looking for them. Unless it was all an act."

"But that's a risky bluff. The more people the security personnel questioned, the greater the chance word would spread about the theft, which would inevitably get back to the military base."

"That's exactly what Isaac said. And the illogic of that drove him bonkers. He was a very logical, kind of regimented guy. Like, anal-retentive, I guess you'd say."

The reasonably prudent person.

"I could see that bothering him. Yeah, when he called me, he made me walk through everything we knew one last time, trying to see whether we'd missed something, but we couldn't think of anything."

He fell silent for a moment, and she listened to him breathing.

Then he said, "Finally, Isaac decided that he'd leave the sleuthing to the FBI or whoever. He told me he was going to give you the spreadsheets and try to forget about the whole thing."

"Spreadsheets?" She sat up straighter and tried to stay calm. Joe had been right about Isaac.

"Yeah. He said they'd show you everything you needed to know to trace the—You didn't find spreadsheets at his house?"

"No. I'm not sure how thoroughly the police searched it, though. They were looking for a gun, not a pile of papers."

The man laughed. "They won't be a bunch of printouts. Isaac would have stored them electronically, on a flash drive or something."

"Are you sure?"

"Lady, I'm positive. Isaac considered hard copies to be nothing but clutter—it didn't matter what it was. But something important, yeah, totally. He would have put it on one of his crazy, indestructible USB drives. He used these drives made out of some kind of metal alloy that's fireproof, waterproof, and crushproof. That's all he used; he wouldn't trust those cheap ones you get for five bucks at the office supply store."

She asked, "If you had to guess, where do you think he would have hidden it?"

"I dunno." The man thought for a moment. "Maybe his car?"

"His car?"

"Yeah, he loved that old thing. He called it his favorite thing in the whole world."

Hope and anticipation electrified her. Her left leg jittered. Pent-up energy and impatience were taking over.

"His car. Great. Let me search his car. I'll call you back if I don't find it."

"You can if you want to, but I don't have any other ideas, and I told you everything I know."

"Okay, thank you." The words poured out in a rush, and she hurried to end the call. She grabbed the car keys from the desk and ran out of the room.

She skidded to a stop just outside the door and stared down at the heavy, metal keychain ornament in her hand.

A metal alloy. Indestructible. He loved his car.

Heart thudding, she turned and walked slowly back into the conference room. She examined the cylinder. On first glance, it appeared to be a single piece of metal. But when she looked closely, she noticed a thin seam running around the bottom. She turned the bottom of the cylinder, below the seam, to the left. It moved. It made two whole revolutions and then unscrewed in her hand. The cylinder was a hollow tube. Attached to the base was a solid metal USB drive, made from the same material as the cylinder.

She stared at her palm. All this time, she and Joe had been carrying around the evidence that had cost Isaac his life.

CHAPTER TWENTY-EIGHT

Aroostine slept in. She rarely slept past sunrise, but when she rolled over to eyeball the clock on the bedside table, she thought she'd misread it. She blinked. No, it really was nearly ten o'clock.

She threw back the light blanket and padded out into the kitchen.

"Morning, sunshine," Joe said in an entirely too-chipper tone. He slid a mug of tea across the counter toward her.

"Thanks." She raised it to her lips, and the unmistakable, warm smell of cinnamon filled her nose. "Where'd you get this?"

"Boom asked me yesterday what your comfort foods were. I told him cinnamon tea, oatmeal with blueberries, and dark chocolate." He ticked off the items and gestured to a small basket near the stove. Then he placed a bowl of oatmeal in front of her. "How'd I do?"

She smiled up at him, and mixed the fat blueberries floating on top of the oatmeal into the hot oats. "A-plus. That was nice of Boom."

He perched on the stool next to hers.

"It was. He said he wanted to give us a token of appreciation. I got a basket, too, for helping him with his office project."

"Oh, yeah? What'd you get?"

"Fresh roasted coffee, a six-pack of local beers, and an éclair the size of your face. The éclair's long gone, but I figure we can take the chocolate and the beer back to the hotel with us tomorrow." He sipped his coffee.

"What did you do for him, anyway?"

When she'd finally dragged herself home the night before, she collapsed into bed and was asleep within seconds. There'd been little time for chitchat.

"I built a bunch of shelves. Easy stuff. He had all the materials there. He just needed someone to put them together."

"Well at least one of us was productive." She frowned down at the oatmeal and pushed the bowl away.

"I thought you said those spreadsheets prove the embezzlement case against Buckmount?"

She nodded. "They do." As the man had promised, Isaac's documents provided a perfect road map. All she had to do was connect the dots.

"And Buckmount's going to plead guilty to Isaac's murder and Ruby's abduction?"

"He is."

"So, it sounds like you're in pretty good shape."

"Except for the drones. I have nothing on him for the drones. Or the break-in at Ruby's."

He tilted her chin up. "Hey, you have to go to court with the facts you have. You aren't a miracle worker."

He was right, but that didn't change the fact that a stone of dread had lodged itself in her stomach. She had to shake her mood.

"Let's take a walk."

They hiked through the meadow. The day they fled their burning rental vehicle, they'd run straight through it until they hit the woods and then they turned right. This time, they made an immediate left and followed a narrow footpath.

The path wound through the fields and then snaked down behind the police station. Joe and Aroostine didn't speak. When the path was flat and wide, they walked side by side, hand in hand. When it narrowed or grew steeper, by unspoken agreement, Aroostine forged ahead and Joe followed.

At the bottom, they reached a stream. Two men in their mid-twenties were fishing. They were shirtless despite the cool breeze. A cooler of beer sat between them.

The men turned when they heard Joe and Aroostine approaching. One raised a hand in greeting.

The other said, "You're the attorney?"

"Yes."

"Thank you."

She tilted her head. "For what?"

"Judge Carole said you're giving up your vacation to help us clean our house. You're going to make it possible for us to heal a wound."

"Isaac's death?" she asked.

The man shook his head. "That, yes. But more than that. There's been a rift between people like Lee and those who want a more traditional way—lots of fighting over whether we should sell shares in the casino, make a private offering, that sort of thing."

"I don't know if what I do today will help repair that divide," she told him.

"It will," his friend said. "You'll see."

His line tightened, something beneath the surface of the water pulled it taut, and the men returned their attention to their fishing.

"Good luck," she said, as she and Joe started to walk on.

"Thanks. We're fishing for the dinner tonight. Hope we catch a bunch—otherwise, we'll be contributing silverbacks." He pointed down at the shiny beer cans and laughed.

Aroostine walked on in silence for a few moments, then she turned to Joe.

"These people are counting on me to do more than deliver a guilty verdict, Joe. They're looking for justice to be restored."

He nodded. "That's what it sounds like."

"But that's not what I do—that's not what the *law* does." A plaintive note crept into her voice. The law was a set of rules and procedures, a tool. It wasn't magic.

"Well maybe it should be."

CHAPTER TWENTY-NINE

Aroostine smoothed back her hair and secured it in a low ponytail. Then she turned to Joe, who was sitting in the driver's seat. He'd pulled into the spot next to Gordon's BMW and killed the engine.

"Ready?" he asked.

"Ready as I'll ever be."

He leaned over and brushed her lips with a quick kiss. "You'll knock 'em dead."

She managed a wan smile and grabbed her bag. She waited while he locked the car and then walked into the police station.

She'd realized during their morning hike that she didn't know where the courthouse was. When she called Boom to ask, he'd nearly dropped the phone, convulsing in laughter. Evidently, Carole convened court at her favorite picnic table. Unsure what one wears to a judgment circle held on the lawn, but fairly sure "a suit" was the wrong answer, she settled on a black skirt and a silver-and-white linen blouse.

Joe took her hand as they mounted the stairs to the station. The doors were propped open. Inside, people were milling around. Kids chased each other up and down the hallways, laughing and shouting, while adults gripping reusable plastic containers full of salads, sides, and desserts gathered in clusters, chattering over the din of voices.

Officer Hunt waved and pointed toward the back door. "Go on out," he mouthed.

The young female officer staffing the door greeted her with a wide smile and yanked it open.

Aroostine took a deep breath and stepped outside. Joe tried to follow, but the officer held out a hand.

"I'm sorry, sir. Carole asked us to have everyone wait inside so she can speak to the attorneys for a moment."

He nodded to Aroostine. "You've got this, Roo."

She winked at him and walked out onto the lawn.

Carole was seated at the picnic bench, deep in conversation with Lee Buckmount. Apparently, the court had no problem with *ex parte* communications. Meanwhile, Gordon was flipping through a stack of papers, frowning down at them.

Aroostine walked over and stood near his shoulder. He was looking at a printout of Isaac's spreadsheets. She could only imagine the heartburn they were causing her opponent.

"Good afternoon, Gordon."

He glanced up. "Aroostine. How are you this afternoon?"

"Tired. A little bit apprehensive," she answered honestly.

He arched a brow at the admission. But then—perhaps because she'd broken the trial attorney's creed of "never show weakness," he nodded and said, "Me, too. These documents—these are bad."

"Is your client going to change his plea on the embezzlement charge?"

Gordon pursed his lips like he tasted something sour. "I don't think so. Carole's talking to him about that right now."

They turned and watched the judge. She leaned forward and gestured with her hands, clearly trying to convince Buckmount of something. But his mouth was a hard line. He sat ramrod straight, arms crossed, neck stiff. Beside Aroostine, Gordon emitted a small sigh.

The judge shook her head sadly and sat back. She looked over at Aroostine and Gordon and gestured for them to join the conversation.

When they approached, she announced, "Lee's steadfast in his position. You're going to have to object to admission of the documents."

"Now or when everyone's here?" Gordon asked mildly.

She arched a silver eyebrow. "I'd normally do that in a sidebar before we start, but I'm inclined to let the circle decide the issue."

"The judgment circle makes evidentiary determinations?" Aroostine asked, hoping that she hadn't actually gasped aloud. She'd hoped that she'd at least be able to argue the law to the judge on issues of what evidence could be considered, but apparently this was going to be a free-for-all.

"Not ordinarily," Carole explained. "But sometimes."

Aroostine decided no response was her best response to that, so she nodded mutely.

Carole waved a hand at the officer on door duty, and people began to stream out of the building. They formed a large circle on the lawn and sat down, legs crossed, shoulder to shoulder. The closest spots to the picnic table were reserved for the members of the tribe most impacted by Buckmount's actions. Ruby, a tense-looking Lily, and a mournful woman whom Aroostine took to be Cathy Palmer, filed in. Boom sat next to the bereaved mother and waved Joe into the spot next to him.

Aroostine scanned the circle. She saw some familiar faces—including the fishermen from earlier in the day—but the assembled group was primarily strangers. Chief Johnson walked through the door, and the officer closed it behind him.

"Is this everyone?" Carole asked, making eye contact with the chief.

"Everyone who didn't have to work and was able to get here. Mae-Ann and Wren are watching the little ones inside," Chief Johnson said.

Aroostine scanned the crowd. With the exception of Lily, everyone appeared to be about thirteen or older. Lily, meanwhile, had crawled into her mother's lap and was staring at Lee Buckmount wide-eyed. Aroostine resisted the urge to pick up Lily and run, to spare her from hearing what happened to her mother.

Carole nodded and raised her hands, palms up.

"Friends, let us begin with the invocation."

Aroostine side-eyed Gordon, who shrugged. "I only know the refrain," he whispered.

The judge began to incant, "We call upon the earth, our planet home, with its beautiful depths and soaring heights, its vitality and abundance of life and together we ask that it . . ."

The circle joined in, "Teach us and show us the Way." Gordon mumbled along.

Carole nodded and continued, her voice gaining strength, "We call upon the mountains of the Cascades and the Olympics, the high green valleys and meadows filled with wildflowers, the snows that never melt, the summits of intense silence, and together we ask that it . . ."

This time Aroostine was ready. "Teach us and show us the Way."

The judge went on to call upon the water, the land, the forests, animals, and the Chinook ancestors in her clear voice. Each time, the circle chanted the refrain. Finally, she said, "And we call upon all that we hold most sacred, the presence and power of the Great Spirit of love and truth, which flows through all Nature to be with us and . . ."

"Teach us and show us the Way," Aroostine recited with the others.

A collective quiet settled over the circle. Carole looked around, searching the faces looking back at her. Apparently satisfied by what she saw, she nodded. "We convene this sentencing circle to heal the breaks in our community caused by Lee Buckmount. This circle will include three outsiders. Attorneys Gordon Lane and Aroostine Higgins, and Aroostine's husband, Joe. This court *sua sponte* orders the *pro hac vice* admissions of Mr. Lane and Ms. Higgins, permitting them to appear before the White Springs Tribal Court for this matter. The decision of this circle will constitute a binding order of this court, appealable under the Appellate Rules of the Ninth Circuit Court of Appeals."

Aroostine could only imagine how much the Ninth Circuit enjoyed handling appeals from Native American rituals.

The judge held up a large, smooth stone. It was translucent and banded with ribbons of red and brown.

"What's that?" Aroostine stage-whispered to Gordon.

"The speaking piece. You have to be holding it to talk. Well, not you and me or the judge—everyone else."

Aroostine didn't know whether to laugh, cry, or start screaming, "Are you freaking *kidding* me?" She considered making a snide comment to Gordon, but he seemed to be rolling with the special stone, so she held her tongue.

The judge said, "Lee has been accused of several crimes. He has agreed to take responsibility for two of them." She handed the stone to Buckmount, who took it with visible reluctance.

His eyes darted around the circle and then returned to the judge. "I accept responsibility for my actions and the harm they caused. Specifically, I am responsible for the death of Isaac Palmer."

Cathy Palmer inhaled sharply. Boom placed a steady hand on her back.

Buckmount looked directly at the woman. "I'm sorry for the pain I caused you, Cathy. Isaac was a good man and a hard worker."

The judge spoke in a soft voice. "Cathy, do you want to speak?" Isaac's mother shook her head no, unable or unwilling to speak. Ruby cleared her throat.

"You have something to say, Ruby?"

"Yes, judge."

Buckmount passed her the stone. Ruby's voice wavered as she said, "Isaac Palmer was my neighbor and friend. He was smart and kind, and he was an inspiration to my daughter to strive to improve herself. His absence leaves a hole in my life—and Lily's."

She stroked the stone absently. Suddenly, Lily took it from her hands.

"I miss Isaac," she said.

The pain of loss in her innocent voice was like a knife. The image of her own grandfather dying in his bed flashed in Aroostine's mind.

Not now.

No one spoke for a long moment. Joe caught Aroostine's eye and gave her a look that said, "this is heavy."

The judge crouched in front of Lily, murmured something to the girl, and took the stone from her hand and pressed it back in Buckmount's hands.

"I also take responsibility for frightening Ruby and threatening her with a gun."

"Ruby?" the judge prompted.

Ruby shook her head.

"Lily?"

"Yes, please," the girl said.

Carole retrieved the stone from Buckmount and handed it to Lily.

The girl took a shaky breath. "I was really scared when my mom called Mr. Cowslip and said Mr. Buckmount tried to hurt her. I was in the car with Mr. Cowslip. He said we had to help my mom, but he was driving really slow. I was so scared we wouldn't get there in time—" She let the stone drop to the ground and covered her face with her hands, then turned and pressed herself into her mother's chest. Her shoulders shook as she sobbed. Ruby stroked the girl's hair and whispered something to soothe her.

Aroostine bent and picked up the stone. It was cool and smooth in her hands. She passed it to the judge.

Carole addressed the circle. "Usually, you know, I would ask you to propose the sentence, and I would merely approve it or suggest alternatives. But Lee's crimes are very serious. I will propose his sentence and ask you to approve it or suggest alternatives. He used the white man's weapon against one of his own. He needs to be removed from the community for our safety and security. Lee, I recommend a sentence of five years in federal prison—the facility to be determined by the Office of Tribal Affairs. It will be a facility that will recognize the Chinook culture and will work with you to restore your spirit, so that some day you may be ready to return to us."

"I accept my sentence," Lee said.

"Brothers and sisters, do you approve?"

A murmur of assent rose from the circle. No one opposed it. Aroostine was beginning to feel altogether superfluous.

"Mr. Lane and Ms. Higgins, do you both agree with the sentence?"

"Yes," Gordon said.

Aroostine hesitated. The sentence was light and not in keeping with the typical sentencing guidelines. But this was not a typical proceeding. And Lee Buckmount was not a young man. "Yes."

A wave of chatter spread throughout the circle.

Carole raised a hand. "We are not finished. There are two additional crimes for which Lee does not take responsibility. However, they may be connected to the death of Isaac Palmer and the attack on Ruby Smith. The attorneys will explain. Aroostine, you may speak first."

Aroostine cleared her throat and smoothed her skirt over her hips, then clasped her hands in front of her.

"I'm an attorney with the Department of Justice. I came to Oregon on a vacation with my husband." She paused and pointed at Joe, who waved to the circle. "My boss called and asked me to stop by and visit Isaac because Isaac had information that showed someone was embezzling a lot of money from your casino. When I arrived at Isaac's house, he was dead. But he had the foresight to make a copy of the documents that showed the embezzlement. He hid the documents on a computer drive in his car."

She stopped and dug out a copy of the files.

"I can pass them around if you like, but they show that each week forty thousand dollars was transferred from the casino's coffers to an account in the Cayman Islands. The entry had a code number that didn't match any of the categories the casino used for accounts payable—for example, employee salaries, payments to vendors, insurance carriers, or utility suppliers. Isaac was able to trace the creation of that category code to Lee Buckmount's employee ID."

She waved the spreadsheets in the air and let her gaze travel around the circle for a beat before she went on.

"Mr. Buckmount denies that he stole this money—which totals nearly a million dollars. Over the course of the year, more than two million dollars would have gone missing. Money that should be staying in *your* community, funding programs."

She waited until heads began to bob in silent agreement with the injustice of the theft.

"But ask yourselves why would he kill Isaac if not to silence him and perpetuate his crimes? And why else would he threaten Ruby, demanding to know what Isaac told her?"

She looked around the circle again. Anger clouded some faces, sadness others.

"Before Lee responds to the charge, I'd like his attorney to address the documents," Carole said.

Gordon nodded. "Ms. Higgins makes a serious accusation against my client. And the documents are complicated financial spreadsheets that she found on a disk that Mr. Palmer used as a keychain. The law requires that evidence, documents, used against a person be found to be reliable. We can't test the reliability of these spreadsheets. The only person who could explain them is, unfortunately, dead. So I ask the circle not to consider the spreadsheets."

A man sitting to the left of Joe raised his hand. The judge gave him the stone.

"Eli Nicholas," he said, identifying himself mainly for Aroostine and Gordon's benefit. "I don't think it's fair to say we can't take these documents into account because Isaac isn't here to explain them. The reason he isn't here is because Lee killed him. And he probably killed him for this very reason, so he couldn't tell anyone about those documents." The man stopped abruptly. His face darkened. "And if it is the federal law that people who kill to prevent their bad deeds coming to light are rewarded, then I for one am glad we have the Tribal Court and not such a backward, savage system."

Aroostine found herself nodding along with Eli's logic.

"I agree," Carole said. "The documents tell the story that Lee tried to silence. Lee, what do you want to say?"

"Nothing."

"Lee does not accept responsibility. Does the circle wish to question him?"

Eli, still gripping the stone, asked, "Does the bank account in the Cayman Islands belong to you?"

Aroostine watched Buckmount's eyes as he calculated his options. He knew that within days, the Department of Justice would receive a subpoena response that would prove he owned the account. Finally, he nodded reluctantly. "Yes, it does."

"Well, that's easy. He should return that money to the tribe," Eli said.

A chorus of agreement sounded.

The judge raised her hand. "Please, take the stone if you wish to speak."

One of the fishermen raised his hand, and Eli passed him the stone.

"Ethan Chessman. I've been on the waiting list for the computer career training program for over a year. All that money could clear the backlog of people waiting for vocational training with plenty left over."

Carole said, "I agree. I reviewed the cultural board's budget with Matthew Cowslip. Those funds would fill many gaps in the programs and support the expansion that the cultural board and the Tribal Board have proposed. Does anyone *disagree* with restitution?"

No one spoke. Finally, Lee raised his hand. The stone made its way around the circle to him. He closed his fist around it and said petulantly, "That's my money. I'm entitled to it for all the work I've done. I created a viable casino. I provide jobs through my security company. I secured the testing facility contract. I've earned that money."

A few people hissed. Gordon shut his eyes for a moment as if to block out his client's behavior.

Aroostine reflected that there was a reason most criminal defense attorneys encouraged their clients to exercise their Fifth Amendment rights.

Carole shook her head. "The Court approves the circle's sentence of full restitution."

Buckmount squeezed the stone but didn't speak. Gordon spread his hands and gave his client the old "told ya" look.

"That leaves just one more charge—the theft of US military equipment," the judge said.

Aroostine had earlier agreed with Ruby not to proceed regarding the break-in at her home because there was no real evidence to support it. Ruby assured her that, as long as Buckmount went to prison for the murder and the kidnapping, she did not feel the need to prosecute the break-in. Now she was about to advance a charge that had even less support than the break-in.

She looked around the circle again. "As you probably heard, I found two unmanned aerial weapons, or drones, in a cave. They had been taken from the testing facility. Isaac Palmer believed that Mr. Buckmount arranged for their theft." She paused and took a deep breath then exhaled slowly. "Sadly, he died before he was able to amass conclusive proof. But ask yourself, if not Lee Buckmount—who owns the company providing security services to the testing facility and who has stolen over a million dollars—then who among you would steal those drones? I don't know you very well, but I'm fairly certain the answer is no one. Only Mr. Buckmount had the means, the funds, and the motive to commit this serious federal crime."

Buckmount was shaking his head furiously.

Gordon spoke. "I have advised Mr. Buckmount not to respond to this charge. He's accused of a national security offense. Respectfully, it is not this circle's place to judge him for that."

Privately, Aroostine thought Gordon's assessment was dead on. But, she wasn't the judge.

Boom raised his hand, and the stone was rolled along the circle, hand to hand, until it reached him.

"I have to disagree. Lee brought the contract to test military drones to our people. Think about that—he brought the military onto our reservation, *our* land. And for what? Greed. Simple, deadly greed. And with the drones came danger. Danger to our lives, to our autonomy, to our peace. It is our place to judge him. And I do judge him for his avarice and the effect it's had on our people, especially our young people."

Officer Hunt raised his hand and received the speaking piece.

"I disagree. I mean, I agree with the sentiment but we cannot sentence people on such weak evidence. Imagine if it were you."

Aroostine barely managed to stifle her gasp. A police officer with empathy for an admitted murderer. It was so unusual as to be unheard of.

"Recommendation, please. Shall we vote?" Carole asked. "Does the circle wish to impute guilt for the theft of the drones to Lee? If yes, raise your hand."

Most of the hands—not all, but a solid majority—shot upward. But several did not. Aroostine saw Officer Hunt, one of the fishermen, Cathy, and Eli all sitting on their hands.

The judge made a sad little *ooh* sound. "The circle wishes to sentence Mr. Buckmount. However, the Court finds insufficient evidence tying him to the drone thefts. He will not stand for this charge."

Aroostine groaned inwardly, disappointed but unsurprised. It didn't really matter in the end. Someone—the Defense Department, most likely—would bring charges in federal court. The government wouldn't let the theft of military weapons go unpunished.

Carole raised her arms. "This circle is closed. We ask the Great Spirit to mend our break and make our circle stronger. We ask the Great Spirit to mend the break that exists inside Lee Buckmount and make him whole again. Brothers and sisters, let's break bread together to strengthen our community."

People stood and began to walk around.

"That's it?" Aroostine asked Gordon.

"Appears so. It was a pleasure to meet you, Aroostine."

"You as well. Aren't you staying for the meal?"

Gordon's eyes drooped. "No, I'm afraid not. There's a federal marshal parked out front. I've arranged for him to escort us to the federal prison in Salmon Run. There's a decent-sized Chinook population there, and the prison will house him at least temporarily while he's processed."

"Escort us? You're going, too?"

He smiled tiredly. "He's my client. He needs me. Now, if you'll excuse me. I really do want to get him settled so I can get back before . . . you know, it gets dark."

Aroostine shook his hand. "I wish you the best, Gordon."

"Thank you. The same to you."

He trudged over to Buckmount to collect his reluctant client.

Joe walked over and swooped her up in a hug.

"Well done!"

"I don't know about that. I didn't *do* much."

"Buckmount's going to prison. A million dollars is coming back to the reservation. I think you did a fair amount, Roo."

She smiled. Joe had never taken much interest in the outcomes of her cases. But then he'd never been so personally involved, either. Joe lifted his eyes from hers and looked over her shoulder. She turned to see Boom standing nearby, just far enough to give them their privacy.

"I'm sorry I didn't have better evidence about the drones, Boom. He must have been very careful," she called to him.

Boom walked over, shaking his head. "Nonsense. Don't apologize. You've done us a great service. Your grandfather would have been proud."

At the thought of her grandfather, seeing her here, among the Chinook, helping them in her small way, her eyes filled with tears.

"Thank you."

"What are your plans now?"

"I think we'll stay one more night at the cottage and then return to our hotel for the last night of our trip. We have a return flight already booked for Sunday. I'm glad I never got around to canceling it."

Lily ran up to them. "Can we all sit together at the dinner? Please?"

"Yes, child," Boom said.

"Sure thing," Joe agreed.

Aroostine squatted so she was eye to eye with the girl. "I'd be honored to sit near you. You were so brave, Lily, telling everyone how you felt."

Lily's eyes were solemn, but a hint of pink pride bloomed on her cheeks. "Thank you. I really was so scared we wouldn't get there in time to help my mom. Boom really, really does drive slowly. Like a tortoise."

Boom and Joe roared with laughter. Aroostine smiled but a chill ran through her—Lily's comment niggled at her. There was something wrong about it. Something that didn't make sense. She tried to shake it off, but it clung to her and lodged itself into her mind.

"You don't drive much?" she asked Boom.

"Not in years. I haven't driven regularly since I was a young man." Joe eyed her curiously.

"Come on," Ruby called, gesturing them to a picnic blanket that she had stretched across a patch of grass.

"Roo?" Joe asked.

"You go ahead and eat. I need to check in with Sid and just take care of a few quick things." She knelt beside the girl. "Save me a good dessert, okay?"

She walked through the sea of people carrying plates and covered dishes. She bumped into Carole, whose arms were wrapped around an enormous salad bowl.

"You aren't leaving?" the judge asked.

"I'll be back in a bit." She started through the doorway then turned back. "Carole?"

"Yes?"

"Why do you think Lee Buckmount wouldn't take responsibility for the drones?"

The judge shook her head, and her hair fell around her face like a silver curtain. "I've known Lee a long time. His refusal to admit the embezzlement makes a certain sort of sense—he's motivated by money, he always has been. I think he hoped he could somehow keep that money even if he went to prison. But I don't understand why he wouldn't allow us to judge the accusation of breaking into Ruby's home or why he refused to admit to stealing the drones. There's no gain for him there. Unless . . ."

"Unless what?"

"Unless he truly didn't do it."

CHAPTER THIRTY

Boom was waiting for her. He watched through his front window as she trudged from the guest house, her shoulders bent as though they carried a great weight. As she stepped up onto his porch, he turned the doorknob and opened the door. She froze, her fist stopping midknock, and blinked at him with sad, fatigued eyes. Dark circles rimmed her eye sockets.

"There you are, Aroostine."

He stepped aside to let her in. She hesitated.

"It's okay, come in. I know why you're here."

She stiffened at that but then her face relaxed, as if she also found comfort in it. He knew what was about to pass between them would wound her. He wished it didn't have to be so.

She walked past him into the living area but didn't sit. He closed the door and locked it.

"Can I offer you some tea? Toast?"

She shook her head.

"You should eat," he urged.

"I'm not hungry." She inhaled deeply, gathered herself, and then exhaled and asked the question he'd been dreading. "Why?" Her voice broke.

He found it difficult to speak around the lump in his throat. "Please, Aroostine. Sit down. I'm making tea. I'll bring it in and we can talk. I'll tell you what you need to hear. But, sit. You look like you're going to collapse."

She started to protest but stopped herself and sank into the love seat.

She still wanted to trust him, he realized with a start. He hadn't expected that. Perhaps she was willing to listen with an open heart and be persuaded.

He hurried to the kitchen to pour the tea before she reconsidered. When he carried the cups into the living room on their saucers, he was pleased to see that his hands didn't shake.

"Thank you," she said. Then she set aside the cup and saucer without taking a sip.

He lowered himself into the chair across from her and waited, wondering where she would begin.

"Does she know—Carole Orr?"

"Does she know what? About my past? Or my present?"

She gripped her hands together, almost as if she were praying. Her interlocked fingers turned white from the pressure.

"All of it."

He sighed, blowing air across the surface of his tea. "Any Chinook on this reservation who's of a certain age remembers AIM and what things were like then."

"The American Indian Movement?"

"Yes. You're too young, and the Lenape didn't have a recognized reservation, so you may not fully understand our history. In the late sixties, early seventies, the country—the entire country—was in upheaval. White, black, red, yellow, brown. No matter the skin color, the people were rising up. Leaders were killed. The government, *your* government, was brutal." He heard his voice take on power. He sounded like a younger version of himself, the man who rallied the people.

"Your history books teach about the Black Panthers, the Kent State massacre, and the assassinations of civil rights leaders. Have you read about the Trail of Broken Treaties or the standoff at Wounded Knee?"

She shook her head no.

"I would guess you haven't. Our people were being executed, stabbed, shot, mutilated by federal government agents. Evidence was manufactured. People went to jail. Women, mothers, were beaten on the courthouse steps for daring to demand justice for their dead sons—"

He stopped himself abruptly and reached for his tea. Now his hands were shaking. The china cup banged against the saucer with each tremor. He drank and tried to slow his heartbeat.

"So, you were in AIM," she said softly, encouraging him to continue.

His voice was weaker now, even to his own ears. "Yes. I was in AIM. So was Carole. So were many others. But I was a young man, full of fight. I grew frustrated; I felt that the leadership was losing sight of the people. Splinter Red Power groups began to form—other natives who felt as I did. Some were angrier than others. I got involved with the wrong people. I made mistakes." He stared down at the teacup for a moment then lifted his head.

She glared at him, her brown eyes flashing. "Mistakes like bombing the IRS building in Salem?"

"Yes."

They sat in silence for what seemed like a very long time. He had to decide how much to tell her and whether he could accept the consequences of telling her.

"You feel betrayed by me, daughter?"

She set her mouth in a hard slash. "I'm not your daughter."

His heart squeezed in his chest at the rebuke. "So you researched my background and you learned that I spent eight years in prison."

She said nothing.

"No one was injured, you know. We bombed the building on a weekend. It was a protest."

She whipped her head up at that. "Was it a protest when you tried to blow me up?"

"I panicked. Please try to understand. Lee Buckmount and his supports were destroying our culture. They were happy to turn a profit on the backs of gamblers and drinkers, but at least we struck a deal with Lee to fund some of our cultural initiatives and to set up a scholarship fund. But then he brought the drones. That was sheer greed. Blood money. He had to be stopped. When Isaac discovered Lee's financial shenanigans, it created an opportunity for me to try to help our community. Lee was distracted, worried, not focused on his businesses. I was able to convince a sympathetic security guard to look the other way while a couple military drones disappeared."

"What was the plan? Were you going to sell them or what?"

"Sell them to whom? Terrorists? My word, no. I don't want *any-one* to have them. They're death machines. I planned to destroy them. The Department of Defense would learn that the testing facility wasn't secure and cancel the contract. That's all I wanted to achieve."

He thought he sensed her beginning to soften toward him—she seemed to have less stiffness in her shoulders, less anger in her gaze. He plowed ahead, hopeful that she would understand. "You know in your heart that those drones are evil. That's why you had the vision that first night."

"Who told you that I heard about the drones from Ruby?"

"You did."

She recoiled. "I did no such thing," she spat.

"Your spirit guide showed you Lily in the vision with the drone. It seemed odd that you felt such a connection to a girl who you'd just met. Unless . . ."

"Unless Ruby told me about the drones? You were comfortable acting on that hunch?"

He shrugged. "You call it a hunch because you deny your background, Aroostine—"

"Please, no more spiritual mumbo jumbo from you. You broke into Ruby's, and you tried to kill me and Joe."

"One life, two lives—this is nothing in the face of an entire people's history." He said the words coldly, even though the truth was he'd struggled over the decision, consulted his own spirit guide, asked the ancestors for guidance. She may not have considered herself his daughter, but he felt a connection to her, and it had pained him to do what he'd done—what he'd had to do.

"As one of the lives you found so disposable, I have to disagree."

He allowed her reproach to wash over him in a wave.

"My turn to ask a question. How did you put it all together?"

"Something Lily said at the sentencing circle about your driving. You're a cautious, out of practice driver, but you got to the scene so quickly when Lee was attacking Ruby. Lily said you drove slowly, though. You were already off the reservation grounds when Ruby called—weren't you? You snatched Lily from school as an insurance policy to keep Ruby from talking to anyone else about the drones."

"Partially correct. I knew Lee was going to beat information out of Ruby. It's his way. I didn't want him to harm the child, but I also didn't want Ruby and Lily to talk to the government. I didn't plan to harm Lily. I just needed to keep the theft of the drones quiet until I could arrange for their destruction."

She scrunched up her face and looked at him as though he were abhorrent. He didn't know how to convince her that she did matter to him—but the Nation mattered more. She was a pure spirit, a fighter for good. Of course she mattered.

But he knew he wouldn't be able to get her to see. It was a battle he'd lost once before: when a young Carole Orr had told him to choose Red Power or her. Of course, his warm feelings for Aroostine were only paternal, unlike the heady first love that he and Carole had shared a lifetime ago.

"But you let me—you *helped* me—try to convict Buckmount for your crimes. You aren't the mystic sage you pretend to be. You're just an old coward and a fraud."

He drained his tea and stood. He looked down at the young woman—ablaze with anger—sitting on his old corduroy divan and felt something like pity. "I'm sorry it has to be this way."

Aroostine wasn't sure what she'd hoped to accomplish by confronting Boom. He was unrepentant and committed to rationalizing his crimes as somehow being in furtherance of some amorphous, greater Indian good. She'd wasted her time coming here. She should have followed her first instinct and gone straight to Chief Johnson.

I'm sorry it has to be this way—that's the best explanation he could manage for attempted murder?

She pushed herself up and out of the sunken love seat cushion.

"I'm sorry, too. I shouldn't have come."

She started toward the door, but he blocked her path. She moved to her left, he moved with her. She moved right. Again, he followed. She stopped.

"I don't have anything else to say to you. I'm leaving." She forced the words out between clenched teeth.

"I can't let you do that."

"I'm not asking permission. Now, please get out of my way."

Something about the sad smile he wore and the hooded expression in his eyes chilled her.

"You can't leave." He raised his right arm and made a sweeping gesture that encompassed the door and windows. "I watched you as you left the circle. I could see in your face that you were beginning to suspect what I had done. At that point, I had a choice. Run or stay and face you. I'm too old to run, Aroostine. I don't want to start a new life away from White Springs. But I'm not going back to prison."

She stared at him, trying to make sense of his words, but his impassive face gave her no clues. She swept her gaze around the room. When she strained her eyes and squinted, she could just make out a thin ribbon of wire dancing around the door and window frames—as if he'd strung a line of Christmas lights that had no bulbs.

Her chest tightened.

"What've you done?"

"I didn't have a lot of time, so I won't pretend it's my best handiwork. But it should suffice. I left the potluck and came back here to wire all the windows and doors to a series of incendiary devices. When I locked the door after you got here, it activated the final bomb. Try to open the door and you and I go sky high. Same for the windows. The only way out is in pieces."

She surveyed the first floor. Two windows in the small front room, one in the kitchen, a front door, and a back door. No basement. A set of stairs, offset from the front door, led to the second floor.

He guessed what she was thinking and shook his head. "Second-floor windows are rigged, too."

She wet her lips. "What's your plan—you want to live in here forever, the two of us?"

"Don't be ridiculous. I'm not crazy, Aroostine, but I am desperate. I'm not going to die in a cage. So you pick: forget we had this conversation, let the drone thing go, and walk out of here to live the rest of your life, or die with me in what promises to be an impressive explosion. I'm at peace with either decision."

She believed him. He looked relaxed and loose. When he spoke, his tone was calm, almost hypnotic.

"And what if I do neither. What if I just settle in, decide being your captive beats either alternative?"

"If you make that decision, then I'll open the door and decide for you."

Her breath caught in her dry throat. She started babbling, the sort of stuff movie police officers say to insane, dangerous men with nothing left to lose, even though it never sways them. She knew he didn't intend to let her live, no matter what promises she made. He'd decided to die in a blaze and to take her with him.

"Boom, you don't want to do this. We can work something out. Disarm the bomb and let me go."

Just like a central-casting villain, he threw back his head and laughed.

"Be serious."

She mentally inventoried the contents of her pockets: pen; nearly dead cell phone; Isaac's keychain; and a lip balm. Someone could likely make a creditable weapon out of those items—unfortunately, she was not that person.

She smiled. Boom smiled back, although his eyes registered distrust. She breathed in, breathed out, and took a step closer to him. Gave him another smile.

"Boom, please." As she said the words, she kept her eyes locked on his and took another step toward him. She was close enough to smell the fabric softener on his shirt.

"Your fate is yours to decide, daughter."

She nodded. Inched one step closer, until their foreheads were nearly touching.

Don't back up, she pled silently, willing him to stay right where he was standing.

As if he heard her thought, he obliged, planting himself more firmly and leaning slightly forward.

"You know what to do," he whispered in a low voice.

She did, in fact, know what to do. She just had to force herself to do it. She stared into his gold-flecked eyes and readied herself.

"Aroostine?"

She snaked both hands out and grabbed his shirt in her fists and pushed him backward, hard. As he lost balance, his torso went back, but his head whipped forward. She lowered her head, tucked her chin into her chest, and pulled him toward her. He flopped forward, and the center of his face smashed into the crown of her head with all the force of his one hundred and eighty pounds and the momentum of her push and pull. Her head instantly screamed with pain; the reverberation of pain began on the top of her head and ran to the base of her skull.

She released the fabric from his shirt and let him fall to the ground. Then she pounded up the stairs without looking to see if he was unconscious, dead, or alive. She simply ignored the thumping pain on the top of her head and ran.

As she hit the landing at the top of the second floor, she fumbled for the cell phone. She pressed herself against the wall, her legs shaking, and hit the speed-dial button for Joe's temporary phone.

He answered on the second ring. "Where are you? You disappeared on me," he grumbled.

"This is important. Do not try to get into Boom's house."

"What? Where are you?"

She panted, trying to catch her breath. "I'm at Boom's. He's booby-trapped the doors and windows. If any of them open, the house will blow up."

"What?"

"I'll explain later, just please, get Chief Johnson, call Sid, call Carole Orr—do something, but do not try to enter the house. Make sure you tell them."

"Okay, I got it. Why's he letting you use the phone?"

She leaned and peered down the stairs but saw no movement below. Was he conscious down there?

"I head butted him. I think I knocked him out, maybe?"

"You did what?"

Impatience vied with panic. She didn't have time for this.

"I head-butted him." She had never done such a thing, but after prosecuting a felony murder case in which a suspected drug dealer had head-butted the arresting officer, who fell, hitting his head on the ground and sustaining a subdural hematoma, she knew the physics behind an effective head butt.

"Whoa."

"Listen, Joe. Really, we can't stay on the phone."

"How are we going to get you out of there?"

"I think I have an idea. But first make those calls." She cocked her head, listening for any sound from downstairs. Silence.

"I will. Roo?"

"Yes?" She couldn't keep the irritation out of her voice. Why wouldn't he just hang up already?

"I love you." His voice cracked as if he were crying.

She stopped pacing and pressed her forehead against the wall. "And I love you." She waited a beat, just listening to his ragged breathing on the other end of the phone, and then couldn't wait any longer. She ended the call.

She pocketed the phone and stared up at the drop ceiling in the hallway. It looked to be the same as the one on the first floor—a collection of inexpensive pop-up tiles that hid the wires, pipes, and other house guts inside. *Just like Grandfather's house.*

She had been five years old. And her parents had left her at Grandfather's house—again. But she couldn't sleep because there was a loud rustling noise over her head. She'd squeezed her eyes shut for hours and pressed a pillow over her ears, but she could still hear it. Finally she'd padded across the hall to her grandfather's room.

In the moonlight streaming through the window, she could see him clearly. He was sleeping, his mouth slightly ajar.

"Grandfather," she'd whispered.

His eyes opened immediately.

"What is it, child?"

She told him about the sound. He clicked on his bedside lamp and sat up. He slid his feet into the slippers lined up beside the bed and took her hand.

They could hear the frantic noise from the hall outside the room in which she slept. She gripped his hand harder. He cocked his head, listening.

"It's a bird."

"Why is it trying to get in?"

"It's trying to get out," he corrected her gently.

He led her back into the bedroom and settled her in the bed. Then he turned on the light and walked in a slow square around the perimeter of the room. He completed one circuit and began another. A third of the way through, he stopped and stood at the foot of the bed. His presence was like a blanket of peace.

She held her breath while he reached a hand up and popped out the square above his head. A terrified bluebird swooped into the room and made a rapid circle. She knelt on the bed and forced the window sash up. The bird circled again, squawking, and flew out the open window. The next morning, he took her out on the roof and showed her the hole near the fan vent. They'd patched it together.

Now she just had to hope she could be as lucky as a bird.

She followed the hallway to the small green-and-white bathroom at the end of the hall. She closed the toilet lid, stepped up on it, and steadied herself with a hand against the wallpapered wall. Then she pushed up on the ceiling tile overhead and slid it out. She climbed onto the toilet tank, gripped the corners of the space the missing tile had occupied, and hoisted herself up.

She army crawled through a nest of foamy pink insulation and angled pipes. Her pulse was trapped in her throat, fluttering just as that bluebird's wings had fluttered so long ago. She reached the end of the crawl space and smacked into a wall.

She rubbed her cheek to stop the stinging and then raised herself to her feet. She straightened an inch at a time. The last thing she needed was another good crack on her head. She'd end up like Boom downstairs. When she was still bent at the waist, her hand hit the vent pipe that jutted out onto the roof.

She pushed. Nothing.

She pushed again, harder. The vent wiggled in her hand, but the roof tile held tight.

Tears pricked at her eyes. She punched up with both hands. More wiggling, but still the tile held.

Frustration and despair clawed at her. She was going to die like this. Boom was going to wake up and detonate the bomb in his rage.

No. She might die here, but it wouldn't be because she gave up. She owed it to Joe to keep fighting. Unbidden, the thought of their dog flitted into her mind. She owed it to Joe and Rufus.

Think.

She needed a tool. She dropped down to her hands and knees and slowly crawled backward to the opening she'd created. It felt like it took an hour, no, a week, to get there.

Hurry.

She jumped down and spun through the bathroom, surveying its contents. The towel bar would be ideal. She gripped it, two handed, and pulled but it was tightly affixed to the wall. She yanked harder but it didn't yield.

She wrenched open the narrow linen cabinet. Towels, washcloths, extra soap lined the shelves in neat rows.

The cell phone chirped in her pocket. *Joe.*

"What?"

"I made all the calls. I'm outside Boom's. Ruby's with me. Where are you?"

"I have access to the exhaust vent on the roof. But I can't break through it. It wiggles but that's all." Her voice cracked, and a raw sob escaped.

Cry when it's over, she ordered herself.

"Okay, let me think."

Twenty long seconds of silence ticked by.

"Forget the vent. It's going to be sturdier than the roof itself."

"You think?"

"Yeah. Old house, not well constructed. Find a piece of ceiling tile that has air leaking through. It'll be loose. And then go to town on it."

"I'll try."

"Don't try. Do it."

Another sob caught in her throat. She wanted to tell him she was terrified. She wanted to tell him to come save her. But no words came.

She ended the call and pulled herself back up into the hot, cramped space, moving faster this time. She wiped sweat from her brow when she reached the end and crouched, running her hands overhead, feeling for air.

There. A cool breeze tickled her fingers. She laughed.

She lay on her back and braced her legs against the roof. Then she pulled them back to her knees and kicked out, like a jackknife, both feet kicking hard. She smashed into the roof.

Wood splintered and a shingle fell sideways, hanging crookedly and letting sunlight flood over her. She blinked and turned her face to the sky. She hadn't been sure she'd ever see it again. Hope bubbled up in her chest.

She scrabbled out onto the roof and scanned the ground below in the fading daylight.

Joe spotted her and waved his arms overhead, joy and relief beaming from his face like a ray. Ruby stood beside him, her face pale and drawn.

Aroostine shuffled a little closer to the edge.

"You're not really going to jump, are you?" Joe yelled up to her.

She shook her head. No, jumping was definitely Plan B. But she could climb like a squirrel.

She worked her way to the spot where the gutter met the downspout and lowered herself onto the downspout. There was no way it would hold her weight, but she could use it to stabilize herself while she worked her way down the side of the house.

As plans went, it was terrible. But it was the one she had.

She jammed her fingers around the downspout and swung herself out so her feet dug into the crevice between two sheets of siding. With her free hand, she clung to the roof line. And then she started to back herself down one piece of vinyl siding at a time. She didn't look down. She could hear Joe and Ruby calling to her. She couldn't make out the words. She wanted to stop and listen to what they were saying. But she forced herself to keep moving.

After the fourth panel of siding, the downspout groaned and pulled loose from the house. She let go of it and dug both hands into the siding, clinging to it with both arms and legs. She squeezed her eyes shut.

"Let go. I'll catch you," Joe's voice promised from below.

It sounded closer than she dared hope. She opened one eye and craned her neck. She was probably nine feet from the ground.

Just nine feet, she told herself. But she was frozen. She'd fallen out of trees higher than this as a kid. But she couldn't peel her fingers off the side of the house.

"Roo, listen to me. I promise, I'll catch you. You have to trust me."

The break in his voice on the last two words tore her in half. Her husband was begging her to trust him.

She closed her eyes and pictured herself falling, falling, and landing in Joe's waiting arms.

"Okay. On three."

"One."

She pulled her toes away from the house and let her feet dangle free.

"Two."

She loosened her grip overhead.

"Three."

She let go and allowed herself to fall. Down, down, down. And then she was jolted and jarred. She opened her eyes. Joe's arms were wrapped around her torso. Tears shone in his eyes.

It was over. She buried her face in his chest and breathed a ragged sigh.

CHAPTER THIRTY-ONE

Ruby and Lily pulled into the drop-off circle in Isaac's Tercel a few minutes before Aroostine and Joe walked through the spotless glass doors with their wheeled suitcases on a luggage cart. Aroostine glanced at the car, but didn't register who they were because they were so out of context. She was about to climb aboard the resort's airport shuttle, when Joe yanked her arm back.

"What's wrong?"

He smiled and pointed at the red car. Lily was on her knees waving frantically out the window.

"I think we've got a ride."

"Oh!" She grabbed her suitcase and hurried toward the car.

Ruby popped the trunk and came around to help them load their bags.

"This is a nice surprise," Joe said.

"Lily insisted we had to see you off. I hope you don't mind?"

"Don't be silly," Aroostine assured her. "We're touched."

She grinned. "That's a relief. I thought if I were you I'd never want to see anyone connected to White Springs ever again." The grin faded, and Aroostine knew she was thinking of Boom.

She rubbed Ruby's shoulder in what she hoped was a consoling gesture. At least he would live to be judged. Sid had told her Carole had managed to talk him out of the house after a sixteen-hour standoff. By then, she and Joe were back at the resort, soaking in the oversized bathtub.

"You'll come back from this—the tribe will pull together."

Ruby blinked and plastered her smile back on. "Yeah, I'm sure we will. Let's get you two to the airport." She slammed shut the trunk and hopped back in the car.

Joe sat in the passenger seat, and Aroostine joined Lily in the backseat. The girl's nonstop chatter as she pointed out every sight worth seeing on the way to the airport—and more than a few that weren't worth seeing—filled the car, sparing the adults from having to make conversation. She was bouncing and giggling the entire trip, but, as her mother slowed the car in front of the drop-off for Delta flights, she suddenly burst into tears.

"Hey, Lily, it's okay," Aroostine soothed.

Lily launched herself at Aroostine and squeezed her arms tight around her waist. The gesture surprised her, and she tensed, quickly recovered, and hugged the girl back.

"I'm going to miss you," Lily cried.

"I'll miss you, too. I don't know any fairies back home," she told her.

That earned her a wan smile. She wiped the tears from Lily's face.

"Can I visit you—in Pennsylvania?"

"If your mom says it's okay, of course. Or you could even bring her with you," Aroostine promised.

Joe unbuckled his seat belt and peered over the headrest at them.

"You can definitely come visit us, Lily, but I have a feeling you'll be coming to Washington, DC," Joe told her.

Aroostine wasn't sure whose eyes widened more—hers or Lily's.

"Where the president lives?"

"Yep. Aroostine's going to get a big promotion, but I know she'll take a day off work to visit the White House with me and you. Right, Roo?" Joe nudged her.

"Uh—tell you what. If you come visit us in Washington, we'll try to swing a tour of the office where the president works," she said slowly, her mind still trying to catch up. Could he be saying what she thought he was saying?

"Really?" Lily's tears were ancient history, as she squealed with excitement. "Can we go, Mom?" She caught Aroostine in another hug.

"Someday, baby. Maybe over Thanksgiving break. Now let go of Aroostine's neck so she can get out of the car before they miss their flight."

Ruby caught Aroostine's eye in the rearview mirror and smiled.

After another flurry of hugs, they lifted their bags out of the trunk and stood at the curbside waving good-bye to the mother and daughter.

As the car went around a curve and disappeared from view, Joe slung an arm around her shoulder. He raised his wrist and checked his watch.

"We have time for a drink before we board. I think your promotion merits a beer for me and some fruity concoction for you."

She wrinkled her brow but allowed him to lead her into the airport. Inside, they stopped at an electronic kiosk that spit out their boarding passes, and he consulted the directory of terminal side shops and restaurants.

"Here we go—The Pineapple Man. That sounds like a place that will have an umbrella drink that'll suit you."

As they glided up to the second floor on the crowded escalator, she leaned close to him.

"This promotion and move back to DC you're talking about, do you know something I don't know?"

"Maybe." He tried to hide his smile but failed.

He guided her toward a restaurant decorated like a tiki bar, and the smiling hostess bestowed them each with a plastic lei before leading them to a high top table for two.

She left them with laminated flip book drink menus. Joe picked up his menu immediately and starting turning the pages.

"No way." She put her hand down on his menu and forced it back to the table. "Come on, what's going on?"

He rested his elbows on the table and leaned across it. "Fine. You're no fun. Sid called me this morning while you were in the bath—"

"He called you? Or he called me and you answered my phone?"

"Well, counselor, I stand by my answer. He called me."

She narrowed her eyes. He went on, "Look, I mean, they're DOJ-issued cell phones. It probably didn't take a lot of brainpower to find me."

"True. But why?"

Joe traced a circle on the table with his index finger. After a moment, he cleared his throat. "I know you're pretty private about, uh . . . everything. But I guess Sid got wind of your jackass husband who refused to honor his wedding vows and support your dream when you moved to DC for the job."

The sight of his downcast eyes and miserable expression tore at her heart. She covered her hand with his and squeezed his fingers.

"Joe, I swear, I didn't say anything negative about you—actually, I didn't say anything at all about you."

"I know, Roo. Trust me, I know you play your cards close to your vest. Maybe Rosie said something or whatever. Listen, that's not the point."

"Okay."

He looked up at her. "The point is, they want you back. And he wanted to talk to me first to make sure I understood how important this is."

Her stomach did a flip. A complete upside-down flip. First, it leapt up in excitement, then it lurched all the way around and landed somewhere near her toes.

"I'm not sure I want to go back. You and Rufus aren't cut out for city living. And maybe I'm not either. I don't know. Besides, it's pretty wrong of Sid to go behind my back and talk to you first."

He weaved his fingers between hers.

"Before you get yourself into a feminist tizzy, you should hear him out."

She tilted her head. "This must be some job if you're trying to talk me *into* it."

"It is. And it's perfect for you. You'd be working at the Department of Justice but in the Office of Tribal Affairs. They want to create an interagency thingy between the Criminal Division and Tribal Affairs where you would consult to a whole bunch of departments on Native American issues and tribal justice and then basically do what you just did at White Springs—you would swoop in and handle particularly sensitive prosecutions and, uh, stuff. You could help set up tribal courts where there aren't any and train the judges and lawyers."

That did sort of sound like her dream job.

It was a role she didn't even know there was a need for a week earlier. And had she known about it, she would have scoffed at the idea of working with Native American tribes in that capacity. But now . . . now she wanted to pick up Carole Orr's mantle and restore justice to her people.

Her people.

Even thinking of Native Americans that way was new. But what were Lily and Ruby, Eli and Ethan, Cathy Palmer, if not her people?

"But DC?" she asked. She had to be convinced in her heart that he was sure this time.

"Well, obviously, you'd do some traveling around, but you'd be based out of DC. *We'd* be based out of DC. But Sid seemed to think that a lot of things could be handled remotely. We could more or less split our time between the farmhouse and an apartment or condo in the city. It'd be the best of both worlds. Who knows? Maybe Rufus will turn out to be a city dog."

Her stomach was inching its way back out of the nausea zone and into excitement jitters.

"It sounds . . . intriguing."

"Right?"

"Are you sure about this?"

He was about to answer when a grass-skirt-clad waitress hulaed her way over to take their drink orders.

"You folks ready?"

"You know, we haven't even looked at the drinks yet. What would you recommend for a celebratory toast before we run to catch our plane?"

Her green eyes lit up. "Oh, definitely a Maui Wowie!"

"Great, bring us two of those, please." He handed her the menus, and she went off to put in their drink order.

"Maui Wowies, huh?" Aroostine could feel her headache forming already.

He waved the topic away. "You asked me if I'm sure. I've never been more sure about anything, other than marrying you. You're a talented lawyer, Roo. And you really want to make a difference. This is a way you can make a difference for *your* people."

"And what about you? What's changed so much that you're willing to do this now?"

"I want to do this with you. I mean, I can't do the lawyer part, obviously. But I want to help you solve problems and bring justice to Native Americans who've been getting the short end. As crazy and demented as Boom turned out to be, I feel like *we*—our culture—played a big role in making him that way. This is my way of trying to turn it around. And I think we make a pretty good team." He grinned at her.

"Really?"

He pinned her with his intense blue eyes. "Really. And, there's one more piece to this. It's my way of turning around our relationship. I love you. I love us together. And I want to be here for you. Starting right here, right now."

A smile crossed her lips.

"Right here, huh? So the watershed moment in our relationship is going to happen at The Pineapple Man in the Redmond Fields Airport?"

"Yep. When we're old and gray, and we're looking back on your career of distinguished government service and how you brought restorative justice to Native American tribes throughout the country, we can say, 'and to think it all started with The Pineapple Man.'"

She burst out laughing at the ridiculous turn of phrase as all the exuberance and joy that had been building in her during their conversation reached a crescendo. The waitress returned with two hollowed-out pineapples full of Lord knew what.

He raised his. "To The Pineapple Man."

She mirrored the gesture. "To us."

ACKNOWLEDGMENTS

My sincere and unending thanks to Alison Dasho, who plucked Roo out of the pile, Mallory Braus, who may love my characters as much as I do and who certainly helped them to grow, James Pierce and Sara Peterson, who applied their eagle eyes to put a polish on the book, as well as to the entire Thomas & Mercer team for the care and attention they've provided to my characters and me along the way.

ABOUT THE AUTHOR

Melissa F. Miller is the *USA Today* bestselling author of more than half a dozen novels, including the legal thrillers *Irreparable Harm*, *Inadvertent Disclosure*, *Irretrievably Broken*, and *Critical Vulnerability*. She is a commercial litigator who has practiced in the offices of international law firms in Pittsburgh and Washington, DC. She and her husband now practice law together in their two-person firm in south central Pennsylvania, where they live with their three children.